Books by April Wilson

McIntyre Security, Inc. Bodyguard Series:

Vulnerable

Fearless

Shane (a novella)

Broken

Shattered

Imperfect

Ruined

Hostage

Redeemed

Marry Me (a novella)

Snowbound (a novella)

Regret

With This Ring (a novella)

Collateral Damage

A Tyler Jamison Novel:

Somebody to Love

A British Billionaire Romance:

Charmed (co-written with Laura Riley)

Collateral Damage

McIntyre Security Bodyguard Series
Book 13

by

April Wilson

Copyright © 2020 April E. Barnswell/
Wilson Publishing LLC
All rights reserved.

Cover Artist: Steamy Designs
Photographer: Reggie Deanching
Models: Tionna Petramalo-Bos and Robert Kelly
Editor: Christina Hart (Savage Hart Book Services)
Proofreaders: Sue Vaughan Boudreaux and Amanda Cuff

Published by
April E. Barnswell
Wilson Publishing LLC
P.O. Box 292913
Dayton, OH 45429
www.aprilwilsonauthor.com

ISBN: 9798666231890

No part of this publication may be reproduced, stored in a retrieval system, copied, shared, or transmitted in any form or by any means without the prior written permission of the author. The only exception is brief quotations to be used in book reviews. Please don't steal e-books.

This novel is entirely a work of fiction. All places and locations are used fictitiously. The characters are figments of the author's imagination, and any resemblance to real people is purely a coincidence.

1

Sophie McIntyre

I hate blind dates. They make me nervous. And as I'm standing here half-naked, surveying the clothes in my closet and debating what to wear tonight, I'm kicking myself for letting Amber talk me into this.

"Just pick something, Sophie," she says as she plops down on my bed with an exasperated sigh. "You'll look amazing no matter what you wear. It's not that big a deal."

"You make it sound so easy."

"It is! A handsome guy picks you up, takes you out for a nice dinner at a five-star restaurant, and then maybe you let him get to second base afterward—or even third. And that's *if* you like him."

I met Amber two years ago when she hired me to remodel her penthouse apartment. We hit it off right away, like we were sisters from different misters. And she's made it her life mission to *fix* me.

"Sophie, you have way too much to offer to sit on the sidelines. You need to get out there again and take a chance on someone new."

I roll my eyes at her. "Look what happened the last time I took a chance."

"What do they say about falling off a horse? You have to climb right back on. Not all guys are like Jeremy. Forget about him. He was a controlling, narcissistic bastard, and you are so much better off without him."

I wasted two years of my life on a relationship that ended in disaster and a badly bruised heart. Since then, I've been more than a little gun shy.

Sighing, I pull yet another sequined cocktail dress off a hanger and hold it in front of me, staring woefully into the full-length mirror in my dressing room.

I've never had a problem getting dates. Quite the contrary. It's just that every man I've ever dated has turned out to be a huge disappointment in one way or another. I'm tired of self-centered assholes who think women are only good for two things—sucking their dicks and looking pretty on their arms. We're worth more, and I refuse to settle for less.

I check the time—it's ten after seven. Kent will be here in twenty minutes. We have reservations tonight at Renaldo's—a five-star Italian restaurant in the city. The only reason I was able to get a reservation on such short notice is because the owner is a good friend of my eldest brother, Shane. Normally it takes months to get one.

Finally, I settle on a mid-thigh, cobalt cocktail dress. The bold color enhances the blue of my eyes, and the deep hue complements my skin tones. I'm definitely a jewel tones kind of girl.

Tonight, I'm wearing my hair down, although I did put a few curls in it. I'm keeping the jewelry light this evening—just a pair of diamond teardrops dangling from my ear lobes and a slender gold chain with a matching diamond pendant around my neck.

After slipping on a matching pair of Louboutin's, I step back to assess the effect.

"I guess it'll have to do," I mutter, because it's twenty after, Kent will be here in ten minutes, and I still need to brush my teeth.

Amber comes up beside me and peers at my reflection in the mirror. The top of her curly blonde head doesn't even reach my shoulder.

"You look stunning, Soph. Kent's going to die when he sees you."

Right on time, the intercom buzzes as the security guard announces his arrival.

The older man's voice booms over the crackling intercom. "Ms. McIntyre, there's a gentleman here to see you." He pauses.

"By the name of Kent Martinez."

"Thank you. Please let him come up."

Five minutes later, there's a knock at my door.

I'm an accursedly tall woman. Barefoot, I'm exactly six feet tall, almost every bit as tall as my four brothers. Add on a pair of four-inch heels, and I'm a contender for professional basketball. This fact is the bane of my existence, because I *love* wearing heels. They make me feel feminine, dainty even, which is rare for me because I usually tower over everyone around me.

Taking a deep breath, I steel myself and open the door. There stands my companion for the night. He looks just as I expected. Average height for a man—probably five-ten—which means I'm towering over him by six inches.

Maybe I shouldn't have worn the heels.

He's wearing a finely-tailored, navy blue pinstriped suit with a crisp white dress shirt and an emerald tie. His black hair is trimmed fashionably short, and he's clean shaven. There's a cute dimple in his chin. He's about my age, early thirties, an attorney in the DA's office.

He has to look up to meet my gaze, and for a fleeting moment, I see a mix of disappointment and discomfort in his dark eyes.

"Sophie?" he says, scanning me from head to toe. He frowns when he sees my spiky heels.

Yeah, I shouldn't have worn the heels.

I nod. "You must be Kent."

Nervously, he nods and clears his throat. "Yes." He steps inside my apartment and offers me his hand.

As we shake, he keeps glancing down at my feet.

I'm tempted to offer to change my shoes, but at the last second I decide against it. If a man can't handle me in heels, then we have no business going out. Instead, I say, "I'll just grab my wrap and we can be off."

After I say a quick goodbye to Amber, who promises to lock up on her way out, we head down in the elevator to the underground parking garage. Just moments after we step out into the garage, my life careens off course in the most horrific way imaginable.

We're halfway to his car—a sleek, black BMW—when a car with heavily-tinted windows comes barreling around the corner, tires squealing on the pavement. Kent throws a protective arm in front of me to stop me, but I'm already stumbling backward. As the front passenger window lowers, a chunky black gun appears in the opening, pointed directly at us. Three deafening cracks in rapid succession rent the air, and then my date crumples to the ground.

I scream.

Then I look directly into the face of the man who just murdered a Chicago assistant district attorney. My blood runs cold. His face—his very *distinctive* face, with a smashed-in nose and a long, jagged scar bisecting his left eyebrow—is one I'll never forget. He has a blood-red tattoo just beneath his right eye—in the shape of a teardrop.

That face is emblazoned in my mind.

As I stare at him, his expression contorts angrily.

"You're a dead woman!" he shouts, pointing the gun at me.

Just as I expect my life to end, a security car comes around the corner, its lights flashing. The killer's eyes widen, and he ducks back into his vehicle and rolls up the window. The car speeds away, tires squealing on the cement.

A uniformed security guard jumps out of his vehicle and comes running toward us.

I'm shaking so badly I lose my balance and drop to the ground, finding myself kneeling in the pool of warm blood flowing from beneath Kent's body. I glance down at his face, which is frozen in a surprised grimace. His eyes are wide open, fixedly staring upward. Already, his complexion is turning a sickly gray as blood continues to ooze out of the bullet holes in his chest.

I press my hands to his chest in an attempt to stop the bleeding, but in the back of my mind, I know it won't do any good.

He's dead.

This man, whom I'd met only moments before, is dead. My heart breaks for him. It's so unfair. His last act was an effort to protect *me*, not himself.

The security guard is already on his radio, calling dispatch and requesting police and ambulances. It's not long before I hear the sirens approaching, getting closer with every thundering beat of my heart.

As I stare at my bloody hands, all I can think is that I need my brothers. They'd know what to do.

I need my brothers.

* * *

"Sophie? Honey, can you hear me?"

I glance at the dark-haired man crouching beside me. "Tyler? What are you doing here?"

Tyler Jamison's sister is married to my brother Shane. How did he—oh. Of course. He's a homicide detective. He's here on official business.

Tyler looks me over thoroughly. "Are you hurt?"

I shake my head as I glance down at my bloody hands and dress. "The blood's not mine." I feel numb, completely detached from the situation.

I watch as a uniformed police officer covers Kent's body with a black tarp. Several officers are at the scene cordoning off the area with bright orange traffic cones and yellow police tape. There's a small gathering of bystanders just beyond the barrier, watching and whispering.

"Did you see who did this?" Tyler asks me.

I nod.

"Did you get a good look at him?"

"I saw his face." A shudder wracks me. "His nose looked smashed in, and there was a scar on his face. And a tattoo of a tear drop."

"Do you think you could ID him from a photograph?"

"Yes. I'll never forget that face."

Tyler lays a comforting hand on my back. "Shane's on his way. He'll be here any minute."

Hot tears start falling, burning my icy cheeks. "Thank you." And then I collapse onto my butt, sitting in a pool of congealing blood.

Tyler helps me to my feet. "Come sit down over here."

* * *

"She's in shock," Tyler says from somewhere behind me.

A moment later, someone crouches down in front of the bench I'm sitting on and reaches for my hand. "Sophie?"

He's here—my brother. "Shane?"

He nods. "I'm here, sweetheart."

An ambulance pulls up and one of the paramedics comes over to do a quick assessment. He recommends that I go to the ER to get checked out.

"But I'm not hurt," I say.

"I know," Shane says. "But you're going to the hospital anyway, just as a precaution. You're in shock. Can you stand?"

After that, everything's a blur. Shane rides with me in the ambulance. When we arrive at the hospital, I'm wheeled into the ER. Immediately, I'm taken back to the treatment area, and a nurse comes in to take my vitals.

Shortly after, two more of my brothers show up—Jake and Liam. Jamie's on his way, they tell me.

And then my parents are there. My mom is sobbing in my dad's arms, and my dad looks like he wants to kill someone.

Tyler's arguing out in the hallway with Shane—something

about wanting to ask me questions.

Shane says, "Damn it, Tyler, she's in shock. Give her some time."

As I lie shaking on a hospital bed, a nurse places a heated blanket over me. But it doesn't stop the quaking in my bones.

He's dead.

Murdered.

Right in front of me.

Without warning, my stomach lurches, and I turn my face to the side and vomit. Nothing but hot liquid comes out since my stomach is empty. The nurse wipes up the mess and pats my shoulder consolingly.

When the argument in the hallways ends, both Shane and Tyler enter my room.

Tyler shows me a photograph of a man. "I'm sorry, Sophie, but I need to ask you. Is this the man who shot Kent Martinez?"

I look at the photograph—at that hideous face—and nod. "Yes. That's him. How did you know?"

"Let's just say he's been on our radar screen for a long time. Are you absolutely sure?" he says.

"Yes. I could never forget that face."

"Thanks, Sophie." Tyler's expression is dark as he exits the room.

I look up at Shane, whose expression is equally unhappy. "What?" I ask him.

He blows out a breath. "This was a mob hit."

My stomach lurches once more. "Mob?"

He nods. "And you're the only eye-witness."

"Oh." The ramifications of that statement hit me hard. I'm the only one standing between the shooter and a long prison sentence.

What are the chances I'll live long enough to testify?

2

Dominic Zaretti

After a long, exhausting day of surveillance, I walk into a dive bar on the seedy side of town and wave at the bartender. "Hey, Steve."

As I sit on my favorite barstool, he hands me a draft beer.

"Thanks, man," I tell him.

"You look like shit," he says, grinning at me. "Rough day at the office?"

"You could say that."

I finished a job today—surveillance on a cheating husband. He didn't even bother to close the curtains while he was bang-ing his secretary doggy style on a motel bed. I got all the video evidence his wife needs to take him to the cleaners.

Now I get to kick back and relax for the evening, maybe even hook up. There are two blondes across the room who've been eyeing me since I walked into the place. Given how cozy they are with each other, I'm thinking a threesome isn't out of the question.

When my phone starts vibrating, I pull it out of my pocket to find a text from Shane McIntyre. He must have a job for me.

Shane: I need to see you at the penthouse. It's urgent.

Well, shit. There goes my chance for a threesome.

I gulp down half my beer and drop a twenty on the counter. "See ya, Steve," I call to him, pointing at the money. "Duty calls."

He waves, and I head outside to my '88 Bronco, which is parked in the rear lot.

I can't imagine what has Shane McIntyre calling me out this late at night, but with him, you never know.

I'm a freelancer—a jack of all trades. The last time I did a job for Shane was when he asked me to help Mack Donovan track down the motherfucker who sexually assaulted Donovan's girlfriend, Erin O'Connor.

I drive northeast toward the Gold Coast, where Shane's apartment building is located. I text him en route.

Me: On my way.

Shane: Thx. Elevator code 5249

Of course his private elevator requires a damn code. It must be nice to be loaded.

As for me? I've got a rundown loft apartment in a former industrial building in a sketchy part of town. I've got my Harley and my Bronco, and that's it. That's all I need. I certainly don't need to live at the top of a luxury apartment building overlooking Lake Michigan, on the most expensive street in all of Chicago.

When the elevator doors open into Shane's foyer, he's standing there waiting for me, leaning against a marble-topped table. His arms are folded over his chest, his ankles crossed. On the surface, his posture is relaxed, but his expression tells a very different story.

I have to duck as I step out of the elevator. "What's wrong?"

"A lot." He pushes away from the table and heads for the door that leads into his apartment. "Come to my office."

I follow him through an open door into a spacious room that looks like something out of a magazine. The back wall is all glass, overlooking the Chicago nighttime skyline. The space is quiet, hushed even, and dimly lit. But I can still make out his wife, Beth, seated on a sofa, rocking a blond baby boy in her arms. She looks... unhappy. And clearly pregnant. Even from here I can see that her belly is huge.

Beside her is her red-haired bodyguard—Sam, I think his name is. And beside him is an older guy with close-cropped silver hair. Sam's partner.

I nod in greeting at the three seated on the sofa. Then I follow Shane down a hallway to his office.

He ushers me inside and closes the door behind us. "Have a seat."

I sit, although I'd rather stand. "Why does everyone look like they're planning a funeral?"

And then he tells me why. He tells me about the shooting, about his sister, about the perp.

"Mikey Alessio?" My gut cramps. "Are you sure?"

Shane's jaw tightens. "Unfortunately, yes. She got a good look at his face. Tyler Jamison showed her a photo, and she ID'd him."

"That's not a face anyone is likely to forget. Fuck."

Shane nods. "Exactly. I'm sorry to call you in on this, but you know better than anyone what we're dealing with here."

"Mikey's gonna kill her, or at least do his damn best trying. And Franco will put out a hit on your sister—in fact, I'm sure he already has. He'll do anything to protect his only heir."

"That's why I called you."

"What do you want me to do? Talk to Franco?"

"No. It's too risky. I want you to get Sophie out of Chicago—tonight. Disappear with her. Take her far, far away, off-grid, and keep her there until it's time for the trial. Testifying is her only hope of surviving this nightmare."

I lean back in my chair and cross my arms over my chest as I swiftly run through my options. There's not much time. I have no doubt Alessio's organization is already mobilizing.

"Can you do it?" Shane says, impatient for an answer.

This isn't just any client we're talking about—this is his *sister*. The McIntyres are a close-knit family. You fuck with one of them, you have to deal with the whole bunch.

I nod. "Where is she? We've got to move fast."

"She's here, asleep in one of the guest rooms. She's still in shock."

I stand. "Take me to her so we can get this show on the road."

"Can we at least wait until morning?" he says, frowning. "She needs sleep."

"She can sleep when she's dead," I say, heading for the door.

I know Franco. He won't hesitate to put out a hit on a socialite if it will save his son.

We leave Shane's office and head back toward the great room. As soon as she spots us, Beth gets up from the sofa and hands the sleeping baby to Sam. Then she joins us in the hallway, her hands cupping her big belly as she glances up at me.

Next, she turns to her husband. "Is he going to do it?"

Shane nods. "We need to wake Sophie. They're leaving."

"What, *now*? But she's sleeping. She needs to rest."

"She can sleep on the way, Mrs. McIntyre," I tell her, hoping to cut the discussion short. "We've got to leave—*now*. Every minute counts."

Beth looks far from mollified. "At least let me go in first and wake her. I'll explain."

"Fine," I say. "But make it quick. I want to be on the road in fifteen minutes."

Beth frowns up at me. "She'll need to stop at her apartment

first so she can pack her things."

I shake my head. "Absolutely not. They're already staking out her apartment building. The only things she needs are the clothes on her back. Everything else stays behind."

"You can't be serious," she says. "Sophie will never stand for that."

I tap my watch. "Thirteen minutes. We're wasting time."

Shane reaches out to caress his pretty wife's cheek. "Go wake her, sweetheart. Tell her Dominic is going to get her out of Chicago and that they need to leave right away."

We both watch as Beth waddles down a long hallway. She stops at a door on the left and quietly slips into the room. Shane and I follow and wait outside in the hall.

All is quiet for a few moments, and then we hear a screeching, "What!"

I wince. I can already tell this is going to be fun.

Shane gives me a commiserating look. "My sister is a bit high-maintenance," he admits. "Her idea of roughing it is eating fast food."

"She's in for a rude awakening then." I check my watch. "Ten minutes."

Shane nods. "Wait here. I'll go talk to her."

For the next seven minutes, I listen to the muffled sounds of an argument through the closed door. Shane and a female voice—I'm assuming it's his sister's—go at it.

Finally, when I've heard enough, I rap my knuckles on the door—hard. Then I open it and walk in. "We don't have time for this."

There's a woman sitting up in bed, wearing a man's t-shirt and a pair of gray sweatpants. Her long, dark hair is disheveled, and there are mascara smudges beneath her smoky-blue eyes. At the sight of her generous breasts pressed against the t-shirt—clearly she's not wearing a bra—my pulse starts racing.

Damn.

She's a looker.

Scowling at me, she pulls the bedding up to cover her chest. "Do you mind?"

There's no time for drama either. "You have three minutes."

Her mouth drops open, and she sputters in indignation. "I'm not going anywhere with *you*. Not like this. Not on such short notice. I have to go back to my apartment, make arrangements, pack my bags, call my friends, notify my clients, stop my mail—"

I stride forward and scoop her out of bed and into my arms. She's a handful, that's for sure. I have to readjust my hold on her so I don't drop her. I notice she's cradling a phone in her hand—that's going to be a problem—but I'll deal with that later.

As Sophie squirms in my arms and calls me every name in the book, I turn to Shane and say, "I'll be in touch."

He nods. "Thank you."

Flustered, Beth reaches for a pair of men's running shoes on the floor and hands them to Sophie. "These are Shane's. They'll have to do for now, until you can get some proper shoes."

As I carry Sophie out the bedroom door, she fights me all the way, squirming and bitching up a storm. "Put me down, right this minute."

Shane barks, "Stop it, Sophie! Do as he says, and we'll all get through this in one piece."

"Beth, my purse!" she snaps, holding out her hand. "It's on the nightstand."

I keep walking. "Forget it."

She smacks my shoulder hard. "I need my purse, damn it! Are you out of your mind?"

"Apparently, I am, for agreeing to this in the first place."

* * *

As we pull out of the parking garage and hit the highway, heading south on Lake Shore Drive and cruising along Lake Michigan, Sophie McIntyre sits quietly in the front passenger seat. She's holding the running shoes in her lap, and I see there's a pair of gym socks stuffed in one of them. Her earlier outburst seems to have sapped her energy. Now she seems almost numb.

She's trying so hard to put up a good front—to look strong instead of scared shitless, but she's not fooling me. Her hands are shaking, and she keeps glancing at the sideview mirror at the traffic behind us, as if she's looking to see if we're being tailed.

Don't worry, baby. That's my job.

I don't blame her for being scared. She witnessed a horrific, cold-blooded murder just hours ago. She's lucky she wasn't killed herself. If the security guard hadn't shown up when he did, and scared Mikey off, Sophie would be dead. I'm not sure that has sunk in yet, but it will.

I have to admit, Sophie McIntyre is one helluva woman. At the moment, despite the fact that she's shaking in her seat, she's alternately glaring at me and watching the traffic around us. Her cheeks are flushed from the adrenaline, and she's on edge. She's no simpering wallflower, that's for sure. And I find that hot as hell.

I have to admit I enjoyed carrying her off like a caveman. I got away with it until we reached the elevator, when she made me set her down.

But until that moment, I got a feel for the woman in my arms. She's a big girl, damn tall for a woman, with supple limbs and amazing curves. Man, those thighs were made to cradle a big man like me.

Get a grip, asshole. She's a client.

I steal another glance in her direction and catch her texting, her fingers flying on the keypad.

Damn it.

I hold out my hand. "Let me see that."

"See what?"

"Your phone."

"Why?"

"Because I said so." I snatch it out of her hands and toss it out my window into oncoming traffic.

"What the hell!" she screeches, nearly shattering my eardrums. "Why did you do that?"

"To prevent you from doing something stupid. What else do you have on you?"

"What do you mean? Nothing—just these clothes." She grimaces as she looks down at herself. "These are my brother's workout clothes. Mine were ruined in the accident."

"It wasn't an *accident*, Sophie. It was an assassination. You don't have anything else on you? Just the clothes?"

"Nothing." She crosses her arms over her chest as if she's just now realized she's not wearing a bra. She glances out her window. "Where are we going?"

"Out of town."

"I know that. I asked *where*."

"It doesn't matter where. We're disappearing. The fewer who know our plans, the better."

"For how long?"

I shrug. "As long as it takes to put Mikey Alessio on the stand. A week, a month, six months. There's no telling. Justice moves at its own pace."

Jesus, I hope this isn't going to drag on that long.

Her tone changes quickly, softening, as she tries to appease me. "Look. Dominic, right? I really need to stop at my apartment. There are things I need."

"Like what?"

"Personal things."

"Things that you can't live without? Like life-saving medication?"

"No, nothing like that. Just… things."

"Then, no. Sorry. We'll pick up what you need on the way."

Fuming, she sits back in her seat. "You're an asshole, you know that?"

I shoot her a glance. "I'm the asshole who's going to keep you alive."

She looks away again, out the damn window, and sulks.

It's all I can do not to laugh. Even when she's pissing me off, it's entertaining.

I have a feeling this might be fun after all.

* * *

About two hours later, somewhere in Indiana, Sophie finally falls asleep, her head lulled back against the headrest. I know this because I've been aware of every little movement she's made since we left—every little sound, every single aggrieved sigh and huff of annoyance.

Not surprisingly, she's pissed.

I don't blame her. Her entire life has been upended without warning. Of course she's angry and resentful. But reality is going to sink in soon, once the shock wears off, and she'll realize how much danger she's in.

I know I'm being hard on her, but it's for her own good. She has no idea what she's up against. No idea how ruthless Franco Alessio can be, especially where his boy Mikey is concerned. Sophie's only chance of surviving this is if we hunker down someplace where the Alessio organization can't find her.

And I have just the place.

With a cry, Sophie wakes with a start, shooting upright in her seat and grabbing the door handle. She's breathing like she just ran a marathon.

"You're okay," I tell her, as I reach over and pat her thigh. "Relax." I shoot her a quick glance, not surprised to see her eyes wide with fright.

She looks around as if trying to orient herself. "Where are we?"

"Indiana."

Gradually, she leans back in her seat and relaxes.

"Bad dream?" I ask her.

She nods, but doesn't say anything.

We drive on through the night, heading farther south. I stop in Kentucky at an out-of-the-way exit with little more than a gas station and a mom-and-pop fast food joint.

I wouldn't mind going inside to take a piss and buy some snacks and drinks, but she's asleep and I don't want to wake her. She's exhausted, and I'm sure as hell not leaving her alone out here and unprotected. She may think I'm an asshole—that's fine, I don't care what she thinks of me—but I'm not about to let her get hurt.

After pumping the gas, I climb back into the Bronco and shut the driver's door as quietly as I can, so as not to wake her. But when I start the engine, she stirs, straightening in her seat with a groan.

She cocks her head, her hand going to her neck, and peers

out the window at a dark parking lot. "Where are we?"

"Gas station in Kentucky."

She sighs as she meets my gaze. "Kentucky? I need to pee. Badly."

With a sigh, I pull into one of the parking spots in front of the convenience store and shut off the engine, pocketing the keys. "All right. Let's go in. We can pick up some food and drinks while we're at it."

I'm out of the vehicle and at her door before she even has her seatbelt unfastened. I open her door for her, but she hesitates as she scans the dark lot.

"It's okay," I tell her, offering her a hand. "There's no one here but us. I made sure of it."

When she takes my hand, I can feel her shaking.

Reality's starting to sink in.

"I'm not going to let anything happen to you, Sophie."

She looks at me, her expression pained as she whispers, "I feel like there's a target on my back."

"There is." I step closer. "But I won't let anyone hurt you."

Her gaze locks on mine, as if she's trying to read my thoughts. Finally, she hops out of the vehicle.

We walk across the lot and inside the gas station shop. She stays close as we head for the only bathroom. I nudge the door open, and we both peer inside to make sure it's clear. It's a single occupant facility with both a toilet and a urinal. The floor is littered with wadded up paper towels, and there are a couple of puddles that look questionable.

It's not the cleanest, but at least it's single occupant, and there's no other way in or out other than this door.

I motion for her to go in. "I'll be right here, guarding the door."

She hesitates for a minute, then slips into the room and closes the door behind her, locking it.

I lean against the door, like a sentry on guard, canvassing the store from my location. Besides us, there are only two individuals in the place, both employees. A young male clerk stands behind the counter reading a comic book, while a middle-aged woman mops the floor in aisle two.

It's a typical little convenience store. The shelves are filled with chips, nuts, microwavable food, candy, pop, beer, batteries, maps, over-the-counter medicines. And there's hot food available—burgers, hotdogs, and pizza. And of course, there's coffee, thank god.

My stomach growls. I need food, and I need caffeine to keep me alert until we reach our destination. We still have a good six-hour drive ahead of us.

I hear the toilet flush, followed by the sound of running water. A moment later, the bathroom door opens, and Sophie's standing there looking no more relaxed than she did before she went in. As I step into the room, she steps back.

I'm six-eight, and the top of her head comes up to my chin—that's got to put her at a full six feet tall. I'm itching to brush my hand over her lustrous brown hair, which is a tangled mess thanks to her nap in the SUV.

Her blue eyes look almost bruised from exhaustion and worry. "Would you mind if I wait in here with you?" She turns to face the corner, offering me some privacy.

I chuckle as I walk over to the urinal and lower my zipper. "I don't mind."

I don't blame her for being cautious. If the mafia had a target painted on me, I'd be cautious, too.

3

Sophie

I feel terribly self-conscious staring at the dingy gray bathroom walls as Dominic takes care of business. I try to ignore the sound of him urinating. Then I hear his zipper go back up—thank god.

This is all so surreal. I'm in a gas station restroom in the middle of nowhere while a man I hardly know is taking a leak not ten feet away from me.

I try hard not to pay attention to what he's doing. Finally, he's washing his hands.

Then, he's at my side, unlocking the door. "Grab what you

need," he says as he opens the door and scans the shop. "Food, drink, candy, chips, whatever. Just make it quick. We need to get back on the road."

As we walk out of the restroom, the woman mopping the floors gives us the evil eye. She scowls, like she's assuming we were doing something illicit in the bathroom.

As if.

I do my best to ignore her and grab the items I need—a toothbrush, toothpaste, aspirin, chewing gum, mints, a hairbrush, and a package of scrunchy hair ties. I grab a jumbo box of tampons because I'm due to start in about a week or so and need to be prepared.

And then it hits me.

My birth control pills!

They're in my purse, which is back in Chicago.

How in the hell could I have forgotten them? I've already missed one pill this evening, and now I'm about to miss a whole bunch of them, which means my protection is screwed. Of course, I won't be having sex anytime soon, so I guess it's not the end of the world. I'll just have to restart a new pack as soon as I get back home.

As I approach the hot food area, Dominic asks me what I want, probably because he sees my hands are full.

"Coffee with creamer and sugar," I say. "And a cheeseburger, please. I'm starving."

He pours two large coffees, his black and mine the way I requested, *five* cheeseburgers, and a hot dog. He also picks up a few cans of energy drinks, a six-pack of beer, and four jumbo-size chocolate bars.

I eye the loot as he sets it down on the sales counter. "Hungry?"

He cocks an eyebrow at me. "Lady, you have no idea."

I set my personal items as discreetly as possible next to the food. "I don't have any money with me," I whisper. "No purse, remember?"

"That's okay. I'll take care of it." He pulls his wallet out of his back pocket and pays with cash.

We carry our goods out to his vehicle and climb back in. I sip my coffee, which is burning hot, and eat my lukewarm cheeseburger. I'm so hungry, even this dried-out burger tastes good.

I watch him wolf down the hot dog and three cheeseburgers. Before he unwraps the fourth one, he offers it to me.

"No thanks," I say. That man sure can pack away a lot of food. "I'm good."

"Suit yourself." He eats the last burger in four big bites, and then he guzzles an energy drink.

I'm sure it takes a lot of calories to maintain his body mass. He's a mountain of a man—all muscle, with bulging biceps and triceps. I doubt he has an ounce of flab anywhere on him. I wouldn't mind finding out, though.

"Where do you put all that food?" I ask him as he balls up the wrapper from the last burger and tosses it into an empty bag.

He thumps his rock-hard abdomen. "Right here," he says, with a surprising hint of a southern drawl. Then he starts the engine.

I watch him scan the parking lot before we take off. "Where are we going now?"

He pulls out onto a gravel road. "I have a cabin in the mountains. You'll be safe there."

"Mountains? *What* mountains?" As we're heading south, the only mountains I can think of are The Smoky Mountains. "We're going to Tennessee?"

"I guess you'll find out when we get there, won't you?" And then he winks at me.

I go back to staring out the passenger window, but it's too dark to see anything. The landscape is just a shadowy blur. At least we're the only ones on the road this late at night. It doesn't seem likely that anyone's following us.

* * *

Refreshed by my earlier nap, some food, and hot coffee, I'm too wired to fall back to sleep. I almost wish I could sleep, because being awake means being very much aware of the big man seated beside me. I notice his every movement, from the way his hands grip the steering wheel to how he occasionally shifts in his seat in an attempt to stretch his back and legs.

Dominic's not a complete stranger to me. I know he's done work in the past for my brother Shane, but other than that, I really don't know much about him.

"I'm sorry my brother dragged you into this," I finally say.

"I'm sure there are a million other things you'd rather be doing right now."

He shrugs. "Shane's a good friend. I don't mind."

"Have you done much work for him?"

"He calls me from time to time."

What he's not saying is that my brother calls him in for the dirty jobs.

I finish my coffee and put the empty cup in our makeshift trash bag. "The man who murdered Kent—Mikey Alessio—he's with the mob?"

Dominic scoffs. "He's *heir* to the throne. He's Franco Alessio's son."

I can almost feel the blood drain from my face. "And if I testify against him, he'll spend the rest of his life in jail."

"Most likely."

"They're going to try to stop me from testifying, aren't they? The mob, I mean."

"Yes."

And how they'll attempt to do that is rather obvious. "They're going to try to kill me."

He tosses me a dark look, his expression illuminated by the faint glow coming from the dashboard. "They can try all they want, Sophie, but I won't let them succeed."

The strength of conviction in his tone sends a shiver down my spine. I almost believe him capable of anything.

* * *

We drive south for hours, not following the main interstate but instead taking small country roads that seem to lead nowhere. The farther south we go, the more rural the landscape becomes. We pass farm after farm, large open tracts of land as far as the eye can see. Dominic's not using GPS. He seems to know this roundabout route by heart.

Despite all the uncertainty, there's something about him that puts me at ease. He's just so damn *confident*.

Even so, I'm still annoyed that he destroyed my phone. My phone is my lifeline—to my family, my friends, my clients. I have several decorating jobs underway right now.

"My clients are going to wonder why I dropped off the face of the Earth," I say. "I have a reputation to uphold, you know. I can't just disappear without an explanation."

"Make a list, and I'll get the info to your brother. He'll inform them that you're taking an unexpected and unavoidable sabbatical."

"Does Shane know where we're going?"

He shakes his head. "No one knows about this place. We'll be completely off-grid. No one will be able to trace your whereabouts."

"Not even my family?"

He shakes his head. "No."

"That seems a little extreme."

"Not as extreme as burying your body."

"Good point."

Eventually, the sun begins to rise, chasing away the darkness. We stop for gas again and take a potty break. Just like last time, there's only one bathroom. Dominic stands guard outside while I use it, and then I wait inside the room while takes his turn. We grab more coffee and some hot breakfast sandwiches. Dominic eats four of them.

The terrain changes gradually from rolling farmland to hills and valleys, and finally to the foothills of The Smoky Mountains. We left Indiana long ago, passed through Kentucky, and now we're deep into Tennessee. We're a long way from Chicago.

Around nine o'clock in the morning, we reach a small town tucked in the Smoky Mountains—Millerton, Tennessee, population nine hundred and four. It's a small berg that time pretty much forgot. The tiny, old-fashioned downtown has about three blocks of shops.

I'm surprised when Dominic parks in front of a thrift shop.

"Time to go shopping," he says as he shuts off the engine and pockets the keys.

I stare out the window at the storefront. "Here?"

"Yes, here. Don't be such a snob." He gets out of the vehicle and walks around to my side, opening my door and motioning for me to jump down. "I'm sorry it's not Macy's or Saks Fifth Avenue, but you need proper clothes, boots, and a jacket."

"But I can't get clothes here."

He raises an eyebrow. "Why not? Do you have a problem with secondhand clothes?"

I roll my eyes at him. "Of course not! I come from a family of seven kids. We *all* wore hand-me-downs. It's not that. In case you haven't noticed, I'm six feet tall. I can't wear most regular women's sizes. And I doubt they have a women's tall or plus-size department."

He chuckles. "Don't worry, we'll find you something. I promise."

When Dominic opens the front door for me, a bell rings overhead announcing our arrival. The shop is practically empty, except for a middle-aged woman standing behind the sales counter folding a pile of brightly-colored towels.

She gives us a fleeting smile. "Mornin' folks." Her southern twang is strong.

Dominic returns the nod. "Mornin', ma'am."

"Anything specific you're lookin' for?" she asks.

"No, ma'am. We're just looking around," he says.

As she goes back to folding towels, Dominic steers me to the men's section. "Find a few pairs of jeans that fit, some t-shirts, and a couple of long-sleeve shirts. Oh, and grab a jacket. It gets chilly up in the mountains at night."

He stares down at my feet. "You look like you'd wear a men's size ten, or ten-and-a-half boot. I'll see if I can find some."

As he turns away, I grab his arm. "But these are *men's* clothes," I say, keeping my voice down.

"You said it yourself, you're too tall for most women's clothes. At least these will fit."

"I'm not wearing men's clothing!" I hiss.

"Hey, beggars can't be choosers. You either find something here or keep wearing your brother's sweatpants for the foreseeable future." He takes a few steps away before pausing to look back. "You have thirty minutes, Sophie. Get *everything* you need in that time. Underwear, bras, socks, pajamas—everything."

"Are you kidding me? You expect me to wear *used* underwear?" I look around for an underwear department. "Is that even a thing?"

He gives me a smug smile. "You're not very observant, are you? On our way in, we passed a table piled high with brand-new panties, socks, and bras, all with the tags still on. I'm sure you can find something." And then his gaze drops to my breasts. "If they carry your size, that is."

With a devilish grin, he walks away.

Taking him at his word, I work fast. If he says we're leaving in thirty minutes, I'm sure he means exactly that. I grab a few sweatshirts, a handful of t-shirts, and several long-sleeve flannel shirts. Sure enough, there's a table near the entrance with new undergarments. Miracle of miracles, I find a bra in my size. I grab a handful of panties and a package of socks.

Then I head for the ladies' department and locate a rack of women's plus-size garments. I find some nightgowns that might work, a flannel pajama set, a couple of casual dresses, and a few tops. I even luck out and find a white terrycloth robe in my size—with the retail tags still on it. There's no time to try anything on, so I just have to hope they'll fit.

A moment later, Dominic reappears holding a pair of men's brown hiking boots. He bends down and removes the running shoe from my left foot.

"Step into the boot," he says.

I do as instructed, and he laces it up.

He crouches down and feels for my big toe. "How does that feel?"

I test it out, surprised that my toes aren't being squished, and take a few steps. "I think it'll do."

At home, I have a closet full of designer shoes in every style and color imaginable. Now, I'm considering buying a five-dollar pair of worn-out hiking boots.

While we're at the sales counter checking out, Dominic grabs a pair of women's dark sunglasses and adds them to the pile, along with a baseball cap.

"That'll be seventy-eight dollars," the woman says.

Dominic pays her in cash. Afterward, he carries our bags out to the SUV and tosses them into the backseat.

"Now where?" I ask him as we climb into the cab.

"Now we go home."

"Home? Whose home?"

"Mine. And now yours, for the foreseeable future."

4

Dominic

My pulse quickens when we reach the turn-off to my road. It's the only way in and out of my mountain homestead, and it's wired to the hilt. Motion detectors, video cameras, two-way communication—every bit of it hidden from sight. We're talking top-of-the-line surveillance, courtesy of my electronics buddy, Owen Ramsey. And it's entirely off-grid, powered by solar, wind, and propane. There are no electrical lines running up this mountain, no phone lines.

My road.

My mountain.

Sophie will be safe here, not just from coyotes, black bears, and bobcats, but from Chicago hitmen. No one ever comes up here except for me and Owen. I called him in the night while Sophie was sleeping and gave him the rundown. I'm sure he's got the cabin fully stocked by now.

We pass the hand-made wooden sign that says:

**PRIVATE PROPERTY.
KEEP OUT OR DIE.**

The gravel road meanders uphill, threading its way through the dense forest. The Bronco has four-wheel drive; otherwise we wouldn't make it up the steep, rutted incline. The road is barely wide enough for us to pass. It's a rough, jolting drive, and Sophie's white-knuckling her door handle with one hand and bracing herself on the glovebox with the other.

"Are you sure this is a good idea?" she says, her voice strained as the vehicle shudders.

Since I'm pretty sure it was a rhetorical question, I don't bother answering.

It's a good twenty-minute drive uphill before the road finally evens out and widens, just before leading into a clearing in front of a rustic, one-and-a-half story wood cabin. There are lights on inside, and the front door is open. Just seeing the place settles me. I've always been happy here. It feels more like home to me than Chicago ever has.

When I park the Bronco, Sophie unbuckles her seatbelt as she surveys the cabin and the yard. "This place is yours?"

"Yep. Home sweet home. I built it myself. Well, with the help of a friend."

We both hop out, and I grab our stuff from the backseat—her thrift shop purchases and the bug-out bag I keep in my vehicle for just situations like this.

"Let me go in first," I say, moving to block her path. "Stay behind me."

I step up onto the porch and call out, "Owen!"

A tattooed, grizzled man with shaggy hair and an even shaggier beard appears at the screen door, a semi-automatic rifle cradled in his arms. "It's about time you got here," he says in a gruff voice.

I'll bet he hasn't spoken to another human since I was here last, about six months ago.

I smile and say, "It's good to see you, too." I step aside. "Come on in, Sophie."

Since my arms are full, Owen opens the screen door for the

two of us. His gaze migrates to Sophie, and he gives her a quick once-over.

I follow Sophie inside. "It's not the Ritz-Carlton," I tell her as she looks around. "There's no room service, but it's clean and comfortable."

She surveys the large open space, looking less than thrilled.

Owen and I built this cabin about ten years ago, log by log, board by board. The downstairs is one big room, with a kitchen on one side and a sitting area on the other. The place is heated by a black potbelly wood stove and a stone hearth. There's a door that leads to a bathroom in the rear, and a small pantry off the kitchen. Up the wooden steps is a half-floor with two small bedrooms. It's barebones. But as I said, it's clean.

Owen already has a fire going in the hearth, mostly for effect I'd guess, as it's not that chilly tonight. It's mid-summer, so at least we're spared the biting cold of winter.

I nod toward the wooden steps that bisect the downstairs. "The bedrooms are upstairs. I'll carry your things up."

Sophie clears her throat and nods not-so-subtly to Owen. "Aren't you going to introduce us?"

"Oh, right. Owen, this is Sophie. Sophie, that's Owen."

Owen produces a rare smile as he gives her an appraising scan from head to toe. "Nice to meet you, ma'am."

Ma'am?

His southern drawl seems more pronounced than usual. He's from these parts, born and raised, while I'm a Yankee transplant. I followed Owen here after our stints in the Marines.

She nods. "Thanks. Same to you."

Then she turns to me. "I'd really love to freshen up a bit."

I nod past the staircase. "Bathroom is back there. You can't miss it."

When Sophie disappears into the bathroom with her bag of toiletries from the gas station, Owen whistles long and low. "What a looker."

My pulse kicks into overdrive. "She's off limits, pal, so don't even think about it."

Owen strokes his hideous beard. "I think I need a trim."

I laugh. "You do look a bit rough. Total isolation's not good for you, man."

He scoffs. "It suits me just fine." Then he waves a hand toward the kitchen. "Pantry is stocked. So is the fridge. There's plenty of wood stacked outside. The propane tanks are full. The batteries are full. The ammo stores are full. You're set for a good six-month siege."

"Thanks, but I certainly hope it won't come to that."

"So, what's her story?" he says.

"She witnessed a mob hit in Chicago. Mikey Alessio offed an assistant DA."

Owen looks impressed. "Damn."

"Yeah. And Franco has put out a hit on her."

"As long as you weren't followed here and she can't be tracked, you'll be fine," he says. "The mountain is wired, as always. A stray dog couldn't get up here without me knowing about it. You expectin' anyone to join you?"

"No. Anyone who comes up this mountain is likely a hostile and should be treated as such."

He nods. "Copy that."

I clap Owen on the back. "Thanks. I owe you."

He shrugs off my gesture. "Nah. It gave me something to do. I was getting tired of my own company. It'll be nice having neighbors for a while. I'll run patrols, keep an eye out for unwanted visitors."

Owen leaves then, closing the solid wood door behind him. I throw the deadbolt, lower the crossbar, and set the alarm. No one's getting in through this door.

A moment later, the bathroom door opens, and the light switches off. Sophie comes out of the bathroom looking tired, but smelling like mint toothpaste. Her hair is freshly brushed and pulled back into a ponytail. She looks stunning.

My breath catches in my chest.

I pick up our bags. "I'll carry your stuff up to your room. You should try to get some sleep."

She nods. "I'm tired. I could use a nap."

With that, she heads up the stairs, pausing on the landing at the top.

"Your room is to the left," I tell her, following her up the stairs. "The other one's mine."

Her bedroom door is already open, and I can tell Owen must have opened the windows for a while to freshen up the room. I follow her in. There's a double bed, one nightstand with a lamp, and a small closet. I notice the bed looks freshly made.

"Sorry it's not what you're used to," I say as she studies the room.

She shrugs, but doesn't say anything. She's probably too tired to care.

I set her bags on the bed. "Get some sleep, Sophie. You can deal with this stuff after you've rested. If you need anything, just holler. I'll hear you."

She turns to me, looking up to meet my gaze. There are soft shadows beneath her expressive eyes. "Thanks."

"No problem." I turn to leave her to it but stop once more. "Sophie?"

"Yes?"

"Don't leave this cabin without me for any reason."

"Okay."

"I mean it. Owen's likely to shoot you if you do."

Her eyes widen. "Are you serious?"

"Yeah. He can be trigger happy sometimes, and he's not used to folks being up here. He's likely to shoot first and ask questions later. Got it?"

I can tell she's still not sure if I'm pulling her leg. I'm not.

But she nods anyway. "I'll keep that in mind."

And then, before I say something stupid, like *sleep well, beautiful,* I take my leave, closing her door behind me.

My job is to keep her alive, not be her friend or coddle her. She's a big girl. She can take care of herself.

* * *

After rechecking all the locks and bolts downstairs, I check the armory. There's a false panel in the back of the pantry that opens up to a veritable arsenal—handguns, shotguns, automatic rifles, knives, flash bangs, hand grenades, and lots and lots of ammo.

Owen wasn't kidding when he said it was well-stocked. The ex-Marine leaves nothing to chance.

Once I'm sure the downstairs is secured, I head to the bathroom to clean up. It feels surprisingly good to be back here, but maybe not under these circumstances. I like to spend my time here hunting and fishing, even sleeping rough outdoors, but that's not likely to happen on this trip. Not while I'm guarding her highness.

I know I'm probably not being fair to her. This has got to be a shock to her, and she hasn't complained all that much.

I need a few hours of sleep, too, so I head upstairs to my bedroom. I've got a California King in here to accommodate my height, but the rest of the room is as sparsely furnished as the other bedroom. I keep clothes and outdoor gear here, so I have everything I need.

I leave my bedroom window cracked open so I can hear any ambient noise outside the cabin, and I leave my door open in case Sophie needs something. I'll be sure to hear her.

And then, I'm out like a light.

5

Sophie

As tired as I am from a ten-hour road trip, I can't sleep. My mind is racing. Was it really only just last night that Kent Martinez was murdered right in front of me? I can't stop thinking about him—how unfair it all is! And I can't stop thinking about my family and my friend Amber. She must be worried out of her mind that I haven't been in touch with her since the shooting. I just hope Shane will let her know I'm all right.

After pacing until my legs ache, I end up sitting at the foot of the bed. It's not even noon yet, so it's too bright for me to sleep.

I've always been terrible at napping. I don't know how Dominic can fall asleep in the middle of the day.

The shooting keeps replaying in my mind, over and over, in full technicolor. One minute I was picking out an outfit to wear to dinner, and the next I was kneeling in a pool of blood with a dead man lying on the ground in front of me.

That poor man.

I close my eyes and press my palms to my face, attempting to take deep, measured breaths and calm my pulse.

Surely I could have stayed in Chicago. If Shane and the police were so worried about the mob, couldn't I have had police protection instead of going to this extreme? Instead of leaving my family and my home—everything I know and love? Now I'm stranded in the middle of god knows where with a virtual stranger. Not to mention his shaggy, gun-toting friend.

Feeling restless, I resume pacing the small bedroom. There are two small windows in the room, one overlooking the side yard, and another overlooking the rear of the cabin. The ground all around the cabin has been cleared and freshly mowed, and in the back there are two rows of huge solar panels, all facing in the same direction. Beneath a rough, lean-to are neat stacks of firewood.

Other than that, it's all forest as far as the eye can see.

At least there's electricity and running water. For that, I'm grateful. I hope I can have a hot shower later today.

Finally, when my energy runs out, I lie down on the bed. The mattress is old, but comfortable. The bedding smells like fresh air and sunshine, as if it just came off a clothesline. If I had my phone, I'd read or watch something on Netflix, but I don't even have that, thanks to Dominic.

Great.

* * *

As I kneel in thick, warm blood, my stomach heaves. My date's eyes are frozen wide in shock, his face screwed up in a grimace of pain. When I look into the car in front of us, a scarred man stares back at me as if he's memorizing my face—just like I'm memorizing his. Suddenly, he opens his door and gets out, stalking right toward me, a black handgun in his grasp. He points the gun at me, just inches from my forehead. "You're dead, too, bitch!" he growls as he pulls the trigger.

Screaming, I shoot up in bed. The room is dark, and I don't know where I am. Panic sets in, my pulse racing. My chest hurts as I struggle to breathe.

A moment later, my door crashes open, letting in light from the hallway as Dominic rushes in, a gun in his hand. "Are you okay? I heard you scream."

Everything comes rushing back. The shooting. Leaving Chicago. The mountains. I'm in Tennessee with Dominic. I nod. "I'm fine. I had a nightmare."

He relaxes visibly. "That's not surprising, given what you've been through. Dinner's ready. Why don't you come downstairs and eat?"

At the mention of food, my stomach rumbles. I reach down for my borrowed sneakers and put them on. The instant I step out onto the upstairs landing, I get a whiff of something delicious.

Dominic cooks?

I don't know what he made, but I want some.

Once I'm downstairs, I make a pit stop in the bathroom to pee and brush my teeth and hair.

I walk into the kitchen just as he's placing two ribeye steaks on plates, and right next to each steak is a huge baked potato.

"There's butter and sour cream on the table," he says, nodding to a small wooden table for two. "Have a seat."

He sets a plate in front of me. My steak looks perfectly seared, medium rare.

"You cooked this?" I ask him.

He nods. "Outside on the grill. Everything tastes better when it's grilled."

I chuckle, knowing my brothers would agree with that statement.

I butter my potato and add a scoop of sour cream, then sprinkle salt and pepper over it.

He sets a mug of black coffee in front of me. "Cream and sugar, right?"

"Yes, please. I can get it."

He shrugs off my offer and disappears through a door, returning a moment later with a brand-new carton of French vanilla powdered creamer and a porcelain sugar bowl.

He sets the creamer and sugar in front of me, and I make my coffee. Then I take a bite of my potato because I'm starving and can't wait another second. The potato melts in my mouth, warm and buttery, and my taste buds sing for joy. "This is fantastic." I cut into the steak and take a bite, surprised to find it tender and full of flavor. "You're a good cook."

He shrugs. "My grandma didn't want me to starve."

"Your grandma?" I ask, hoping to find out more about him. "She taught you to cook?"

He sits across the table from me and cuts into his steak. "Yeah. My mom died when I was ten, and my grandparents raised me."

"I'm so sorry about your mom. Are your grandparents still alive?"

With a frown, he shakes his head. "They both passed a few years back."

As we eat in silence, I occasionally sneak a peek at him when he isn't looking. He's a very striking man, so incredibly... big. All over. Everything about him is oversized, from his hands to his powerful arms, his chest and broad shoulders. His legs are like tree trunks. He's also rather good-looking, with his brown hair trimmed short on the sides, a bit longer on the top, thick and wavy. His strong jaw is covered by a trim beard.

For a self-indulgent moment, I imagine threading my fingers through those thick, brown waves and tugging hard.

He's wearing a t-shirt, and I can see part of a tattoo peeking out beneath the sleeve. What I find most alluring are the thick tendons and veins running the length of his arms and onto the backs of his hands. He's got very sexy hands.

"The pantry is stocked with canned goods," he says after swallowing a bite of his steak. "And the fridge and freezer are stocked with chicken and beef. Owen keeps chickens down at his place, so we'll have plenty of fresh eggs."

"Your friend, Owen—where do you know him from?"

"US Marines Corp. We served two tours together in Afghanistan."

"And he lives close by?"

Dominic nods. "His cabin is halfway down the mountain."

"I don't remember seeing any other cabins on our drive up the lane."

"You wouldn't be able to see it. It's way back in the woods. I'll show you tomorrow, in case you ever need to find it on your own."

I take another bite of my potato and mull over his words. "Why would I need to find it?"

He turns his head to meet my gaze. "In case something happens to me."

I don't know how to respond to that, so I don't say anything. *What could possibly happen to him?*

He finishes eating first and carries his dishes to the sink.

"I'll do the dishes," I offer. "You cooked dinner. The least I can do is wash up."

But he just shrugs and carries on. I have a feeling he's so used to being self-sufficient and doing everything on his own that it doesn't occur to him to ask for help.

As soon as I finish eating, he collects my plate, silverware, and coffee mug and sets them in the sink of hot, soapy water.

I grab a hand towel and start drying the wet dishes in the dish rack. "I'm not completely helpless, you know."

Standing beside him is a novel experience for me. I'm not used to someone towering over me. Beside him, I almost feel small. It's a nice feeling.

He grins. "Good to know. I wasn't quite sure."

It takes me a second to realize that his words are in response to me telling him I'm not helpless. Laughing, I bump my shoulder into his firm, unyielding bicep. *Ouch.* "Thanks a lot."

"Well, you're a city girl, and clearly a high-maintenance one at that."

I smile at his response. It wasn't meant to be mean-spirited. I just think he doesn't know what to make of me.

As he washes each item, he hands it to me to dry. Then, he shows me where everything goes.

"Time for a tour," he says as he dries his hands on a towel.

We start with the pantry, which is just off the kitchen. There's an ancient washer and dryer set in there that are probably older than I am. Wooden shelves line the wall, filled with every type of dry good and nonperishable staple imaginable—flour, sugar, cans of meat and beans and fish. Canned vegetables galore.

"The armory is in here," he says, nodding toward the back wall. There's a single hook nailed into the wall, and when he pulls on it, a section of the wall swings forward, like a secret door. He steps inside and pulls a chain hanging overhead, turning on a bare light bulb.

I follow him in, stunned at the array of weapons and ammunition on display. "Good god," I say. "Are those hand grenades?" I point to a box of small, gray oblong objects with pins sticking out of them.

"Yes, and flashbangs." He points at another box. "Do you know how to shoot?"

"Yes. My brothers made sure my sisters and I learned how to shoot."

He gives me an amused look. "I'll test you on that later."

We leave the armory, switching off the light and closing the door behind us. If I didn't know better, I'd never guess that secret back room existed.

"I don't think anyone followed us from Chicago," he says, "and they can't trace us here, so we should be all right. But if not, and if something happens to me, you need to be able to defend yourself."

He says that last little bit ominously, as if he thinks something might happen to him.

"You're serious, aren't you?" I say.

He gives me a droll look. "I'm always serious."

I suspect he's right about that.

* * *

After the tour of the cabin—which didn't take long as there

wasn't much else to see—Dominic goes outside and returns a few minutes later with an armful of logs, which he stacks beside the hearth. He makes several more trips, accumulating an impressive supply of wood. All I can think is that he's probably bringing in hordes of spiders.

As the sun sets outside, the air grows distinctly chillier.

Dominic builds a fire in the hearth, and then another one in the wood-burning stove. I sit on a comfortable old sofa and watch him work, his movements quick and efficient. Obviously, he's done this before.

"I take it there's no central heating?" I ask.

"No. Just this wood stove and the hearth. This high up, once the sun goes down, the temperature does too, even in summer."

Once he's got a fire going, he lights two oil lamps. The resulting light is warm and adds to the rustic ambience. It's really quite charming. If I weren't on the run for my life, I might actually enjoy this cozy little cabin.

I pull a fleece blanket off the back of the sofa and curl up with it. "If only I had something to read, this would be perfect," I muse. "Oh, that's right, I had about a *thousand* books on my phone—not to mention movies, music, and TV shows—but someone tossed it out the window of a moving vehicle."

He rises from the stove, hands on his hips as he watches the flames blaze behind the protective screen. "I'm sorry about your phone."

"I don't see how having my phone would have hurt anything."

He tosses me a glance that clearly shows he disagrees. "You

want a beer?" he offers, heading for the kitchen.

"Is that my only choice?"

"Yeah, sorry. I'm fresh out of caviar and champagne. There's water, and I think there are some soft drinks in the pantry."

"Beer's fine." Actually, I'm not a big fan of the stuff—I'd much rather have a glass of red wine—but I don't want him thinking I'm a sissy. He already thinks I'm high-maintenance.

He pops the caps off two chilled bottles and carries them to the living room, handing one to me. He sits in a wooden rocking chair opposite the sofa and takes a long pull on his beer. Then he sighs as he runs his fingers through his hair.

I find myself watching him, distracted.

"Are you tired?" I ask him. "It's been a crazy twenty-four hours."

"No. I'm just glad to be back here. The city drives me nuts."

"Then why do you live there? Couldn't you live here?"

He shrugs. "I have a few aunts and uncles in the city, and some cousins. We're not close, but they're family. Family is everything."

"I can certainly toast to that." I lift my bottle in his direction. "To family."

He nods as well, then takes another long pull on his beer. "I'll see about getting you some books. And there's a satellite radio in the pantry, so you can listen to music."

I perk up at that. "Do you have a phone? A satellite phone?" I doubt there's any cell signal out this far, but I bet a satellite phone would work. "I want to call my family and my friend

Amber. They must be worried to death."

He shakes his head. "No phone calls. It's not safe."

"But you do have a satellite phone, right? In case of emergencies?"

He nods. "I do, but you can forget about it. No phone calls, Sophie. I mean it."

"How do you get in touch with Owen?"

He nods to the kitchen counter, where I spot a walkie-talkie seated in a charging cradle. "Short-wave radio."

Finished with his beer, he gets up from the rocking chair and heads to the kitchen to toss his empty and grab another from the fridge. On his way back, he resets the security system.

"Do you know how to turn off the oil lamps?" he says.

"Yes."

"Good. Then turn them off when you turn in. I'm going to bed now."

"What about the wood stove?"

"It's fine. I'll get up in the night to add some more wood. It should keep us comfortable in the night. There are extra blankets in your bedroom closet if you get cold."

And then he's gone, stomping up the wooden steps in his chunky work boots, leaving me alone downstairs.

Because of my nap, I'm not sleepy. I don't think it's even that late yet, but of course I wouldn't know the time as I don't have my phone, and I don't see any clocks.

After I toss my empty beer bottle, I search the downstairs for the satellite phone—just in case of an emergency—but I don't find it. I do, however, find a stash of old paperback books in a box on the top shelf in the closet. They're all westerns, but at this point, I'm desperate and I'll take anything.

I curl up on the sofa with my blanket and watch the flames flickering wildly through the glass door on the wood stove. I crack open a worn copy of *Ride the River* by Louis L'Amour and start reading.

At least it's a romance of sorts.

But I find it difficult to keep my mind on the book because my thoughts keep straying to the man upstairs. I've never known anyone like him. He's nothing like the men I've dated, and he's certainly not my type. And yet, I can't seem to stop thinking about him.

As I lean my head back and close my eyes, I start imagining what those hands would feel like on my body.

6

Dominic

I'm not afraid to go up against a black bear with nothing more than a hunting knife in my hand. I'm not afraid of standing my ground against organized crime in Chicago. I'm not even afraid of terrorists with sniper rifles. But I am scared to death of that woman downstairs.

Or rather, I'm scared of my body's reaction when I'm around her.

If I could teach her to shoot, hunt, and fish, she'd be the most amazing woman on god's green earth.

She's a city girl, though, through and through. That much

is obvious. I'd heard things before about Shane's eldest sister. Some highfalutin' female who remodels million-dollar penthouses for rich folk in Chicago. She dates assistant DAs, so I'm sure she has no use for a yahoo like me.

My ma would have loved her. Ma was a big woman, too—six feet tall. Of course, my dad is even taller, about my height.

Like a coward, I high-tailed it upstairs to hide out in my bedroom for the rest of the evening. I was afraid if I stayed downstairs I'd end up staring at her all evening, and probably end up making her uncomfortable. Or worse yet, she might get ideas about having a bit of fun with the hired help. And that's not acceptable. She's a client, and that means *handsoff*.

Shane McIntyre entrusted me with his sister's safety. It's my job to keep her safe—even from her own impetuous self—not chase after her like a buck in rutting season.

But god I want to—chase after her, I mean. She's like an Amazon goddess—statuesque, with meat on her bones and curves that just won't quit. Those breasts of hers would more than fill my big hands. And those *hips*! I want to clutch them tightly as I pin her beneath me and drive into—*fuck*!

This is Shane's sister! She's off limits. Even if she wanted me to, I can't make a move on her. He'd kill me. He's trusting me with her, and that means something.

So now I'm up here in my room, hiding out like a fucking coward because I didn't think I could get through the evening without a hard-on straining to bust out of my jeans.

I need to stay focused on our current predicament. Yes,

there's a satellite phone—she'll never find it—and Shane has the number. When it's time for us to return to Chicago, he'll call me and leave a message with instructions. And then, I'll deliver her to Chicago, safe and sound.

But until that day arrives, she's under my protection, and I take that responsibility seriously. I will protect her—even from myself.

* * *

I'm lying on my bed, still wide awake, when I hear her come up the stairs. I've got my fist wrapped around my cock, attempting to distract myself. I throw the sheet and blanket over me in case she gets the bright idea to open my bedroom door.

But she doesn't. She disappears into the other bedroom and closes her door. I listen to the sounds of her settling in for the night—pulling her blankets back, taking off her shoes and her clothes, and finally climbing into bed.

I wonder what she's wearing to bed. Is it one of the t-shirts she bought at the thrift shop? Or one of the nightgowns? Or better yet, nothing at all? I don't know her sleeping habits, although I sure as hell would like to.

I sleep in the buff. Maybe she does too. Or maybe I could convince her to sleep naked, because then it would be so easy for me to press up against her in the night and slip inside her from behind. Just the idea of sinking into the lush, sweet body—

Fuck.

I hear her bed creaking as she gets comfortable. Then, nothing but silence.

I squeeze my cock, the full length of it turgid and thick. After grabbing some lotion from the nightstand drawer, I stroke myself from root to tip and back again. My thumb runs over the head, skimming that round knob and collecting the bit of precum seeping out.

Wishful thinking, buddy.

I work myself thoroughly, wishing like hell it was her hand on me and not mine. Or better yet, her mouth. Or her pussy.

Just the thought of sliding into her lush wetness—

Damn it.

I grit my teeth as I come, catching my jizz in a tissue. And then I lie there for god knows how long, wondering what Sophie's wearing to bed. I wonder what her breasts look like. What color and size her nipples are. I wonder what her pussy looks like. Hair or bare?

Just the thought of finding out makes me hard again.

* * *

The next morning, I wake at sunrise, dress, and head downstairs to put on a pot of coffee. Thanks to a boatload of sexual frustration, I didn't get much sleep last night. I kept dreaming about going down on Sophie, licking and sucking on her until she was a wet, trembling mess.

The object of my lust seems to have slept just fine, because I didn't hear a peep from her room all night long.

I carry my second cup of coffee out onto the front porch and sit on the swing to drink it. The morning songbirds serenade me, as squirrels chase each other up and down the tree trunks before disappearing into the upper canopy of leaves.

Owen walks through the yard, a hunting rifle perched over his shoulder and one of his dogs at his heel. He gives me a nod, which I return, and then he melts back into the forest, silent as a wraith.

I have to wonder if it's a good idea for him to spend so much time alone out here in the woods. I know he prefers solitude, and I know he suffers from PTSD, as do many vets. Maybe we should ask him to join us for dinner one of these evenings. It might do him good to practice his conversational skills.

The screen door opens and closes with a bang as Sophie steps out onto the front porch, a cup of steaming hot coffee in her hand. She's wearing a pair of ripped jeans she picked up from the thrift shop and a long-sleeve t-shirt. The jeans cup her amazing ass like nobody's business. What I wouldn't give for the privilege of peeling them down her long, long legs.

"Good morning," she says in a sleepy voice that makes me want to take her right back upstairs to bed.

I shift my position to give my cock room. "Mornin'."

"Was that Owen I saw just now from the kitchen window?"

"Yeah. He's making his morning rounds."

Her brow furrows in concern. "Why?"

"It's all right. He's just patrolling. Security has been heightened under the circumstances."

"You mean because of me."

I shrug. The answer is yes, but there's no need to rub her nose in it.

She walks past me and takes a seat on the steps leading down to the ground, sipping her coffee as she gazes out over the yard.

"I'd like to run into town today, if you don't mind," she says casually. "I need to pick up a few things."

"I can have Owen make a trip into town. He can get you whatever you want."

She glances back at me beneath thick, dark lashes that shield the most remarkable blue eyes I've ever beheld, the color of soft denim. "I need things, Dominic."

"I told you, Owen—"

"I'm not about to ask a stranger to pick up *personal* items, if you know what I mean. Do I have to spell it out?"

"Didn't you buy *personal* items at the gas station? I seem to remember a box of tampons."

She shudders—literally shudders—at the reminder. "Yes. But I didn't get everything I need. Look, either you drive me into town or give me the keys to your Bronco and I'll drive myself."

Hell, this woman isn't going to make my life easy. "Fine. I'll drive you. After breakfast." I stand and head back inside. "And just to be perfectly clear, Sophie, you do *not* leave this cabin without me. You got that?"

Looking more than a little pleased with herself, she nods before taking a sip of her coffee. "Got it."

As I fire up the gas stove and set a skillet on the burner, I mull over the fact that she just played me. Smiling, I get out a package of bacon from the fridge and a carton of eggs and get to making breakfast. Before long, she joins me in the kitchen, sets the table for the two of us, and drops two slices of bread into the toaster.

"Did you sleep well last night?" I ask her, making small talk just so I can hear her voice again.

She hums as she butters the toast. "Yeah. I did get a little chilly in the night, though. I had to get up and grab another blanket."

I refrain from saying that if she slept in my bed, she'd have been plenty warm.

She finds a jar of strawberry preserves in the pantry. "Can I open this?"

I nod. "Sure. Help yourself to anything you find."

She gives me a cocky grin. "Including the satellite phone?"

"Anything but that."

And then we're both sitting down at the table to eat breakfast.

"After I eat," she says, "I'll take a quick shower, and then we can head into town."

"Sure." I smile.

Yep, she played me.

* * *

On the drive down the mountain, I'm seriously tempted to

blindfold Sophie. I know it's stupid, but I'd just feel better if she didn't know how to find her way back to civilization without me. It's not that I think she'd be stupid enough to run off on her own—without protection—but I made a promise to Shane. It's not one I take lightly.

By the time we make it down the mountain, I turn left onto a state road and head for Millerton. I park in front of the general store and toss some quarters in the meter.

"Where to first?" I ask Sophie as she climbs down from the Bronco.

She points to a storefront across the street. "The pharmacy."

"All right."

She pauses with her hand on the door. "Thanks to you, I have no money on me." She gives me a glare. "You're going to have to advance me some cash. I'll pay you back as soon as I can."

I pull my wallet out of my back pocket and hand her two twenties. "Is that enough?"

She snickers. "Hardly. But I guess it'll have to do for now."

Out of habit, I scan the street—both sides, up and down—looking for nondescript sedans with Illinois plates and dark, tinted windows. It sounds like a cliché, but it's accurate. It's what they'll be driving.

I see nothing amiss, so I follow Ms. McIntyre across the street and into the small pharmacy. Just inside the door, she picks up a red shopping basket and hooks it over her arm. Almost immediately, she disappears from sight—a woman on a mission—but it's not hard for me to keep track of her. She's so tall I can spot the top of her head easily over the shelves. Besides, the place isn't all that big.

I find her looking over a selection of razors and shaving cream. I keep back, out of sight—I'm not even sure she knows I'm within view—and watch her select an expensive, high-end razor and a pink can of shaving cream. She drops the items into her shopping basket.

Like the pervert I am, I mentally catalog all the places on her body that she might want to shave—her legs, obviously, and her armpits. But beyond that is pure speculation, and I have no business even going there.

She turns the corner and meanders down the hair care aisle, spending the next ten minutes debating between two different shampoos.

When she stops in front of a display of blow dryers and curling irons, I have to put my foot down.

I walk up behind her. "No hair dryers."

She jumps, one hand going to her chest. "Jesus, Dominic. You scared the shit out of me."

"Sorry, but no hair dryers. It'll put too much strain on the solar batteries."

She puts the hair dryer back on the shelf. "Fine. How about a flatiron at least?"

I shake my head. "Sorry."

With a huff, she walks off muttering something about her hair getting frizzy.

I follow her, of course. She picks up a few other things—a

bottle of bodywash and some colorful scrubby shower things, as well as a few other items in the female department. I try not to look too closely.

When she pauses in front of the condoms, looking them over, my heart rate shoots up.

Don't worry, baby. I've got condoms.

Eventually, she ends up in an aisle containing paperbacks and magazines. She grabs a few of each.

And then, on her way to the check-out, she picks up a giant bag of peanut M&Ms and a big bag of Skittles.

"Is that everything?" I ask her, as I join her at the sales counter.

"For now."

The total exceeds the forty bucks in cash I gave her, so I pull out my wallet and toss another twenty onto the counter. The cashier rings us up and lays the change on the counter. Before I can take it, Sophie grabs it and pockets it before sashaying out of the store without a backward glance.

Why the fuck does that turn me on so much?

"Anything else?" I ask her as we stow her bags in the back of the Bronco.

She nods. "I'd like to pick up a few things at the grocery store."

"All right. Lead the way."

We head to the small mom-and-pop grocery store and pick up a few items. She grabs two bottles of red wine, some fresh corn-on-the-cob, a pint of local strawberries, and a few other items.

"Anything else?" I ask her once I store the groceries in the Bronco.

She glances across the street at the diner, a hopeful look on her pretty face. "Are you hungry?"

Ah, that's my girl.

"Sure, I could eat," I say. Hell, I can always eat. It takes a lot of calories to maintain my weight.

We cross the street and walk inside the diner.

"Hi, y'all," says a pretty red-haired woman standing behind the counter. She's dressed in a gray uniform dress with a white apron over top. "Have a seat wherever you like. I'll be right with you."

There are several booths available at the front of the restaurant. Sophie heads for the closest one, but I reach out and steer her toward the last booth. It's more strategically positioned to give me the best view of the dining room. I take the far bench, so that I'm facing the rest of the room. Sophie slides into the bench opposite mine and picks up a menu.

I scan the restaurant. It's half-filled, with mostly retired couples and a few families with young kids. A guy wearing dirty overalls is seated at the counter, trying to pretend he's not checking Sophie out.

I guess I can't blame him.

Sophie looks up from her menu. "I think I'll get the turkey bacon melt and fries. What about you?"

I don't bother looking at the menu. Diner food is the same

everywhere. "Pot roast and mashed potatoes."

She nods. "Good choice. I thought about that, too, but the bacon won me over."

I grin as I contemplate the joys of spending time with a woman who appreciates bacon.

After taking one last, long look at Sophie, the guy at the counter tosses money next to his plate and heads for the men's room. He's clearly a local, and no threat to Sophie, but I don't like how he was looking at her.

After we place our orders with the red-haired waitress—Sandy, according to her nametag—Sophie slides out of the booth. "I need to visit the ladies' room."

I get up, too.

"Don't bother," she says. "The restrooms are right over there."

But, of course, I do bother.

"Suit yourself," she says, and then she makes her way across the room to the door marked *Ladies*. I can hear other female voices in there, so I wait outside for her rather than go in and make a scene.

I find a quiet spot next to a gumball machine and lean against the wall. A few minutes later, Sophie comes out of the ladies' room at the same time the guy from the counter comes out of the men's. Not noticing, she practically walks right into him.

"Whoa there, darlin'," the guy says, his hands going to her shoulders as he makes a big deal of steadying her. Then he slowly slides his hands down her arms.

"Get your hands off her," I say, stepping away from the wall.

The guy glances back at me, his eyes widening as he acts all innocent. I swear to god, I'm giving him two seconds to release her before I smash his face in.

Apparently, I'm telegraphing my mood, because he releases Sophie abruptly and steps back, his hands in the air.

"Calm down, buddy," he says, giving me a smug grin. "I meant no disrespect. Just didn't want the little lady to take a spill."

Sophie rolls her eyes at the *little* comment and marches back to our table. I wait for the asshat to exit the restaurant before I join her.

"I can take care of myself, you know," she says as she rips the paper wrapping off her straw and sticks it in her Coke. "You've met my brothers, right?"

I nod. "Some of them."

"They made sure their sisters knew how to defend themselves. I might not be as kickass as my sisters Lia or Hannah, but I've got size on my side. If he'd gotten out of hand, I would have racked him in the balls."

"Ouch." I wince just thinking about it. I'll bet she's got a wicked knee. "I'll keep that in mind."

Our food arrives soon after, and we dig in.

She takes one bite of her sandwich and moans in pleasure. "Oh my god, that's so good." And then she dunks a French fry in ketchup and pops it into her mouth, closing her eyes as she chews.

Damn. Watching her eat is almost as good as foreplay.

When we're nearly done eating, our waitress leaves the check with me and walks away.

Frowning, Sophie reaches across the table and grabs the check. "I hate not having any money, and no way to get some. Thanks to you, I don't have a single credit card on me." She gives me a death glare. "I can't even go to a bank and have someone wire me money because I don't have any freaking identification either."

"I'll loan you some cash."

Her eyes flash murderously. "Look, I appreciate what you're doing—I really do—but this is ridiculous. I'm not a prisoner. I need my own money. I hate not being able to pay my own way. I'm not going to rely on you, or any other man, to pay my way."

"You're not a prisoner, Sophie." Exasperated, I pull my wallet from my back pocket and flip it open. "How much do you want? Consider it an interest-free loan." I proceed to toss twenties on the table. One, two, three, four, five of them. "Come on, Soph, that's a hundred bucks. We're in the middle of nowhere, in case you haven't noticed. How much money do you need?"

"Don't call me *Soph*. My name is So-*phee*."

"All right, *Phee*," I say. "You never answered my question. How much do you need?"

Scowling, she swipes up the money I tossed onto the table and organizes the bills so they're all facing the same way—which I find adorable. Then she smooths out any creases, folds the cash in half, and tucks it into her back pocket. "It's a start."

She grabs the check and marches up to the counter. "I'll pay the check."

With a sigh, I get up to follow her. "You don't have to. I'll get it."

But she ignores me and hands the woman behind the counter the check and pays for it herself.

As we exit the restaurant, I laugh and say, "Okay, so you paid the check with the money *I* gave you. How in the hell is that any different than *me* paying the check?"

She grits her teeth. "It just is."

When we reach the Bronco, I unlock the front passenger door and open it. She climbs up into her seat as I walk around to the driver's side.

"I'm self-sufficient and independent," she says, jerking the seatbelt across her chest and snapping it in place. "I don't like men paying for me. It gives them *ideas*."

I toss her a glance as I start the engine. "Heaven forbid a man get *ideas*." I grin. "You're a real ballbuster, aren't you?"

"I'm sure you're way overdue to have yours busted."

I laugh as I reverse out of our parking spot. "I'm sure you're right."

Sophie doesn't say much on the drive back to the cabin. I hate that she's so frustrated over the loss of her phone and her credit cards, and I can't blame her. But she doesn't realize how easy it would be for her to unwittingly slip up and give away our location. She has no idea how ruthless Franco Alessio's boys are when it comes to hunting for information. If she called the wrong person or shared the wrong bit of information—even the slightest thing—it could mean her death.

And if pissing her off is the price I have to pay to keep her safe, then so be it.

7

Sophie

Once we're back at the cabin, I grab my bags and carry my things up to my room. I make sure I slam my door loud enough that Owen can hear it from his cabin halfway down the mountain. I know I'm acting like a bitch, but I can't help it. I feel powerless, and that drives me insane.

I grab one of the paperback books I bought at the pharmacy—a new release by one of my favorite romance authors—and head back downstairs. I grab a cold bottle of water from the fridge and walk out the front door.

Dominic's outside chopping wood—with his shirt off!

For crying out loud!

Why does he have to show off his ridiculously-ripped torso? I try not to stare at his arms as he brings the ax down hard and splits a log clean down the middle with one swing. His back muscles are well defined and giving me ideas.

He raises his long, muscular arms and does it again. *Thwack!* And again. And again.

Showoff.

Maybe chopping wood is his way of working off stress. He didn't ask to babysit me. And I'm sure this situation is no fun for him either.

Just thinking about Chicago makes me miss my family and my friends. Especially Amber. We had plans to go see *Hamilton* next week for her birthday—our favorite musical—and now I'm sure that's not going to happen. I hope she goes anyway.

I realize I'm a horrible person for sulking over my own life when Kent Martinez lost his.

God, I suck.

My plan was to sit out here on the swing and read, but that's no longer an option. Not with Mr. Six-Pack displaying his physical prowess across the yard. So instead, I take my book and my water bottle and walk around to the back of the cabin.

"Sophie? Where are you going?"

I hear him calling me, but I don't answer. He said I'm not a prisoner, so I'm going for a damn walk. Surely *that's* acceptable. We're in the middle of nowhere, and there's probably not another soul for miles around—well, except for his shaggy-haired friend.

I'll find a quiet spot in the woods where I can sit down on a fallen log and read my book—without having to fend off an eyeful of a half-naked man with bulging muscles.

I find a clearly-marked path leading into the woods behind the cabin, so I take that—the path of least resistance. I walk the trail for about ten minutes, far enough away that I can no longer hear the *thwack* of Dominic's ax. Lo and behold, I do find a fallen log, right next to a shallow stream, and I take a seat on the mossy trunk and crack open my book.

I am barely three pages into my book when I hear a twig snap behind me. Jumping nearly out of my skin, I turn to see what it is.

"Shane's not paying me nearly enough to babysit you," Dominic says, looking annoyed.

I jump up from my seat. "Don't sneak up on me like that! You almost gave me a heart attack."

"I told you not to wander off without me. You're not even armed."

"Oh, please. There's nothing in these woods I need to worry about, except for maybe you."

"No? So, you don't think you need to worry about black bears or bobcats?"

"There aren't any bears in these woods." I sound more sure of myself than I am. "It's too close to town."

He laughs. "Then what made those gouges? A squirrel?"

He points at a tree not more than ten feet from me that has

long, deep grooves carved into the trunk.

Shit.

I hate when he's right.

He comes closer, and that's when I notice the black handgun tucked into a holster strapped around his hips.

"I'm sorry about earlier," he says. "I know you're frustrated, Phee. I get it."

"Don't call me that. My name is Sophie."

"I thought you said it was So-*phee*."

"You know what I meant."

He's so close to me I can feel the heat radiating off his big body. I can also smell him—a combination of warm body and male scent. It's practically an aphrodisiac to my poor sex-starved body.

I try to ignore the fact that he's towering over me, which is unfortunately also a huge turn-on. Curiosity gets the best of me. "Just how tall are you, anyway?"

"Six-eight."

"I'm not used to feeling short around men."

"I'm not used to being around women who are sturdy enough they won't get knocked over by a stiff... wind."

Dear god, for a minute I thought he was going to say a stiff *fuck*. "Sturdy? Is that supposed to be a compliment, because it's not."

"Yeah, it is. Hey, Phee, if you're going to be walking around out in the woods, you need to carry a gun."

"So I can defend myself from black bears and bobcats?"

"No. So you can fire a warning shot if you're in trouble, and I can come running."

I laugh. "I know how to shoot. If I run into something out here that wants to take my head off, I'll plug it between the eyes."

He pats me on the back. "All right, Annie Oakley. Come show me what you can do with a handgun."

"Really?"

"Yeah, really. I need to know you can handle yourself with a firearm. Let's go."

* * *

Back in the cabin, I follow Dominic to the secret door at the back of the pantry. He pulls it open, switches on the light, and ushers me into the small windowless space.

"Pick your weapon," he says, gesturing toward the back wall and its impressive display of guns in every size and style imaginable.

I study the selection of handguns, rifles, shotguns, and semi-automatics. I've shot them all at least once, at my brothers' insistence. My gaze lands on a familiar model, and I point to the small black handgun. "I'll take the three-eighty."

Dominic nods in approval. "Good choice." He pulls the handgun off the wall and checks to see that it isn't loaded. Then he hands it to me and watches me grip it firmly. "It fits your hand well, it's easy to conceal, and the kick's not too bad."

A pang of longing hits me. This gun makes me think of my brothers.

Dominic hands me a box of ammo. "Load it."

I glance up at him. "You're testing me."

He nods. "Do it. Then we'll go outside and do some target practice."

"Fine." I open the box of ammo and pull out a handful of rounds. Then I release the stock and load the rounds, quickly snapping each one into place. Then I pop the stock back into the handle and engage the safety.

Pursing his lips, he pockets a handful of additional rounds. "All right, let's go," he says, nodding toward the door.

Outside, he leads me into the woods a short distance to a small clearing. At the tree line, there's a rope between two trees, and hanging from the rope are empty beer cans with holes drilled through them, strung up in a row like Christmas lights.

"Nice decorating job," I say.

He crosses his arms over his very distracting bare chest. "Show me what you can do."

"Don't you want to put a shirt on first?" I ask him. I noticed he has a t-shirt tucked into his back pocket.

"No. I'm hot."

No kidding.

But it is a warm, humid day, and he was chopping logs not that long ago. I can see sweat glistening on his sun-kissed skin.

Standing in the center of the clearing, about twenty feet from the beer cans, I flip off the safety and raise the handgun in a steady grip. I sight my target, hold my breath, and gently squeeze the trigger, all while trying and failing to ignore the man looming behind me.

When my round hits the lower half of the first can, it spins gloriously on the rope. I move down the line in rapid succession, hitting five of the six cans.

I smile up at him, feeling pretty darn pleased with myself. My aim is quite good, but it's been months since I've shot. I wait for some sarcastic remark, but he says nothing.

Instead, he reaches into his pocket and hands me six more rounds. "Reload."

"Wow, you're a tough crowd," I say, but I do what he asked.

"I'm not going to pat you on the head and tell you you're a good girl, like I'm sure your brothers do." He grips my shoulders and walks me back ten feet. "Again."

I shoot again, probably from thirty feet away now, managing to hit four of the six targets. "Four out of six isn't bad," I say defensively. "Not from this distance."

"Congratulations, Phee. You can hit sixty-six percent of the people trying to kill you. Try again." And then he hands me six more rounds.

We repeat this over and over until my arms are shaking and my hands ache. By my final attempt, I hit only two cans—or at least what's left of them—out of six.

"Have you ever shot a rifle?" he says.

His question surprises me. I was expecting a more acerbic comment. "No."

"I'll teach you. In the event of trouble, you'll be safer shooting from one of the upstairs bedroom windows. Under those circumstances, a rifle will be your best bet." Then he turns and walks back the way we came.

For a moment, I just watch him, admiring his stride as his long legs eat up the ground.

I don't get him. Does he ever loosen up? Does he ever relax? Yes, we're stuck out here in the middle of nowhere under extraordinary circumstances, but that doesn't mean we can't at least try to make the best of a bad situation and have some fun.

I run after him. "Whoa, slow down, Jolly Green Giant."

8

Dominic

I know I'm being an ass, but I can't help it. As I stomp back to the cabin—acutely aware of Sophie's exact location every second as she trails behind me—I contemplate the fact that Shane's sister is one hell of a woman. She's gorgeous, smart, funny, and sexy as hell. And to top it off, her aim's not too bad.

She's got a great eye. At twenty feet, she nailed most of the cans. With a few days of practice, I'm sure she'll hit every damn one. Even when I pulled her back farther from the target and made her shoot until her arms were about to fall off, she didn't complain. With practice… she'll do even better. Now I just have to teach her to shoot a rifle.

The problem is, if I'm going to help her with weapons training, that means spending a lot of time in close proximity to her. That's what I'm worried about. I'm already hiding the fact that she gives me hard-ons at the most inconvenient times. I could have Owen teach her to shoot a rifle—he was a sniper in the Marines, for Christ's sake—but I can't stomach the thought of him spending so much time with her.

Yeah, I'm a possessive, jealous fuck.

I can't stop thinking about how much I want to put my hands on her, my mouth, my tongue. I want to lick and suck every inch of her body. I'm dying to know what she *tastes* like. It's driving me crazy.

When we reach the clearing at the cabin, I wave her inside. "Let's grab a rifle and see how you do."

She grumbles as she climbs the wooden steps to the front porch and follows me in. "My arms are killing me. Can't we wait a bit?"

I turn back to face her. Her cheeks are flushed from the hike in the woods, her hair a bit wild, and she's breathing hard, her chest heaving. Naturally, that calls attention to her breasts, which are magnificent.

"All right." I have to avert my gaze. "We'll do it later."

"Good. I'm wiped out."

She heads for the fridge, opens the door and peers inside. Then she pulls a cold beer out and tosses it to me before getting one for herself. She digs the bottle opener out of the silverware drawer and pops the cap off her bottle, then tosses the opener to me.

Can a woman be any more perfect?

"Let's grill out tonight," she says. "Burgers and corn on the cob?"

And, she just upped the ante.

"Sure. I just need to grab a shower first." After I finish my beer, I toss the bottle into the recycling bin and head for the bathroom.

In the shower, standing beneath a spray of hot water, I jerk off out of desperation for release, fisting my cock and giving it a real workout.

By the time I'm out of the bathroom, with a towel wrapped around my waist, I head up the stairs just as Sophie's coming down. She's changed out of her jeans and t-shirt into a skimpy little dress that ends mid-thigh and showcases her gorgeous figure. I freeze, one hand on the railing.

Dear god in heaven.

She sashays down the stairs and stops in front of me. She's standing one step above me, and that puts us about eye level.

Her gaze flits down to my damp chest before returning to my eyes. "Did you enjoy your shower?"

My skin heats as I wonder if she guesses that I jacked off in the process. I swallow hard. *What the fuck did she ask me?* "Uh, yeah."

"Did you leave enough hot water for me?"

Immediately, I picture her standing naked in the shower,

water sluicing down her curvaceous body, her hands skimming over her breasts, down to her belly, and then lower— "If you're quick about it."

Her full lips quirk downward. "But I don't like it quick. I like to take my time."

Jesus Christ, is she flirting with me?

"Then you'll be taking a cold shower," I tell her. "Consider yourself forewarned."

I step aside so she can pass by, and as soon as the coast is clear, I climb the stairs two at a time and disappear into my bedroom.

Already, my dick is stirring again, as if coming in the shower never happened.

What the fuck is that woman trying to do to me?

* * *

After dressing and going downstairs, I disappear into the armory to do some maintenance. If I'm going to teach her how to shoot a rifle, I want it to be in tip-top shape. I sit at the workbench and clean my favorite Winchester. I bet, with her naturally good aim, she'll master it in no time. She's certainly strong enough to handle it.

When I come out of the armory, the cabin is empty. I glance up the stairs and see that her bedroom door is wide open. "Sophie? Are you upstairs?"

No answer.

"Sophie?"

She's not here.

My heart rate kicks up, as does my adrenaline. I told her never to leave this cabin without me. I rush out onto the front porch, expecting to see her sitting on the swing, perhaps reading, but there's no sign of her.

Until I hear her scream bloody murder from somewhere behind the cabin.

I jump to the ground and take off running—unarmed and unprepared, but ready to tackle anything. I pull up short, though, when I spot Sophie with Owen. She's jumping back frantically, pointing at the ground.

Owen calmly picks up a writhing black snake and carries it to the edge of the woods, where he releases it in the undergrowth.

"It's just a rat snake, Sophie," he tells her calmly. "They're harmless."

"How was I supposed to know that?" she says, her voice raised and agitated. "I'm sorry, but I left my snake identification guide back in Chicago."

Owen laughs, and I stare at him, wondering what he's doing here.

When he catches sight of me watching him, his smile falls. "Hey, Dominic."

If I didn't know better, I'd say he looks guilty.

Sophie turns to me, mad as hell, her hands on her hips. "Did you know there are snakes in these woods?"

I try not to laugh, because that'll only make her madder.

"Well, yeah. Isn't that kind of obvious?"

"Twenty-three species of snakes reside in these mountains, to be exact," Owen says. "But only two are venomous, so your odds of dying by snake bite are low."

Sophie scowls at him. "Gee, thanks, Ranger Rick."

I shake my head at the two of them. "If you two are done foolin' around, Sophie, why don't you get the food ready? I'll fire up the grill."

"I'd be happy to," she says, passing by me as she heads back to the cabin.

I glance at Owen, who's watching Sophie's retreating form. "Hey, Sophie!" he calls to her.

She turns back. "Yes?"

"I'm going into town. Do you need anything?"

"Yes, as a matter of fact I do," she says, giving me a smug look. "Thank you for asking. I'd love some Oreos."

Owen looks perplexed for a minute. "You mean the cookies?"

"Yes, the cookies. And some Pepsi, please." She reaches into her pocket and pulls out some cash. "Here—"

He brushes off her offer. "That's all right. I've got it. I'll see you later." And then he passes us by and heads into the woods.

Owen absolutely hates going into town. He avoids it like the plague—I've known him to put it off for six months. As I head to the grill, I wonder what he's up to. I'm tempted to ask him, but I have a strong suspicion I already know. And I won't like his answer.

* * *

After dinner, I set up a paper target shaped like a man's torso in the yard behind the cabin.

Once I teach her how to load the Winchester, I demonstrate firing it, drilling four holes in rapid succession into the dead center of the target's chest.

"Whoa, cowboy," she says, sounding impressed.

I bite back a grin as I hand her the rifle. "Here. You try."

She loads four rounds into the chamber. Then, she lifts the rifle in her arms and aims. Her first shot goes high and to the right, missing the target altogether. "Shit," she says, frowning.

"Hug it closer." I demonstrate by stepping close behind her, wrapping my arms around hers, and drawing the weapon tighter to her shoulder. "Hold it snug and sight your target." Reluctantly, I release her.

She tries again, and this time when she fires, she hits the edge of the paper target.

"Better," I tell her. "Try again."

She fires again, this time grazing the outline of the figure.

Getting closer.

"Hey, not too shabby," she says, clearly delighted with herself.

She takes another shot, improving yet again, landing a shot in the target's right shoulder. "I think I'm getting the hang of this."

"Sure, at twenty-five yards. Now, let's try fifty yards."

"What?" She looks at me like I'm crazy.

"If someone's sneaking up on the cabin, you want to be able to stop him at a hundred yards. We're just getting warmed up, Phee."

The nickname slipped out, but instead of berating me for it, she smiles.

We practice for another hour, this time at fifty yards. Her first few attempts are pathetic, but after a while, she manages to give the target a few flesh wounds.

"How about trying to do some actual damage?" I tell her. "At this rate, you're just pissing him off. You need to stop him in his tracks."

She scowls, and I wonder if she's thinking back to the shooting in Chicago. I never really asked her about the guy who was killed. Shane just mentioned he was an assistant district attorney—and her date. That's all I know about him. That, and presumably he was prosecuting organized crime.

"Were you two close?" I ask her. "You and the assistant DA?"

Looking surprised by the question, she shakes her head. "Kent? I'd never met him before that night. It was a blind date set up by my friend Amber."

"A blind date? You're kidding." *Why in the world would she go on a blind date?* There must be men beating down her door. For that matter, I find it hard to believe she's still single. She has to be in her early thirties.

Her expression falls as she remembers. "I didn't want to go. I only agreed because Amber wouldn't stop begging me."

"Why didn't you want to go?"

"I don't date much," she says.

"Why not?"

She shrugs. "I just don't."

She shoots another half-dozen rounds, each time getting closer to the bullseye.

"Can we stop now?" she finally asks, handing me the rifle.

I load five rounds into the chamber and fire them off, all five shots piling up on top of one another in the center of the target's chest. "Aim for the center of the chest," I tell her. "It's the largest area. You'll have a better chance of hitting him and doing lethal damage."

As I pick the box of ammo off the ground, I notice that she's quiet all of a sudden. "Everything okay?"

She looks at me like I'm an idiot, and I'm surprised to see tears in her eyes.

Fuck.

"No, Dominic, everything's not okay," she says. And then she heads back to the cabin, leaving me to follow.

But she doesn't go inside, as I was expecting her to. I find her sitting on the porch swing, looking dejected.

I set the rifle and the ammo down. "Mind if I join you?"

She scoots over to make room for me, but doesn't say anything.

"Want a beer?" I ask her.

"No. But I'd love a glass of the red wine we bought."

I go inside and return shortly with a beer for me and a glass of wine for her. I hand her the glass.

She takes a sip. "Thanks."

I sit beside her on the swing once more. It's late evening now, and this high up, dusk sets in early as the sun falls behind the tree line. The temperature has already begun dropping, and I notice her shiver beside me.

I lean closer to her, brushing my arm against hers. "Do you want to go inside? I'll build a fire."

She nods. "That sounds nice." But her voice sounds a bit melancholy.

"What's wrong, Sophie?"

She sips her wine. "I miss my apartment. I miss Amber. I miss my family." She slaps her bare arm. "The mosquitoes are biting. We'd better go inside."

I follow her in, and while she pours herself a second glass of wine, I start a fire in the pot-belly stove to ward off the chill.

I'll make her a fire. Then I'm going up to my room to get the hell away from her. The proximity is getting to me. I hate seeing her sad. It makes me want to wrap her up in my arms and never let her go.

9

Sophie

While Dominic fires up the wood stove, I carry my glass of wine and a paperback book to the sofa, where I get comfortable. I think I'll just sit here a while, read, and enjoy the eye candy on display.

My attention drifts from the words on the page to the man crouched in front of the stove. I watch him arrange the kindling and coax the flames to take hold.

Dominic is bigger than life, literally and figuratively. He's rugged and domineering—everything I always thought I'd hate in a man. But in him, it's downright sexy.

The men I've dated—including my crappy ex, Jeremy—have always been sophisticated, highly-educated men who wear tailored suits and drive BMWs. They're the polar opposite of Dominic. He's nothing like the guys I've been attracted to in the past, and yet I can't stop looking at him.

I watch him load another log into the fire, his muscles flexing beneath the fabric of his t-shirt, and I can't help staring at his long fingers. My brain short circuits when I think of all the places I'd like those fingers to be.

Just watching him turns me on. I feel flushed with arousal. And, also thanks to him, I don't have my vibrator with me. It's back at my apartment in Chicago.

At the sound of a knock at the door, I jump, almost spilling my wine.

Dominic rises to his feet and walks to the door. Peering through the peephole, he growls, "Son of a bitch."

"Who is it?" I ask, my heart suddenly racing. We're certainly not expecting anyone. I jump up from the sofa and join him.

Dominic opens the door, and Owen walks inside holding a grocery bag.

I practically gawk at his new and greatly improved appearance. All that long shaggy hair is gone, and his beard is neatly trimmed. He looks... gorgeous. I had no idea there was such a handsome man lurking under all that scruff. I never noticed how blue his eyes are. "Wow, you clean up well."

Owen shrugs. "I was overdue for a visit to the barber." He sets the sack on the table. "I brought your cookies and soda pop."

"Thank you," I say, still reeling from the change in his appearance.

My gaze bounces from Owen to Dominic, who looks like a disgruntled lumberjack in comparison to his friend. His big arms are crossed over his chest, and he's scowling at Owen.

Owen shifts on his feet, looking... embarrassed, I think. Or at least self-conscious.

I reach into my pocket and pull out the money I've been holding onto. "Here, let me pay you for the supplies."

But Owen shakes his head. "Nah. Don't worry about it."

"Well, thanks for stopping by," Dominic says, his hand still on the door. He opens it wider and nods outside.

Dominic's being rude.

As Owen turns to leave, I say, "Owen, wait!"

He turns back. "Yeah?"

"Would you like to stay for a beer?" I say, mostly to annoy Dominic. "Or join me for a glass of wine?"

I think he's about to accept my invitation when Dominic says pointedly, "It's late, and he was just leaving. Weren't you, Owen?"

Owen frowns. "Yeah, I need to get back and check on the dogs. Thanks anyway. Maybe another time."

"You're welcome anytime," I tell him. "Don't be a stranger."

Dominic closes the door after Owen leaves, throwing the deadbolt and dropping the crossbar into place. Then he turns to me, looking mad as hell.

"What the hell is your problem?" I ask him, feeling my own

anger escalating. "And why were you so rude to Owen?"

He props his hands on his hips and steps closer, looming over me. "Stop flirting with Owen."

"What are you talking about? I wasn't flirting."

He glares down at me, and if this were anyone other than Dominic, I might be a bit afraid.

"Yes, you were," he says between gritted teeth. Then he bats his eyelashes and speaks in a ridiculous falsetto voice, when he adds, "Oh, Owen, you saved me from the big scary snake today. Thank you for my cookies. I couldn't live another minute without them."

I slam my wine glass down on the kitchen table behind me. "Stop being an ass! I wasn't flirting with him. I was just being *nice*, because he was nice to *me!*"

"And I'm *not* nice? Is that it? I grilled you burgers and corn on the cob tonight. And I taught you to shoot a rifle."

I burst into laughter. "Is that supposed to impress me? I have news for you... right now you're *not* being nice. And you certainly weren't being *nice* when you threw my iPhone into traffic."

He stalks closer, his complexion darkening as his blood pressure rises. "You want to know why I tossed your phone? Because it could get you killed, that's why! It would be too easy for you to make a call and inadvertently alert half of Chicago to your whereabouts. If that happened, we'd have mobsters swarming this mountain, with their gun sights set on *you*! So pardon the fuck out of me if I take your safety seriously. Apparently, you don't."

"You don't intimidate me, so stop trying!" I step in his direction and get in his face. I'm barefoot and he's wearing boots, so he's really towering over me. "You are such a fucking Neanderthal, you know that? Apparently, body size doesn't always correlate with brain size."

His eyes narrow for a second, causing my heart to pound. Not because I'm afraid of him, but because he's hot as hell when he's angry. All that fierce energy directed at me is... tantalizing. And he did say he was just trying to protect me. I can *almost* forgive him for destroying my phone.

When his gaze drops down to my mouth, and his nostrils flare, I realize I'm not the only one getting turned on here.

Holy shit.

He grabs me by my upper arms and hauls me against his rock-hard chest. I can practically hear his jaw grinding in frustration.

"Shane should have warned me you were a pain in the ass," he says. "I would have demanded hazard pay."

I stare up into his whiskey-colored eyes, losing myself in their fiery depths. He's angry, resentful, agitated, and so damn hot my panties are melting.

I feel myself growing wet, and the spot between my legs is throbbing. "Dominic, if you can't handle me, you shouldn't have taken the job in the first place."

His eyes narrow on me as he sucks in a breath. "Handle you?" As he inhales, his broad chest expands, pressing against my aching breasts. "I can handle anything you throw at me, little girl."

I laugh. "Baby, there's nothing *little* about me. Surely you've noticed."

"Yeah, actually I have."

The change in his tone catches me off guard, that deep voice dropping an octave, even lower, rich and resonant like fine bourbon.

On impulse, I reach up and skim my fingers over his trim beard, cupping his cheek before brushing my thumb over his lips. His eyes drift shut, and he groans softly. He *is* affected by me! *He's feeling it too.* The thought shakes me to the core.

This has the potential to be far more than just some flirtatious teasing, and I'm desperate to find out. I want him, badly.

I slide my fingers from one hand through his hair and grip the back of his neck, hard. I slip the other beneath his t-shirt and let my fingers glide across his rock-hard muscles.

Without warning, he grabs me, pivots us, and backs me into the wall, pinning my wrists above my head. No one has ever manhandled me like this. I should be furious. I should curse a blue streak at him and ram my knee into his balls. Instead, my body melts, and my nipples tighten, aching for attention.

As I suck in a breath, his gaze latches onto my lips.

He's as turned on as I am.

The thought of having him—of being on the receiving end of all that strength and power—is mind-blowing.

We stare at each other, both of us breathing hard, clearly at an impasse. We could stand here all night yelling at each other, we could walk away, or... I tug one of my hands free and slide it behind his head to coax his mouth down to mine.

He grimaces like he's in pain. "Sophie—no. I can't."

His lips are perfectly framed by his beard, and I'm dying to find out if they're as soft as they look. "Dominic?"

"What?" His terse reply is little more than a breath.

"Kiss me."

His grip on my wrists tightens almost painfully. "I said no."

"Why not?"

"Because, I *can't*. You're Shane's sister, and you're my client. It wouldn't be right."

"Oh, for fuck's sake. The question is, do you *want* to? We're both consenting adults. It doesn't matter whose sister I am."

He winces. "Sophie—"

I press my breasts against his chest, and he sucks in a breath. Then, in the blink of an eye, he releases my wrists and slides his fingers into my hair, pinning my head to the wall. His lips cover mine, hot and demanding, and his tongue invades my mouth, seeking, stroking, tasting.

I run my palms over his pecs, up to his shoulders. Then my fingers trail back down his chest and skim over both of his nipples. I flick the flat discs with my nails.

He shudders, groaning harshly. "*Sophie.*"

I stroke his tongue with mine and slip my hands around his back where I begin kneading those thick, ropy muscles. "I want you, Dominic. Right now."

He growls against my lips, and then he raises his head to stare down at me. "If I fuck you, it won't be just once. It would take at least a month for me to fuck you every way I've been imagining. I won't want to stop."

"Who said anything about stopping?"

I can see the battle going on inside him, the fight he's waging. He tears off his shirt and tosses it aside.

He grips the hem of my sundress and whips it over my head, then tosses it on the table, leaving me in only my underwear and bra. His heated gaze lights up when he sees my belly button piercing—a small pink diamond on a gold hoop. "You've been holding out on me, Phee." He gently toys with the piercing. "Why hasn't this come up in conversation before now?"

I laugh. "That's hardly the thing one brings up in random conversation."

"It sure as hell should be." Chuckling, he picks me up and sets me on the table. I'm swooning from the knowledge that this man is strong enough to lift me without breaking a sweat.

Grinning, he pushes my thighs apart, and when the cool air hits the hot, damp gusset of my panties, I shiver violently.

Dominic drops to his knees and pulls me to the edge of the table. His arms hook beneath my thighs and he draws me close. My pulse skyrockets instantly, and I'm so aroused I can barely breathe.

He doesn't waste any time before he presses his face to the aching spot between my legs, his nose brushing against the fabric, against *me*, as he breathes in deeply. He burrows closer, his nose rubbing against my sensitized clit, and I cry out sharply. I dig my fingers into his hair and fist the wavy strands. He grunts, but he doesn't tell me to stop.

Dear god, I'm already so close to coming.

He rocks back on his heels, separating us, and I groan in disapproval.

"Just a sec, babe," he says. "Cool your jets." He peels my panties down my legs, whipping them off me and tossing them god knows where. Then he moves in again, his gaze locked on my pussy. His eyes darken as he skims a gentle fingertip over my folds. "You're bare."

I can hardly breathe now, let alone speak. I'm so damn glad I waxed last week.

"So soft," he says, as if mesmerized. And then he swipes his tongue between my labia, parting the lips and swirling his tongue around my clit.

"Dom—ahh!" His name devolves into a keening wail as he torments my clit with his tongue, lashing my most sensitive spot. I feel a finger circling my opening, sliding easily through the slick arousal gathering there.

"Lean back," he orders.

I do as he says, bracing myself on my elbows. This angle tilts my pelvis higher, making it easier for him to slowly slide his long finger inside me. I gasp at the sudden intrusion—*damn, even his finger is big.* And then he's stroking me inside as he torments my clit with his tongue—a one-two punch that sends my pulse careening.

My hips are rocking on their own, my thighs shaking, as my body melts. He knows exactly what he's doing—how to drive a woman wild. At this point, I'm absolute putty in his hands and

I'll do anything he asks.

My orgasm hits me hard and fast, with no warning. My thigh muscles tighten as my body shudders. Shamelessly, I cry out, loud and shrill, and I'm just grateful we don't have any neighbors nearby.

He continues to stroke and tease me through my orgasm, drawing it out and keeping me on edge, until my body slowly comes down from the high. Then he shoots to his feet and reaches around me to unfasten my bra.

My bra ends up wherever my panties went, leaving me naked and fully on display. Normally, I'd feel terribly self-conscious to be bare like this, with him still mostly dressed, but the blatant hunger on his face gives me the confidence to feel brazen and daring.

Dominic cups my generous breasts, which overflow even his big hands. He bends down and draws a plump, dark pink nipple into his mouth and sucks. As his mouth pulls at my breast, I feel a corresponding tug between my legs, making me desperate to wrap them around his hips.

My body knows what it wants. It wants Dominic, inside me, thrusting hard. But he doesn't seem to be in any hurry. He presses his face into my cleavage, breathing in deeply as he nestles between the heavy mounds. When he bites down gently on my other nipple, I screech. Not because it hurts, but because it feels so *good*.

"You're a loud one," he observes, grinning as he sucks that nipple into his mouth.

"You bit me!"

Laughter rumbles deep in his chest. "I'll make it better, I promise."

Suddenly, he releases me and steps back to unbuckle his belt and unfasten his jeans. He shoves his jeans down to his knees, revealing the fact that he's commando underneath.

Oh, wow.

He's also hard as a rock, his thick, long cock defying gravity as it strains upward.

He's huge.

I'm not surprised because everything about the man is oversized. The thought of that monster cock tunneling inside me makes me want to weep with joy.

He bends down to retrieve his wallet from the back pocket of his discarded jeans and pulls out a condom packet.

"Thank god," I say. The last thing either of us would want to do is stop this train because we didn't have any condoms.

I stare in awe as he expertly rolls the extra-large condom down his impressive length. Then he grasps my hips and hauls me closer. Spreading my legs wide and looping his arms beneath my knees, he steps close and positions the head of his cock against my drenched opening.

He looks down. "You're soaking wet. Good." Then he meets my gaze. "Let me know if I hurt you. I'll try to slow down."

I wrap my legs around his waist, digging my heels into his ass. "I don't want slow."

"Don't be so sure, Phee," he says, using that damn nickname

again. But because his voice has dropped an octave, low and guttural, it sounds sexy as hell, and I think it's growing on me.

He releases one of my legs just long enough to fist his cock and guide it into me.

I'm already soft and wet from my earlier orgasm, drenched in arousal, but still, I feel the burn of him as he stretches me.

I exhale a long breath. "Jesus, Dominic."

"I warned you." He looks at me. "You okay?"

Gasping, I nod. "Fine. You're a lot to take, though." I adjust the angle and rock my hips in invitation. "Hurry up and shove it in, will you? We don't have all night."

He grins and pats my thigh. "Careful what you wish for, baby."

And then he presses deeper inside me, stretching me with his wide girth. I feel a slight burn as he tunnels deeper. I'm aware of every single inch as he fills me, and it feels so damn good.

He takes his time, sliding inside inch by inch, until he's fully seated. "There," he says.

I am utterly impaled on him.

Overwhelmed.

Taken.

It's earth-shattering and hot as hell.

And then he starts moving—slow, steady strokes—and the bottom falls out of my world, leaving me spinning and reeling. He slides in and out a few times, his jaw clenched, nostrils flaring. I can tell he's holding back, probably afraid of hurting me. But I don't want careful. I want him to *fuck me hard*. I want him to let loose.

As he begins to pick up speed, I reach up and scrape my nails down his chest, gently scoring his flesh. His dark gaze flashes at me, aggressive and slightly out of control.

"You don't have to be careful, Dominic," I remind him. "I want *you*."

With a groan, he explodes into rapid, deep thrusts, tunneling hard in and out of me. His big hands release my thighs and slide beneath me to grip my ass cheeks. He pulls me even closer, tilting me back and holding me pinned in place as he drives into me, hard and fast.

We're both gasping for air now. I grip the edge of the table to brace myself against the force of his thrusts. He digs his fingers into my ass cheeks, squeezing them, molding them, like they're his playthings.

His face and neck muscles tighten as he throws his head back, tossing a deep-throated roar to the rafters. He comes in a heated rush. Even with the condom in place, I can feel the force of his ejaculation as his cock bucks inside me, pulsing and throbbing with each spasm.

He keeps thrusting, his movements slow and languid now as he revels in his pleasure. He presses his forehead to mine for a soul-piercing moment before he kisses me tenderly.

He lowers me back fully onto the table, and I struggle to catch my breath. Then he leans forward, his torso covering mine, dwarfing me, making me feel small and protected. There's something so fundamentally sexual in being physically dominated like this.

When he finally pulls out, his sheathed length is covered in my glistening arousal. He quickly removes the condom and disposes of it in the wastebasket.

"Let's get cleaned up," he says. "And then we'll go to bed."

After we clean up, he takes my hand and leads me up the stairs. When I start to go left to my room, he steers me in the opposite direction, toward his.

He looks down at me, his voice rough when he says, "I told you there'd be no going back. You're sleeping in my bed now. If you think once was enough, you're dreaming."

I could argue if I wanted to, call him presumptuous and an egotistical ass, but surprisingly, I don't do any of that. I want to know what it feels like to sleep in his strong arms, to share his bed. At least for tonight.

I'm curious enough to want to see where this magical feeling takes me.

10

Dominic

As I lie in the dark, with Sophie's warm, naked body pressed against mine, I'm at a complete loss. I thought sex with Sophie would be amazing.

It wasn't.

It was life changing.

As she snuggles against me—her head on my chest, her arm across my abs—I feel something I've never felt before. Something I thought I would never experience... a sense of belonging, of rightness.

I've never really felt like I belonged *anywhere*.

I was born to a single mother—one who struggled to feed us—but she died when I was just a kid. My grandparents raised me after that, but let's be honest, I was a handful back then, and they were getting up there in years. They loved me, and they did the best they could for me, but I was a bit of a hellion.

I've always felt like I was on the outside looking in. I felt like I was a burden to my grandparents, and I never had a meaningful relationship with my father. How could I? Wealthy, powerful men who knock up their maids don't spend time with their bastard kids.

Not even when said man loved the maid.

It just doesn't happen.

Sophie comes from a loving family, with parents who dote on her, not to mention a passel of siblings who'd do anything for her.

I grew up an only child. And after my mom died, I was pretty much left to my own devices, running the streets and getting into all sorts of trouble.

Sophie McIntyre is a princess, and I'm the bastard son of a disgraced maid. There's no future here. The best I can do for us both is put an end to it.

She snuggles closer, throwing her leg over mine. She's a cuddler. I've got one arm around her, and I gently run my fingers up and down her spine. She makes a soft, throaty sound in her sleep and burrows even closer.

My cock is stirring again already, and I want more of her. But it's the middle of the night, and she needs sleep.

There may not be any future for us, but I'm not ready to let her go. Not yet. I meant what I said when I told her there was no going back. Now that I've had her, I only want more.

She's an addiction I never knew I had.

* * *

I wake to the sensation of Sophie rimming my right nipple with the tip of her index finger. Goosebumps prick my skin as instant arousal shoots straight to my cock, which is already stirring.

"You're playing with fire," I warn, my voice rough from sleep.

"I like to live dangerously," she murmurs, flicking the tip, which has tightened into a tiny, hard knot.

I reach behind her and grasp a handful of her ass. "Have you ever done anal before?"

She freezes. "No."

I chuckle. *That shut her up pretty quickly.* "What, no sassy comeback?"

She lifts her head to look at me. "And you have?"

"Sure. Plenty of times. It's fucking hot, and a lot of women dig it."

She peers down at my erection, which is already at full staff, standing straight up. "You've shoved *that thing* in a woman's ass before?" She sounds more than a little skeptical.

I can't help grinning. "Yep."

She pulls away and sits up. "Forget it. I'm not letting you anywhere near my ass with that monster. I'd never be able to walk again."

I laugh as I pull her back down into my arms. "Don't you want to experience an anal orgasm? I hear they're intense."

"That's bullshit."

"No, it's not." I pull her to my chest and slide my fingers down her spine to lightly stroke the crease between her ass cheeks. Gently, I tease her tight little pucker. "Your anus is an erogenous zone. There's a nerve back there that goes straight to your clit. Orgasm time."

"You made that up."

"I did not. If you don't believe me, Google it. I'm surprised you haven't tried it before."

She studies me as if she's waiting for the punch line.

"I'm serious, Phee." I notice she's stopped telling me not to call her that.

"Forget it," she says, as if she's just made up her mind. "You're not sticking your cock in my ass."

"Okay." I rub her back again, trying to soothe her hackles. "How about a finger? I can make you come with just a finger in your ass." I smile as I hold up my longest finger. "It's not that big."

She laughs nervously. "You are a very naughty man, Dominic."

At least she didn't say no. I open the nightstand drawer and grab a condom and some lube. I tear open the condom packet and quickly sheathe myself.

Sophie stares at the lube. "And where do you think you're

putting *that*?" she asks, sounding a little bit tart and a lot judgmental.

I pull her on top of me, spreading her thighs over my hips. When I reach between her legs, I check to see how wet she is, sliding my finger easily through her arousal. "Oh, I'm not the only naughty one," I say. "You're soaking wet, Phee. Were you dreaming about me last night?"

She playfully smacks my shoulder. "Shut up."

I sit her up on me. "Put my cock in your pussy."

Her eyes glitter with mischief as she lifts herself, positioning me at her opening, and then slowly eases down on me.

She moans, biting her bottom lip as she begins to work herself down on me.

I run my hands up her thighs, over her soft abdomen, pausing a moment to tease her belly button piercing and then continuing up to her gorgeous breasts. I hold them in my hand, marveling at their generous size and weight, and at her perfect, *perfect* pink nipples. "I think I'm a breast man, now."

She gasps as she sinks lower onto my cock. She takes a deep breath as she finally seats herself. "What were you before?"

I slip my hands behind her and clutch both of her ass cheeks, spreading them so I can reach between to tease her hole. "You have to ask?"

"If you say an ass man, I'm going to hit you again."

"What do you think the lube is for, darlin'?"

She glances at the tube on the nightstand and frowns. "No way."

I reach for it and unscrew the cap. "Just a finger, that's all. It won't hurt, I promise."

"Are you nuts?"

"Come on, Phee. Aren't you even a *little* bit curious about an anal O? I promise you'll love it. I tell you what. If you don't absolutely love it, I'll take you to town today and buy you anything you want."

"You sound like an infomercial." Then, she gets a smug look on her face. "Anything I want? Even a new cell phone?"

I squeeze her ass hard enough that she winces. "Nice try, but no. Anything but that."

She scowls, but already she's starting to move on me. I think she's getting off just thinking about my finger in her ass. "You'd better not hurt me," she warns, "or I'll castrate you."

I grab the lube and spread a thick line along my finger. "Castration's a little extreme, don't you think?"

"Not in this case. You've been warned."

"Lean forward."

Cautiously, she leans forward until her breasts hang down to my chest.

"Good girl," I say. "Now fuck me and ignore my finger."

She huffs in annoyance, rolling her eyes, but she complies and starts moving slowly on my cock.

"That's it," I tell her as she rides me, searching for the angle she likes.

She closes her eyes—most likely hoping to ignore me—and rides my cock like an angel, rising and falling in a sweet rhythm. Her lips part on a heavy exhale, her cheeks flushing a pretty pink. As she undulates her gorgeous hips, I reward her by cupping one of her breasts in my hand—the one without the lube—gently rolling and tweaking her lush nipple until it tightens into a tight bud.

She groans loudly. "Oh god, yes."

I slip my finger between her ass cheeks and rim her hole, spreading a generous amount of lube at her opening. The last thing I want to do is cause her any discomfort. If I do, I know I'll never hear the end of it, and she'll never let me near her ass again. I just want to give her pleasure—mind-blowing pleasure.

I slip the tip of my lubed finger inside her ass.

"Dominic," she warns in a tight voice.

"Ignore my finger," I remind her.

She laughs. "Yeah, right."

"Now, relax for me, and gently push out."

When she does as I ask—*for once*—I slip my finger inside her, up to the first knuckle, then gently withdraw it. I repeat the process a few times, spreading the lube inside her, going a little farther each time until finally she starts to relax. She's still moving on me, so I don't think she's too concerned about what I'm doing.

I feel her thigh muscles begin to tighten and shake, and I know she's close to finding her own pleasure. But I want to be the one to send her over the edge. Soon, my finger is moving easily inside her ass, sliding through the lube. Her body naturally tightens around my finger, and she groans.

She opens her mouth on a breathy gasp. "Dominic!"

"Shh, just let it happen."

"Dominic." Her voice is a mix of wonder and warning.

I time the strokes of my finger with her movements so that she gets a double dose of stimulation.

She throws her head back, panting, as she rocks herself on my length, moving faster. Her movements increase the pressure of my finger in her ass as I stroke the wall separating her backside from her vagina.

I'm close to coming myself, just from watching her, but I grit my teeth and try to hang on until she comes first. This is for *her*.

Suddenly, she stiffens, her eyes popping open as she stares right into mine. "Dominic!" Her head dips down to my chest as she groans. "Oh, *fuck!*"

Simultaneously, her luscious body tightens around my cock and her ass muscles clamp down on my finger. As her pussy squeezes me, I cry out roughly and shoot my load.

She strains as her body vibrates, breathing hard, gasping for air. Her cry is loud against my chest, her breath hot on my skin. She shudders violently, and then she collapses on me with my throbbing cock still embedded deep inside her.

My finger slips from her backside, and I wipe it on a tissue. Then I wrap my arms around her quivering torso and hug her to me.

"Phee? You okay?"

She's still trying to catch her breath, and I give her time to come down from the high. She finally quiets, going so still that

I'm afraid she's fallen asleep.

"Baby?" I give her a little nudge. "The condom's starting to slip."

She lifts her head. "I'm wrecked. I had no idea." She gingerly separates herself from my cock and rolls off me. "That was the best orgasm I've ever had. It's still tingling."

"What is?"

"My ass, deep inside. You were right, damn it. That was incredible."

Laughing, I lean over to kiss her. "I told you."

11

Sophie

Dominic goes downstairs to dispose of the condom in the bathroom. All I can do is lie here on his bed and wallow in the residual pleasure of what he just did to me. I can still feel his finger in my ass, stroking me back there, teasing me. It didn't hurt at all. There was just a very pleasant feeling of fullness—and then bam! Something detonated inside me, like a happy grenade.

And I can still feel it.

Moaning, I stretch on his bed, gloriously naked, my pussy soaking wet. I roll onto my belly and lay my head on his pillow, which smells like him—outdoorsy and masculine, like pine, leather, and smoke from the wood stove.

As I marvel at the best orgasm I've ever had, I wonder what we're doing together. *Is this for real?* I can't help but be attracted to him. He's just so honest and forthright, straightforward, masculine, domineering, and yet also funny and kind. He's a powerhouse, yet gentle at the same time.

I hear him coming back up the stairs and I smile because I have no idea what he'll do next, or what might come out of his mouth. What does this mean to him? Is this just fun for him? A distraction from the monotony of hiding out in the woods?

And what does this mean to me? What do I want it to mean?

He climbs onto the bed and lies on top of me, his chest against my backside, his hips aligned with mine. His dick is semi-hard again, and I feel it stirring against my ass.

He reaches around beneath me and strokes my clit. "I hope she's not feeling neglected," he says.

I burst into laughter. "*She?* You mean my clit?"

"Yes." He rubs tight little circles around my clitoris, which is slippery as hell at the moment. Then he growls softly into my ear and murmurs, "You are so fucking wet."

More laughter. "Gee, I wonder why."

I realize I've never laughed so much after sex. Dominic has the uncanny ability to make me lower my guard.

He rolls off and turns me onto my back. He kisses me, hot and thoroughly. "I love making you come," he says. "I love the sounds you make. The squeals—"

"I do not *squeal*."

"Yes, you do." He slides down the bed and cozies himself between my thighs. "I want to get you off one more time, and then we'll go take showers and make breakfast. I've worked up an appetite."

I push against his shoulders, but I might as well be trying to move a thousand-pound boulder. "I just came, Dominic. I can't come again."

He chuckles. "You've had some pretty lame sexual partners, if that's what you think."

He pries my thighs apart and buries his face between my legs, zeroing in on my clit with gentle laps of his tongue. His beard rubs the tender skin of my inner thighs, contrasting starkly with the softness of his tongue lapping at me like a big, lazy cat.

When I flinch, my sex too sensitized to handle more, he slows his tongue, softening his touch as if he's petting my clit.

"Dominic, I can't—"

"Shh... relax."

I close my eyes and breathe, and soon my entire focus is on the hot, wet juncture between my legs. He licks me there slowly, gently, like he's coaxing my clit to feel pleasure again.

It does feel good. So damn good. I grasp his hair tightly as my pulse picks up. "Dominic."

But he doesn't respond. He just keeps licking and teasing.

Without warning, a soft wave of exquisite pleasure ripples through me, radiating from my core outward, a soft undulation of pleasure as I come again. My thigh muscles tighten, and

I arch my back off the mattress, keening softly.

Smiling, he comes up beside me and kisses me, his beard and face wet and smelling like me. I feel like I've marked him—or maybe he's marked me. This is all so raw and new.

He kisses me. "Shower, then breakfast."

And then he climbs off the bed, grabs my hand, and pulls me to my feet. I stumble, my legs unsteady, and he catches me. Holding my hand, he leads me out of his room and down the stairs.

I'm not sure of the time, but I can see that it's broad daylight outside. The curtains are open, and I feel exposed as we traipse through the downstairs naked. "What if someone sees us?"

"No one comes up here."

"What about Owen?"

Dominic makes a gruff sound deep in his throat. "He knows better than to peep through windows."

We climb into a hot shower together and take turns washing. When I reach for my bottle of peppermint shampoo, he takes it from me and squirts some into his palm.

He works the suds into my hair, his long fingers firmly massaging my scalp and making me moan shamelessly.

"You have incredible hair," he tells me as he gathers up the long strands.

My eyes drift shut, and I take a moment to enjoy his touch. "Thank you."

Finally, he maneuvers me so that I'm standing beneath the spray and then he rinses my hair.

"My turn," I say, picking up a bar of soap I assume is his. It smells like man soap, outdoorsy and pine. I lather my hands and run them over his chest, exploring all the ridges and valleys of his muscles, down his washboard abs, and lower to his thick, muscular thighs.

I take hold of his penis, which is semi-hard, and marvel at his size as it grows harder by the second. With one hand, I stroke his cock, and with the other, I cup his heavy sac.

"Are you sure you're up to another round?" he asks.

He's got a point. I am feeling rather sore this morning.

* * *

After showering and dressing, we make breakfast together. He fries bacon and sausage while I cook the eggs and make toast. It's all very domestic.

Every once in a while, he brushes against me—closer than necessary—or he presses up against my backside and loops his arms around me. He even kisses the crook of my neck, which is ticklish, sending me into a fit of laughter.

"See? I told you," he says. "You squeal."

When we're done eating at the little kitchen table, he wipes his mouth and lays down his napkin, frowning. "I'll show you how to find Owen's cabin today. You should know, in case of emergency. If something happens to me, he's your lifeline. You'll go to him."

I shudder at the thought of anything happening to Dominic.

"Don't be silly. Nothing's going to happen to you."

Getting up to clear the table, he shrugs, looking far from happy. "I have to plan for every contingency, Phee. I'd be a fool not to."

12

Dominic

As soon as Sophie disappears upstairs into her room to get ready, I leave the cabin and head across the yard to the shed. I need to make a quick call, and I don't have much time.

The shed door is secured with a combination lock. I enter the code and let myself in, flipping on the light after shutting and securing the door. At first glance, the shed looks like any other shed, with spare tools lying on a wooden workbench, some coils of wire hanging on the wall, a gas-powered lawn mower, and a gas can in one corner.

I crouch down in front of the workbench and unlock the small cabinet beneath it—another combination lock. Inside, among other necessities, is a satellite phone.

It's time for me to check in with Shane. If I don't, he's liable to send the troops after us. Despite what I told Sophie, Shane *does* know where we are. He has the coordinates for this cabin—just in case.

I punch in his number, and he answers on the second ring.

"Shane McIntyre."

"Hey, Shane."

"Jesus, Dominic, it's about time you called. How's Sophie? Is she all right?"

"Yeah. Besides being a pain in the ass, she's fine."

He laughs. "Didn't I mention that?"

"No, you didn't."

"Cut her some slack," he says. "This is difficult for her. She's a city girl. She's not used to roughing it."

"No kidding."

"Seriously, though," he says. "How is she?"

"She's fine. She's still sulking about her phone—I destroyed it as we were leaving town. Speaking of Chicago, what's the word on the street?"

"Just like you said, Alessio has mobilized his organization, and his men are scouring the city for any word on Sophie's whereabouts. My brother Jake and his team are keeping tabs on them."

"I'm not surprised." I know full well what Franco is capable of. "Keep your family safe, Shane. Don't underestimate him. Beef up your security, and don't let your wife go wandering around unprotected."

"Don't worry. She's not leaving the penthouse, and I have increased security for all of my family, not just here at the penthouse." He pauses a moment, then says, "Have you told Sophie about your connection to the Alessios?"

"It hasn't come up."

"Are you going to?"

"I wasn't planning on it. I don't think it's relevant."

"Of course it's relevant," he counters. "He's your father, Dominic. You need to tell her. She deserves to understand the predicament you're in."

"It's not a predicament," I say. "Franco Alessio means nothing to me, and Mikey even less. I'll be glad when that reprobate is convicted of first-degree murder and safely behind bars for the rest of his life."

"Tell her, Dominic." Shane's voice has taken on an edge.

"Look, I gotta go, before she starts wondering where I am and comes looking for me. With my luck, she'll wander off and get lost in the woods."

"Call me again in a couple of days. I hope to have some news for you on the trial date by then."

"Right. Later."

After ending the call, I consider calling Franco, but just for a minute. And then I reject the idea. I don't want anything to do with him. He may have fathered me, but he's never been a father. Franco's wife made sure my mother suffered terribly, and he did nothing to stop it, despite the fact that he supposedly loved her.

I stow the sat phone back in the cabinet and secure the door. The last thing I need is Sophie finding this thing and making phone calls to her friends back home.

I meant what I said to Shane. There's no love lost between me and Mikey. I may be his big brother—half-brother, rather—but the family connection means nothing to me. Mikey's a cruel, sadistic son of a bitch, and the thought of him getting his hands on Sophie makes me want to kill. Mikey would take great pleasure in making sure she suffered.

I step inside the cabin just as Sophie's coming down the stairs, dressed in ripped jeans, a sleeveless white tank top with a red plaid shirt tied around her waist, and a well-worn pair of men's hiking boots. She's fucking adorable.

All I can think about is how we fucked on that kitchen table just last night, and how I had her riding me this morning. My cock stirs, wanting to know when we can do it again.

"You ready?" I ask her. "Let's get moving."

"Just a sec. I want to brush my teeth and hair." And then she disappears into the bathroom.

While she's dolling herself up, I grab my chest holster off the hook by the door and check the ammo. Then I head into the armory and pocket some extra rounds. It never hurts to be prepared. When I return to the main room, she's just coming out of the bathroom, her lustrous hair pulled back in a ponytail, making her look even younger.

I watch her hips sway as she approaches, and my dick stirs again for the umpteenth time today.

God, she looks fuckable.

She walks right up to me, a pleased smile on her face, and tilts her face up to mine.

"What are you so happy about?" I ask her, purposely sounding grumpy and fighting a smile.

"Nothing." And then she gives me one of those secret grins women give when they're thinking dirty thoughts about a guy, but they're not willing to let him in on it.

She surprises me by going up on her toes and kissing me.

"What was that for?" I ask. I give up fighting a smile. She's in a playful mood, and I find that a major turn-on. I'm already thinking we should postpone our outing to Owen's cabin. I can think of plenty things I'd rather be doing right here with her.

She leans in close and whispers, "My ass is still tingling."

And then with a wink, she walks past me and out the door.

Holy shit.

Now I want to do a *hell* of a lot more than just finger her ass. And if she continues to tease me like this, I might add in a spanking. I wonder if she's ever been spanked by a lover. Probably not. But there's a first time for everything, and I bet she'd like it.

"Don't tempt me, baby," I mumble as I set the alarm system. I follow her out, jogging down the porch steps to meet her in the yard.

"Lead the way, Daniel Boone," she says, gesturing to the thick woods in front of the cabin.

Shaking my head, I resist the urge to toss her over my shoulder and carry her back inside the cabin for round two. Instead, I head toward the trees.

There's a trail that leads from my cabin directly to Owen's. The trail isn't obvious, but it's there if you know where to look. Sophie follows me, and we disappear into the trees.

The path is narrow, certainly not wide enough for two people, so she has to follow me. It's not much more than a deer path. It's a good thing this isn't a covert operation because Sophie makes enough noise for ten people.

It's easily a twenty-minute trek down the mountain, following a curving path over hard-packed dirt and fallen moss-covered logs until we come to a swiftly-moving creek. The water isn't deep here, only about two feet, but there's no point in getting our boots wet. I walk across a fallen tree that acts as a natural bridge.

When I get to the other side, I glance back expecting to see Sophie following my lead, but she's still standing on the other side of the creek, a scowl on her pretty face.

I plant my hands on my hips and try to look annoyed, rather than amused. "Are you comin'?" I ask her.

She clambers up onto the tree trunk, her arms stretched wide for balance, and wobbles like a top as she stares down at her boots. "I'm not sure this is a good idea," she yells over the sound of rushing water.

I motion her forward. "Don't be silly, Phee. Just walk across."

She looks up at me and glares. "Is there another way?"

"Yeah. There's another path we can take that would add another hour to a five-minute stroll."

She bites her bottom lip as she contemplates the alternative.

"Oh, for Christ's sake." I walk back toward her and offer her my hand. "Come on, baby. You'll be fine."

She clutches my hand with both of hers, holding on for dear life, and takes a tentative step in my direction. Slowly, I lead her across the log, steadying her when she loses her balance.

Her boot slips once on the moss, and she shrieks loud enough to alert everyone in a twenty-mile radius.

But I have a solid hold on her hand. "Relax, I've got you."

When we reach the other side of the creek, I let go of her hand and jump down to the ground. When she reaches for me, holding her arms out expectantly as if she assumes I'll catch her, something weird happens in my chest. There's a shifting sensation, and then some heat. I find myself grasping her around the waist and gently setting her on the ground in front of me.

She clutches my shoulders for dear life. "Thanks." She glances up at me, a bit breathless.

Her cheeks are flushed a pretty pink, and her eyes are a smoky blue—I'm finding it hard to breathe.

"You're welcome," I say, my voice low. Before I do something stupid, like kiss her, I release her and turn away to start walking again. "Try to keep up. Owen will wonder why we're taking so long."

She hurries after me. "He knows we're coming?"

"Sure."

"You told him?" she says.

"No need. He's got these woods wired with sensors. He knows someone's on this path, and he can guess it's us."

We walk a few hundred more yards before I stop her and point down at the dirt path. "Do you know what that is?"

She peers at the dark pellets on the ground. "I'm guessing it's animal poop."

"Bobcat scat," I confirm.

She looks up at me. "You mean shit, right?"

"Yeah."

"So, there really are bobcats in these woods?"

"I told you there were."

"How can you tell this is from a bobcat and not some other animal, like a fox or a raccoon?"

"They're different shapes and sizes."

Sophie rolls her eyes. "You are such a boy scout."

"Hey, if you're going to be in the woods, you need to learn this stuff."

But she's already walked on past me, and now *she's* leading the way. I let her take the lead, figuring as long as she stays on the path, and within my sight, she can hardly get into trouble.

When we near Owen's homestead, I move out in front of Sophie—just as a precaution—and holler a greeting so he knows it's us.

We step out of the trees and into a small clearing, and there's

Owen seated on the front steps leading to his cabin. His is just one story, basically a one-room structure, no bathroom. He uses the woods. His cabin is hardly more than a glorified shed, except for the bank of solar panels on the roof.

He waves at us. "Hey."

"Hi, Owen," Sophie says, joining him on the steps.

"I want her to know how to find you in case she ever needs to," I tell him, although I don't want to think about any circumstances that would require Sophie to seek out Owen's help. It would mean I was somehow incapacitated, or she was in danger—both of which are unacceptable.

"So, how about a tour?" she asks Owen.

He stands. "There's not much to see, but sure, if you want one."

Owen opens the door to his cabin, and Sophie walks inside. I follow her into the one-room cabin. He's right. There's not much to see—a bed, a wood stove, a sink, a mini fridge, and an electric cooktop. That's it. He's as minimal as can be.

The tour takes all of two minutes.

Sophie looks around. "Where's the bathroom?"

Owen nods toward the door. "Outside. In the woods."

She frowns. "You go to the bathroom in the woods?"

He shrugs and nods. "Sure, why not?"

She cringes. "Ew. And I thought Dominic's place was rustic."

Owen hands us each a cold beer, and we go back outside to talk. Sophie sits on the porch steps. I sit near her, on the porch railing, and Owen sits on a tree stump in the yard.

"So, what's going on back in Chicago?" Owen asks me after he takes a long pull on his beer.

Shit.

Sophie perks right up at that and tosses a look my way. "Have you spoken to someone back home? Have you spoken to Shane?"

Thanks, Owen, for opening that can of worms.

I can't bring myself to lie to her, so I say, "Yeah, I spoke to Shane earlier today."

She lights up. "What did he say? Anything about the Alessios? Are they really looking for me?"

"They are." I buy myself some time by guzzling half my beer. I really don't want to be having this conversation with her right now. Or ever.

Her expression falls. "Really?"

Owen stands and joins me at the porch railing. "Have you tried talking to your dad? Maybe Franco would call off his dogs if you asked nicely."

That motherfucker.

"*Dad?*" Sophie repeats, looking stricken.

I nail Owen with a glare. "Thanks for that."

Owen shrugs. "She should know, man."

"Know what?" Sophie looks to me. "What's he talking about? Franco Alessio is your *dad?* Are you serious?"

Since she's bound to find out sooner or later, I figure there's no point denying it. "Yeah."

13

Sophie

Furious, I hand Owen my empty beer bottle and head for the trail that leads back to Dominic's cabin. I need to get away from him before I scream.

He lied to me.

Dominic shoots to his feet. "Sophie, wait!"

When I don't stop, he follows without saying another word, which is good because I can't deal with talking to him right now.

Franco Alessio is Dominic's *father?* The very man who wants me dead? And, my god, that means Mikey is Dominic's *brother.*

Jesus Christ, I can't wrap my mind around any of this.

"Sophie, slow down before you hurt yourself," he says.

I throw up my hand. "Don't talk to me!" I storm ahead, practically tripping over fallen branches and stones in my path.

"Sophie, come on. Let's talk about this."

My heart is pounding as I try to catch my breath. "You lied to me!"

"I didn't lie."

"You didn't tell me the truth, and that's the same thing, asshole!"

"Baby, please."

I stop dead in my tracks and pivot to face him. "Don't you dare call me *baby*. In fact, don't talk to me at all."

I turn to resume my power trek back to the cabin, but he grabs my arm and pulls me back to face him.

"Calm down, Phee," he says.

I dig my nails into the back of his hand, and although he grimaces in pain, he doesn't let go.

"Let go of me," I hiss. "And don't *ever* tell me to calm down, you douchebag."

He grins. "*Douchebag?*"

"Stop laughing. It's not funny."

His lips flatten, but he's still fighting a grin. "Just let me explain."

"Okay, then explain. Why didn't you tell me you're an Alessio?"

His jaw tightens. "Because I'm not."

"He's your father, Dominic. I'm pretty sure that makes you

an Alessio."

His eyes darken as they narrow, and for a second I feel a frisson of unease skate down my spine. He's clearly furious now.

"Franco Alessio isn't my *father*," he says. "He's the monster who used and manipulated a young teenage girl, knocked her up, and kicked her to the curb the minute his bitch of a wife found out. He may have fathered me, Sophie, but he was never my *father*. There's a hell of a difference."

Hearing the underlying hurt in his tone takes the wind out of my sail. My shoulders sag, and I remove my nails from the back of his hand, leaving little half-moon imprints behind. "Sorry."

He shrugs it off. "Owen's right, you deserve to know. Come on. Let's go home, and we'll talk."

Home.

The way he said it makes my heart hurt.

Dominic walks on ahead, and I follow. My mind is racing with all the implications of his relationship to the Alessios. It's not that I don't trust him, or that I don't trust his motives. Shane would never have asked Dominic to protect me from the Alessio organization if he didn't believe wholeheartedly that Dominic would do exactly that. Unless he didn't know about Dominic's connection to the mob.

"Does Shane know Franco's your father?" I ask.

"Yeah, he knows."

When we reach the creek, Dominic waits for me to catch up. Without saying a word, he lifts me up onto the fallen tree and guides me across. Once we reach the other side, I jump down and walk ahead, wanting to put some distance behind us.

This whole situation was complicated enough to begin with, but this changes everything. I can't believe his father is a *mobster*. And not just any old mobster, but the head of an organized crime syndicate.

Once we're back at the cabin, he follows me inside, shutting the door quietly behind him.

I turn to face him. And what I see in his expressions stops the heated words that are poised to come out of my mouth.

He looks so damn conflicted as he stares at me, his jaw clenched, throat muscles working.

And then I realize that it never once occurred to me to ask him how he was doing through all of this. All this time, I've been selfishly focused on myself and how this situation is affecting me, when it has to be hard on him too. Maybe even harder.

I close the distance between us, standing toe-to-toe with him, and look up to meet his gaze. His eyes meet mine, and the uncertainty I see in them makes my chest ache.

"I'm sorry," I say, reaching up to cup the side of his face. To my surprise, he closes his eyes and leans into my hand. "Are you okay?"

His eyes snap open. "Shouldn't I be the one asking you that?"

"Tell me about your dad."

He shakes his head and leads me by the hand toward the sofa, where he sits and pulls me onto his lap so that I'm facing him, my thighs straddling his hips.

He threads his long fingers through my hair and pulls me

close enough that our foreheads are almost touching. "I don't want to talk, Phee. I just want to fuck."

"Ah, sex. The ultimate avoidance tactic."

"Sex first, then we'll talk later. Who doesn't like make-up sex?"

I smile. "Were we fighting?"

"It sure sounded like we were. You called me an asshole and a douchebag."

His thighs are rock hard beneath mine, and I feel the sexual need radiating off him in waves. His hands slide down to my hips, and he presses his erection between my legs. He wants comfort, temporary oblivion.

"You promise we'll talk afterward?" I ask. It seems arousal is contagious. Already my body is heating and softening.

He nods as he brushes his nose against mine. "You are so fucking beautiful."

He pulls my tank top free from my jeans and slides his warm palms underneath the fabric, skimming my torso from my quivering belly to my breasts. He cups them and starts rubbing my nipples through the silky fabric of my bra. My nipples tighten, and instantly I feel an answering ache between my legs.

"Take off your shirt," he says, his voice gruff.

I untie the plaid shirt around my waist and toss it onto the couch.

"Now the tank top," he demands, his voice like gravel. "Take it off. Take it all off. I want you naked."

I'm shocked to find myself getting aroused by his bossy demands. He's such a Neandertal. He thinks he can just tell me what to do, and I'll do it. That arrogant, son of a—

"Take it off, Phee," he says, his voice edged with warning.

I do as he says, tossing my tank onto the cushion next to us.

His gaze locks on my chest, and as he stares at me, I feel my body heat up. At first, he traces the swell of both breasts just above my bra cups, his fingers warm and gentle. Then, with no warning, he pulls my bra straps down off my shoulders and tugs the cups below my breasts, causing them to lift and sit up prettily, begging for attention.

He eyes my breasts hungrily and traces one nipple with his finger. Then he leans forward and sucks it into his mouth. I cry out sharply, shocked at how good it feels.

His other hand unfastens my jeans, and he slips his fingers inside my panties and begins stroking me.

"So soft," he murmurs as he caresses me.

His touch is electric, setting my body on fire. Before I can stop myself, I moan loudly, and he smiles.

As he continues to tongue my nipple, flicking it gently and making me squirm, his middle finger slides between my nether lips and locates my clit.

He makes a growling sound as he strokes me. "God, you're already wet for me." And then, without warning, he nudges me off his lap. "I want you naked."

He bends down to unlace my boots and tugs them off, along with my socks. Then he pulls my jeans and panties off me. "Take off your bra."

Unable to look away from his heated gaze, I reach behind me to unclasp my bra and let it fall.

Here I am, standing in front of him stark naked in broad daylight, while he's fully dressed. I'm shocked by how much this turns me on. I glance over at the window. If someone came by, they'd get quite an eyeful. And that thought only makes me hotter. I'm such a hussy.

He tracks my gaze to the window and grins, the bastard. Then he snags my wrist with one hand as he unfastens his jeans with the other. I watch as his zipper comes down and his penis escapes its confines, already hardening.

He pulls me close, obviously wanting me to return to my former position straddling his lap, but instead I drop down and kneel on the rug between his legs and wrap one hand around his impressive erection. He's had his mouth on me, and now it's my turn.

He eyes me hungrily as he wraps a thick length of my hair around his fist. "You're asking for trouble."

Licking my bottom lip—and capturing his undivided attention in the process—I feel a sense of power I've never felt before. Dominic is a magnificent specimen of a man, a sexual beast, and right now he's all mine. "Maybe I like trouble."

Pulling my hair, he gently tugs me closer to his erection. "That I don't doubt."

I slide back his foreskin to reveal the head of his cock which is a deep, ruddy pink. There's a glistening drop of pre-come at the tip of his cock, beckoning me. He's aroused too, as much as

I am.

I grin up at him, feeling a bit cocky myself. "Don't pretend you're not dying for my mouth on you, because you'd be flat out lying."

He tugs me even closer. "Shut up and put me in your mouth."

Smiling, I take my sweet time, teasing him with the tip of my tongue.

He tightens his fist in my hair and growls a warning. "Sophie."

Lazily, I lick his length from base to tip, then swirl my tongue over the broad crown and beneath the sensitive ridge.

Groaning, he shifts in his seat and tightens his grip on my hair. "Stop teasing and suck me, damn it."

But I'm in charge right now, and I want to make sure he knows it. I continue to tease him, first sucking the head of his cock into my mouth, then swirling my tongue around it. I tease him and torment him, driving his arousal sharply higher. He's right, I am poking the bear.

Taking momentary pity on him, I swallow his shaft as deep as I can, and then I begin to bob my head on his cock with wild abandon, using my mouth, my tongue, and my hands to drive him wild.

With a growl, he grips my head with both hands and urges me to take him deeper. When I do, he throws his head back on the sofa cushion and groans. "God, yes."

With one hand stroking him, I take him as far back in my throat as I can manage. He's too big for me to take all of him, but I use my hands, too, and make the best of it. It's certainly good enough to make his thighs quake and tremble. My head bobs up and down as I fuck him with my mouth.

His fingertips dig into my scalp. "That's enough." He pulls me up onto him, and I'm straddling his hips once more. As I rise up on my knees, he positions himself at my opening, and I lower myself onto him, slowly working him in.

Impatient, he raises his hips and thrusts into me. "Jesus, Phee, you're killing me." When I lean forward and suck his bottom lip before biting it, he growls again. "Fuck!"

Once I'm fully seated on his cock, he cups my butt cheeks and lifts me up, then lets me fall back down. His hips rise to meet me, thrusting deep inside. Faster and faster we move as he bounces me on him effortlessly. His arm muscles bulge and flex, and I'm mesmerized by his sheer strength.

As the delicious heat between us increases, my mouth latches onto his, and we devour each other, lips, tongues, breath. I'm gasping for air, his chest is heaving, and it's wild and glorious and I've never felt so alive or so wanted before. There's nothing pretty or elegant about this; it's just raw, animalistic sex.

He reaches between us, his finger sliding through my wetness. A moment later, I feel his finger at my backside, gently rimming me. Electricity shoots up my spine. And then his finger becomes insistent, nudging its way inside.

"Relax," he mutters hoarsely.

I obey, loosening my muscles, and his finger slides inside easily as he begins thrusting gently, long, slow drags inside me.

"Dominic," I gasp as I press my forehead to his.

He changes his angle so that his cock brushes my clitoris, over and over, stroking it so perfectly. The intense pleasure, combined with the naughtiness going on in my backside, is too much. I cry out shamelessly, the sound high-pitched and needy. I guess I do squeal.

He's relentless, coming at me from both sides, driving my pleasure higher and higher.

"Dom—oh god, Dominic. Please, yes, don't stop—just like that." As my orgasm tears through me, I clamp down on both his cock and his finger. The blinding pleasure is so exquisite, I bury my face in the crook of his neck and gasp for air.

He throws his head back and shouts as he comes hot and furiously inside me. When I feel the unfamiliar sensation of liquid heat inside me, my heart nearly stops. Oh, shit. He's not wearing a condom.

I'm so shocked I can only whisper his name. "Dominic."

"I know," he mutters harshly. "Shit! I'm sorry. I... forgot."

"We both did."

He pulls me to his chest and wraps his arms around me. I can feel him throbbing inside me and with each twitch of his cock, my body reverberates with pleasure. My ass is tingling again, *damn him.*

His lips brush my ear. "I'm sorry. We'll be more careful next time."

His stomach growls loudly then, breaking the tension, and we both laugh.

"Let me guess," I say. "You're hungry."

"It is lunchtime, you know."

He lifts me gently up and off of him, standing me between his knees, and I feel semen trickling down the inside of my thighs. "Oh my. I'm leaking." I've never had sex without a condom before. This is... different.

"Let's get cleaned up and dressed. Then we'll make some lunch."

"You promised you'd tell me about your dad."

He sighs. "I haven't forgotten."

14

Dominic

I can't believe I fucked her without a condom. I've never made such an asinine mistake in my life. The last thing I want to do is get someone pregnant. I'm not like my father, fucking indiscriminately, knocking girls up, and then kicking them to the curb.

Of course, Sophie's not a girl. She's a woman, and a rather sophisticated one at that. Frankly, I'm surprised she even gives me the time of day. I don't know how she feels about me, and I'm not about to ask. Whatever it is we have going on, I don't want it to end. And I sure as hell don't want to ruin it.

While Sophie heads to the bathroom to clean up, I fasten my jeans and wash up in the kitchen sink. I smile when I think about her getting off with my finger in her ass. I think she finds it shocking, and that's part of the allure. I also think she digs it. I'm not kidding myself that she'll ever let me fuck her there, but I do like pushing the envelope with her. Maybe one day she'll let me work her up to something a little bigger, like a small dildo or a butt plug. I can dream, can't I?

I hear the bathroom door open, and then she runs upstairs to her room without saying a word to me. She's been pretty quiet since we fucked, and I imagine she's a bit freaked out that we forgot to use a condom. To be honest, I am too. I've *never* forgotten. That just shows how much she rattles my brain.

I figure we can do something easy for lunch, like make sandwiches. I'll grill steaks later this evening for dinner. By the time she comes back down, wearing a cute little dress held up with tiny straps, I have everything for lunch laid out on the counter.

"Sandwiches and chips okay?" I ask her.

"Sure." She walks to the fridge and pulls out two beers, handing me one.

"Buttering me up?" I say. I know what she's waiting for—my life story. And it's the last thing in the world I want to talk about.

She walks around to the opposite side of the counter and sits on a barstool. Getting comfortable, no doubt.

"Start talking," she says after taking a sip of her beer.

I hand her an empty plate. "Make your sandwich."

I've laid out a loaf of bread, sliced chicken from the deli, swiss and cheddar, lettuce, tomatoes, mayo, and potato chips.

She makes herself a sandwich and dumps a pile of chips on her plate.

"All right, start talking," she says just before she pops a chip into her mouth.

I don't even try to hide my lack of enthusiasm. "My mom's parents emigrated from Italy to the US when they were newly married. My mom was born here, in Chicago, a first generation American. She didn't even graduate high school. She was pretty, though, so she had no trouble getting jobs. Eventually, an employment agency placed her in the Alessio household as a maid. She was just seventeen and gorgeous—I've seen pictures of her. Franco took a liking to her. Hell, he took more than a liking—he got her pregnant. Too bad he was already married."

Sophie picks up her beer, and says, "Did she love him?"

I shrug. "She said she did. She never really talked much about him—certainly not to me. She told me that once she started showing, Franco's wife, Angelica, caught on to the fact that her husband had a little piece on the side.

Angelica told Franco to get rid of my mother. She threatened to have my mom killed if Franco didn't get rid of her, so he did. He fired her immediately and showed her the door. She left with nothing, disgraced, pregnant, and heartbroken."

"You have your mother's last name?"

"Yeah."

"What was her name?"

"Mia."

"Mia Zaretti. That's pretty. Did Franco have any other children at the time? Besides you?"

"No. I was his firstborn. His wife gave birth to Mikey five years after I was born. They never had any other children."

I swallow the last of my beer and toss the bottle into the recycling bin, then grab another from the fridge. I know it's early to be drinking, but I don't give a damn. I just want to get through this.

"I'm sorry," she says. "I know this must be painful for you to talk about."

I take a bite of my sandwich—it tastes like cardboard—and nod. "You have no idea."

"And I take it you don't have a good relationship with your father?"

I shake my head. "Like I said, he may have fathered me, but he's not my father. All my life, I've had as little to do with Franco as humanly possible."

She frowns, her pretty lips turning down. "Has he ever tried to reach out to you?"

Abruptly, I toss my uneaten food in the trash. "This conversation is over." And then I walk out the door, letting it slam shut behind me.

I head for the woodpile, grab the ax, and start swinging. I've split three logs in half by the time I hear the cabin door open and close quietly. I keep my attention on what I'm doing and do my best to ignore the woman who's walking this way.

Two more logs split, and already I'm working up a sweat.

Two more, and my arms are starting to ache. Still, I raise the ax and bring it down with crushing force.

"I'm sorry," she says quietly, standing back a dozen feet behind me.

Smart girl.

I'm not sure exactly what she's apologizing for. For asking me to talk about it? Because my mom died? Or because my father is a fucking criminal? Anyway, it doesn't matter. "Forget it."

Thwack! Another log split in half. At this rate, we'll have enough wood cut to last us a month.

The thought of being stuck here on this mountain—alone with *her* for another month—fills me with dread. It's not because I don't enjoy her company. Quite the opposite. I like it too much. I'm starting to crave it.

She clears her throat and says, "I'm sure it must be difficult to have a father who—"

I hurl the ax across the yard, the blade embedding itself in a tree trunk twenty feet away. Then I turn to face her. "A father who what? Is a fucking criminal? One who makes his money selling drugs and pressuring small business owners to pay him protection money? One who launders dirty, ill-gotten gains and always manages to stay one step ahead of the feds?" Furious, I stalk toward her. "What's so fucking difficult about that, Sophie?"

I get in her face, and by god, she doesn't cower one inch. Her soft cheeks pinken and she starts shaking, but she doesn't back away. She doesn't even look away.

Taking a deep breath, she steels herself, swallowing hard before she says, "I'm sorry you lost your mother, and I'm sorry you have a shit dad." Her voice is quavering, but that doesn't stop her. "I admit I don't know exactly what that's like, but I can guess how I'd feel if it were me."

My hands somehow end up on her shoulders, gripping them firmly as I loom over her. "My dad's been begging me for *years* to join his organization. Mikey's an idiot. He's a mean, narcissistic asshole who's unfit to take over anything. You know what irony is? I'm Franco's bastard son, the one he abandoned decades ago, and yet he would do anything—offer *anything*—to bring me into the fold. But you know what? I don't want to be a fucking criminal. I may never amount to much, but at least I have my integrity. That matters more to me than money, power, *anything*. I've never sacrificed my integrity. And I never will."

She flinches but stands her ground. I realize I'm hurting her—squeezing her shoulders too hard. I release her immediately. "Sorry."

Her expression softens, and then she tears up. Tentatively, she rests a hand on my arm, clutching my bicep. "You're an honorable man, Dominic. You're nothing like your father. You never could be."

"You don't know anything about me," I snap, still angry and wanting to strike out at her. She's the one who dredged this up. I usually manage to keep it buried deep, but she just keeps poking and prodding. She's spoiled rotten and doesn't know when to take *no* for an answer, or when to mind her own business.

"I'm sorry I upset you," she says. "That was never my intention. I just wanted to understand how you could be connected with—" She pauses.

"With a mob boss? With a criminal?"

She nods. "With the man who wants me dead."

A knot lodges in my throat. "Shit, Phee. I'd never let them hurt you. If you believe anything, believe that."

She nods. "I do. I believe you."

I want so badly to pull her into my arms, to hold her tight, but I'm a sweaty mess right now. Sophie makes me feel things I've never felt before. She challenges me, which I like. She excites me, which I *really* like. And she arouses me to no end.

Even now, after my emotional outburst, I'm wondering if she'll sleep in my bed again tonight. But I'm not sure if she wants to fuck the son of a mob boss.

I take a step back. "I need a shower. Then we'll work on your rifle skills."

Her expression falls, as if she's disappointed. "Okay. If that's what you want."

"Yeah, it's what I want. I need to know you can defend yourself."

"They can't find us here, right? Your father—Franco—he doesn't know about this place, does he?"

"He doesn't. But still, I never leave things to chance. If they find out where you are, they'll send a team."

She blanches. "To kill me, you mean."

I'm not going to lie to her or sugarcoat the situation. "Yeah.

To kill you."

"All right," she says. "I'll make you a deal. Go take your shower and teach me how to hit a target with a rifle at a hundred yards. And then afterward, we can go into town for dinner. I have a craving for hot apple pie with vanilla ice cream. How does that sound?"

"All right. It's a deal." I cup her cheek but resist the urge to lean in and kiss her.

She may be many things, but a coward isn't one of them.

15

Sophie

While Dominic takes a shower, I make coffee. I need more caffeine if I'm going to survive being marooned out here in the wilderness. I'd give anything to be back home, maybe out shopping with Amber at Water Tower Place or simply strolling down North Michigan Avenue, stopping at the bridge over Chicago River to watch the boats and kayakers paddling downriver.

Once the coffee is ready, I pour a cup, doctor it up with plenty of sugar and French vanilla creamer, and then sit at the breakfast counter to sip my beverage of choice. As the molecules of caffeine sink into my cells, I survey the cabin. I know Dominic has a phone hidden here somewhere. He admitted as much when he told Owen that he'd spoken to Shane.

There has to be a phone in here. A burner phone at least, if not a satellite phone. The problem is, I have no idea where he's hidden it.

The water is still running in the shower—*what the hell is he doing in there that's taking so long?* In the meantime, I do a quick bit of reconnaissance in the cabin to see if I can find a phone.

I check the small coat closet and each of the kitchen drawers and cupboards. I check the pantry. I know it's not in my bedroom because I've already scoured that room. The only other place I can think to look is Dominic's bedroom, but I don't want to risk getting caught snooping in his private space.

Then I remember the armory! That would be the perfect place to hide a phone. I return to the pantry and open the hidden door. After switching on the light, I scan the room. It's jam-packed with all kinds of weapons, ammo, and god knows what else. I take a quick peek, but don't find anything.

Frustrated, I carry my coffee out to the front porch with the intention of sitting on the swing, but I notice a small wooden shed across the yard. That would be a great hiding place. No one would think to look there. I head over to the shed, intending to search it, but the door is locked with a combination lock that requires three numbers.

I try a few basic combinations, but none of them work. Of course it's not going to be as simple as one-two-three. *Damn it.*

"Need some help?"

I nearly jump out of my skin as I turn to find Owen and his dog just a few feet behind me. "Owen! You startled me."

Owen grins apologetically. "Sorry. Didn't mean to scare you." He looks around the yard. "Where's Dominic?"

"He's in the shower."

"Oh." He frowns. "You need something from the shed?"

Crap.

"Um, no. Not really. I was just curious." I give him a smile that I hope will distract him. "I'm bored, actually. Hey, do you want some coffee? I just made a pot."

He nods. "Sure. I'd love some."

Owen follows me inside, leaving his dog outside. As he sits at the breakfast bar and I pour him a cup of coffee—which he drinks black—Dominic comes down the stairs. He's dressed in jeans and a black t-shirt that clings lovingly to his brawny muscles.

Showoff.

He glowers as he approaches us.

"Want some coffee?" I ask him, smiling sweetly.

"Sure." He comes around to my side of the counter, standing beside me, and reaches for an empty coffee cup in the overhead cabinet. He hands it to me before turning to Owen. "Everything all right?"

Owen takes a sip of his coffee and nods. "The mountain's quiet."

Dominic nods. "Not for long. We're going to do some target

practice this afternoon," he says, tipping his head toward me. "I want her competent with a rifle in case we have visitors."

"Want me to hang around?" Owen says.

"No," Dominic says rather quickly. "There's no need."

Owen finishes his cup and steps off the barstool. "Okay. I'll leave you to it then."

"I promised her I'd take her into town for dinner tonight."

Owen frowns as he looks from Dominic to me and back again. "You think that's a good idea?"

"Why not?" I say, afraid I'm going to lose my evening out. I could use a distraction.

Dominic shrugs. "It'll be fine. It's just dinner."

"Folks are nosy, is all," Owen says, as he gets to his feet. "People will see her. And people talk."

"We'll keep a low profile," Dominic says.

"All right. Suit yourself," Owen says. He takes his leave, disappearing out the door and then into the woods with his dog at his heels.

Dominic and I retrieve my three-eighty and a box of ammo. He makes me stand at the kitchen counter and practice loading and reloading my clip, over and over, until my fingertips are sore.

"How many times do I have to do this?" I say, getting irritated. "I know how to load the fucking gun."

"I know you do. But it needs to become ingrained in your muscle memory. You need to be able to load a gun in the dark, with your eyes closed."

And then, to prove his point, the idiot blindfolds me with a bandana and makes me do it over and over. My first attempt is a bit slow, my fingers fumbling. But after a few more tries, I can do it pretty quickly.

After he's satisfied with my loading skills, we both grab some ear protection and go out back to the little makeshift shooting range and I shoot half a box of rounds, hitting tin cans at various distances, and then paper targets shaped like men.

Then we switch to the rifle, and he makes me practice loading that before having me shoot at paper targets at twenty feet, thirty feet, forty feet.

Fortunately, I have very good hand-eye coordination, so my shots aren't completely horrible.

"You're great at maiming the enemy," Dominic says wryly. "But your goal isn't to piss them off. You need to take them out. Neutralize the targets."

"Don't you think this is overkill?" I ask him. "No one's going to find us way out here."

"That's the plan," he agrees. "But we have to be prepared for anything. If the Alessios get wind of your location, they'll send a carload of hitmen gunning for you."

I shudder, horrified at the reminder that someone could very well want to shoot me—on purpose. And then I remember that the person behind the threat is Dominic's own father. Would he really send a car full of armed men to his own son's location? He'd have to know there'd be a gun fight, and that Dominic could get hurt.

We head back inside, and Dominic takes me up to his bedroom window, which overlooks the front yard. He points toward the spot where the lane emerges from the trees.

"If they come, it'll be by vehicle, probably a nondescript sedan with tinted windows. The car will appear there, coming up the drive. Owen will be alerted first and, theoretically, he'll have time to warn us. Remember, it's a twenty-minute drive up to this cabin. Owen would know the minute they turned onto our lane. If they come, you grab a rifle, plenty of ammo, and head up here to this window. It's got the best vantage point. And as soon as they step out of the car, you fire. Shoot to kill. Do you hear me?"

I don't like this at all. "Why are you telling me this?" I ask him. "If something happens, you'll be right here with me, and then you can order me around all you want."

He turns to face me and looks me in the eye. "Because if something happens to me, I need to know that *you* know how to defend yourself."

Dominic opens the window, kneels in front of it, and aims toward the spot where the lane disappears into the trees. He raises the rifle in his arms, sighting a target and fires. A small branch explodes, obliterated.

There is no screen on the window, and I realize that's intentional.

He hands me the rifle. "Pick a target. Something near the lane."

I hoist the rifle to my shoulder and get a good grip on it.

Closing one eye, I sight the vicinity where he shot before, pick a low-hanging branch, and fire.

Nothing.

"Try again," he says.

For the next hour, he makes me take shot after shot at small-to-medium tree branches. I make a few shots, but not many. He also makes me practice loading and reloading the rifle until my fingers are numb.

Finally, when my shoulders are on fire and my arms ache, I lay the rifle on the floor in front of me and take off my ear protection. "I've had enough. Every muscle in my body hurts, and my ears won't stop ringing. Can we stop now, please?"

He sighs, clearly less than happy, and takes off his own headset. "All right."

I climb to my feet. "I'm going to take a shower and change before we head into town."

He rises to his feet as well, towering over me. "Fine. Just don't take too long. I want to get back before dark."

"It'll take as long as it takes, Dominic," I say, heading for the door. "You can't rush perfection."

He calls after me. "Hey! This isn't a date, it's just dinner. There's no point in getting all dolled up."

I ignore him and walk across the hall to my bedroom, where I go through the clothes I picked up at the thrift shop. I know this isn't a date, but I feel like going out and having fun, and I want to look good doing it. He can be a stick-in-the-mud if he likes, but I'm going to have fun tonight.

I settle on a pair of distressed blue jeans because they hug my ass nicely, and a light-blue, sleeveless blouse with a plunging neckline. I wish I'd picked up a pair of sandals when I had the chance, but I'll have to make do with my funky, chunky man-boots. They'll contrast nicely with the feminine top.

While Dominic's muttering to himself in his bedroom, I jog down the stairs to the bathroom and climb into a hot shower. While I'm washing, I check on the status of my lady garden—still smooth, thank god. I had my last wax about two weeks ago, so I know I'm running on borrowed time.

I'm pretty sure there's not an aesthetician within a hundred-mile radius. I don't know what I'm going to do when my hair starts growing in. The last time I tried shaving down there, I cut myself. I'm not interested in a repeat of that.

After a quick shave of my legs and underarms, I step out of the shower and wrap a threadbare towel around me. *Note to Dominic: buy some new towels.*

After dressing, I put on a light touch of makeup—just enough to look like I'm not wearing any makeup. I towel-dry my hair, leaving the waves in, and then put it up in a high ponytail and let a few strands fall to my shoulders.

Lastly, after applying a bit of rosy-pink lipstick, I stand back to take it all in. *Not bad.*

"Hurry up already," Dominic grouses just as I come out of the bathroom.

He's standing at the kitchen counter nursing a cup of coffee. When he hears me approach, he turns to face me, about to say something, when his eyes nearly bug out of his head. "What in the hell are you wearing?"

I stop mid-step and glance down at my outfit. "What?"

"What d'you mean, *what*?" He stalks toward me and points accusingly at my chest. "You're seriously going to wear *that*?"

"Why not? It's a pretty top."

He scowls. "It shows off your cleavage. Damn near all of it!"

"So?"

"*So?*" He glares at me. "Go change. I mean it, Sophie. Put on that plaid shirt you were wearing earlier."

I start laughing. God, I haven't had a good laugh in a long time. "Sure, *Dad*," I say, embracing my snarky side as I walk past him to the kitchen to pour myself a cup of java. I wave him off. "Finish your coffee and let's go."

"Aren't you going to change?"

"No. I look good. Get over it."

Annoyed, Dominic disappears into the armory and comes out with a black 9mm handgun strapped to his chest. He pulls on a black leather jacket to hide the gun and the holster.

"You're going armed?" I say, a bit surprised.

"Honey, I'm always armed."

The sight of him in black leather is... *hot*.

Dominic sets the alarm, and we leave the cabin and climb into his Bronco. Then it's off we go, heading for town. It's a mind-numbing drive down the rutted, rocky lane to the main road.

"Can't you guys do something about this road?" I say. "It's

horrible."

He laughs. "That's the point, baby. It slows everyone down, coming and going, and gives us plenty of advance warning."

Once we reach the main road, Dominic turns left and heads into town. It's around six o'clock, and my stomach is growling.

"What sounds good to you?" I ask.

He makes a dismissive sound. "I'm not picky."

When we reach the small three blocks of what passes for a downtown here, he pulls to the side of the street.

"There's not much to choose from," he says. "The diner, the tavern, or the gas station convenience store."

I laugh. "The tavern. A big fat juicy burger, fries, and a cold beer sound really good right now. I'll bet they have a jukebox."

"Fine. The tavern it is."

We pull around behind the building and park in the rear lot. There are a number of motorcycles parked back here, pickup trucks, and old clunkers. The lot's nearly full.

"Looks like we're not the only ones hungry," I say, hopping down from the SUV.

We walk to the back door, and Dominic opens it for me.

Immediately, I'm hit with delicious aromas coming from the kitchen. Music's playing loudly on the sound system, and chatter and laughter fill the air. It takes a moment for my eyes to adjust to the dim lighting.

We walk down a narrow hallway, past the restrooms and the kitchen, to the main room in front. Most of the tables are packed, as is the bar area. There's a dance floor in the center of the tavern, and off to the side are a number of pool tables.

A harried blonde in a tight black miniskirt and short cowgirl boots breezes past us, but not so quickly that she doesn't have time to give Dominic a quick once-over. "Seat yourselves, folks," she calls back to us. "I'll be right with you."

Dominic steers me across the room to an available booth along the far wall. I slide into one side, and he sits opposite me. He grabs two menus from the condiment rack and hands me one.

"Let's make this quick," he says. "We eat and get back to the cabin."

I glance around the bar, my eyes fully adjusted now to the dim lighting. Clearly this is where everyone comes for a night out, to let their hair down.

Dominic points to my menu. "Do you know what you want?"

I lay it down. "Yes. I told you—a burger, fries, and a draft beer."

When our server comes, bringing us two glasses of iced water, we place our orders. Dominic orders a burger, onion rings, and a Coke.

"Not drinking tonight?" I ask him.

"No. I'm driving, and I'm armed."

"Good point."

Our drinks come right away, and while we wait for our food, I make a visit to the jukebox and put some coins into the machine. The playlist is all country, and while I'm not a big country music fan, I do find plenty of selections I like.

"Wanna dance?" I ask him, when I return to our table.

He gives me a look. "What do you think?"

"Yes?" I say hopefully. And when he frowns at me, I laugh. "Oh, come on. Let's have some fun. A couple of dances won't kill you."

"I don't dance."

"Do you play pool?"

He gives me an equally unhappy scowl.

"Wow, you're the life of the party, aren't you?" I tease, reaching for my glass. I take a sip of my beer. "Darts? My brothers taught me to play. I'm not bad."

He chugs his soft drink, and a moment later our waitress appears with a refill for him. I swear, she's been keeping tabs on him and waiting for an excuse to come back.

"Here you go, darlin'," she says, setting a fresh Coke in front of him. She picks up his empty glass. "Your food will be right out. Is there anything else I can get you?"

"No, this is fine," he mutters, sounding like a grump.

His eyes are on me, so I don't think he notices how she's looking at him—like she wants to sink her teeth into him. She's petite and curvy as hell, with short, curly blonde hair and big brown eyes.

"You must be new around here," she says. "I've never seen you in here before."

He shrugs, and all I can think is that Dominic needs to work on his social skills.

"This must be your sister," the woman says, giving me an icy smile. "I can see the resemblance."

"Sister?" I say, choking on a mouthful of beer.

Dominic bites back a grin, and I can just guess what he's thinking.

Yeah, if we're siblings, then we're both going to hell.

"She's definitely not my sister," he says, grinning.

"Sorry," the girl replies. "I just thought, you know, since she's so tall."

"Darcy, your order's up!" yells a man from the kitchen.

Our waitress nods toward the kitchen. "Gotta go, but I'll be back soon with your food." She looks directly as Dominic. "If you need anything else, hun, just flag me down."

"Sister, huh?" I say once we're alone. "If she only knew the naughty things we've been up to."

Grinning, Dominic shakes his head.

Darcy is back again in record time with our food, and we dig in.

"I think target practice makes me hungry," I say before popping a fry in my mouth.

As Dominic's gaze locks onto my mouth, I feel a rush of heat. His eyes drop to my cleavage, and I could swear he looks hungry. But he hasn't touched his food.

"Aren't you hungry?" I ask him. "I'm famished."

He nods. "I am."

"Then eat before your food gets cold."

We eat then, both of us focusing on our food and avoiding eye contact. He's in a bad mood, but I'm not sure why. And something weird is happening between us. He's acting miserable, yet he keeps watching me like a hawk who has spotted a mouse.

When I'm done eating, I lean back in my seat. He's nearly finished. He picks up a small onion ring and holds it out to me. I lean forward and snatch it from his fingers with my mouth.

"What's wrong?" I ask him.

He glances around the bar. "Half the guys in here are undressing you with their eyes."

"Ignore them. It's their problem, not ours."

It looks like he's done eating, so I steal the last onion ring off his plate and pop it into my mouth.

He smiles at me. "Ready to go?"

"But we just got here," I argue. One of the songs I programmed into the jukebox comes on—*Body Like a Back Road* by Sam Hunt. "Wanna dance?"

His gaze meets mine. "Definitely not."

"Oh, come on. You're no fun."

He shrugs. "Can we go now? Please?"

Our waitress brings me another beer, and I pick it up to take a big drink. "No! We came here to have fun."

"No, we came here because I promised you dinner in town. I never said anything about having *fun*. Let's go."

I finish off my beer and slip out of the booth. "Fine. You sit here and entertain yourself. I'm going dancing."

And then I head for the dance floor, by myself, and start dancing to one of my favorite songs before it ends.

Not a moment later, some guy appears in front of me. Tall as me, blond, with muscles to spare. He's wearing black jeans and a form-fitting t-shirt advertising a local feed store. "Hey, baby," he says with a low drawl. "You here alone?"

"It sure feels like it," I say.

He holds out his arms. "You're way too pretty to be dancin' alone, sugar. How about you let me join you?"

Before I can reply, Dominic steps between us.

"How about you get lost?" he says, glaring down at the other guy.

The blond hottie stares at Dominic for half a second before he steps back. "Hey, I was just tryin' to be friendly, that's all. She looked to be alone."

"Well, she's not," Dominic says. "She's with me."

The blond walks away, muttering under his breath. Dominic moves to go after him, but I grab his arm and pull him back.

"You're here now, so you might as well dance with me," I tell him.

He looks down at me, far from thrilled. "I don't dance, Phee."

When he calls me that, my heart softens, as does my attitude. "Come here, big guy. I'll teach you."

The next song is also one of mine—*Cruise* by Florida Georgia Line. Grateful it's a slow song, I pull Dominic close. "Put your arms around my waist," I tell him. Then I lift my arms and wrap them around his neck.

"Phee, I really don't—"

"Shut up, Dominic." And then I nudge him into a gentle

sway. "See, it's not hard. Just hold me and move in slow circles."

He leans down, his lips brushing my ear and sending shivers down my spine. "I know all about moving in slow circles, baby."

He pulls me closer, the ridge of his erection pressing against my belly. "No one dances with you," he says, his lips hovering over my ear. "No one but me."

16

Dominic

I lied to Sophie about not knowing how to dance. I've done more than my share of dancing in bars and clubs. The problem is, I wanted to avoid getting this close to her tonight. I'm already having a hell of a problem wanting to get close to her, and the way she looks tonight is proving to be my kryptonite.

She looks fucking gorgeous, and that goddamn top she's wearing is driving me crazy because I can see more than a little cleavage. Standing this close to her, able to smell her sweet scent, with my arms around her and hers around me... it's unbearable. When I glance down at the spot where her chest is pressed against mine, I get an eyeful of plump curves and enticing shadows, and it's enough to make me forget my own name.

I don't know what the fuck I'm doing anymore. I thought this job would be boring and monotonous—you know, babysit a spoiled socialite. But it hasn't been. I can't ever remember having this much fun with a woman. And it's not just the sex—although that's hot as hell because she's comfortable with her body and her needs. It's everything about her. She's fun, strong-willed, and annoyingly feisty. I find that an irresistible combination.

The sex started off as a way to let off steam, but now it's changed into something else. I crave her all the time. I feel possessive where she's concerned, and I don't know how to handle it. I want her in my bed—permanently. I don't want to just blow off steam with her. I want to rock her world. I want her to turn to me when she's feeling needy, or when she's had a bad dream, or when she finds a spider in the shower.

I want her to turn to *me*.

I want her to come to *me*.

I want to keep her safe... especially from my own fucking father.

I think about what will happen when Mikey goes on trial and Shane tells me to bring Sophie back to Chicago to testify. The thought of her returning to Chicago makes my blood run cold, but she has to testify. Once Mikey's convicted and behind bars, there won't be any reason for the Alessios to come after Sophie.

But until then, until Mikey's convicted, they'll stop at nothing to prevent her from testifying. As long as there's a chance they can keep her from showing up in court, they'll do anything. Mikey might be an idiot, but he's Franco's heir, and that means something to Franco.

I know it does, because he's been begging me to join him since I was ten years old.

Technically, I'm his heir because I'm his firstborn son—even if I am a bastard child. That also means something to Franco, but it means jackshit to me.

He's a criminal, and I'd rather die than join his operation—period. End of story.

The current song ends, quickly melding into another one, also a slow song. Sophie's pressed up against me, her supple arms around my neck, and her head resting against my shoulder. She's practically boneless against me, letting me support her. If I didn't know better, I'd think she was enjoying this—I mean *really* enjoying this, and not just killing time until a better offer comes along.

"This isn't so bad, now is it?" she says as she tilts her face up to mine.

"It's not the worst thing I've ever done."

She rolls her eyes at me and then plants a kiss in the center of my chest.

I feel the heat of her lips through my t-shirt, and it stokes a fire in my belly. "Do you still want to play pool?" I ask her, mostly to distract her, but also because if she really wants to play, I want to make her happy. So much for making this a short evening.

She grins. "Really? You'll play?"

"Sure. It beats dancing."

She smacks my chest, and I catch her hand and bring it to my lips. I open her fingers and place a kiss in the center of her palm. Then I link our fingers together and lead her to the back corner of the tavern, to the pool tables. One of them is free, so we stake our claim.

"Eight ball?" I ask her.

She nods. "What are the stakes?"

I raise my brow. "We're playing for stakes?"

"Of course. That's what makes it fun."

I join her at the far end of the table and lean in close so she can hear me over the music. "You don't have any money on you, so what did you have in mind?"

She thinks it over a minute. "If I win... you have to give me an hour-long, full-body massage tonight."

"All right. And if I win..."

"Yes?"

"You let me put something bigger than my finger in your ass."

Her eyes widen as she smacks my arm. "Dominic, be serious! I told you, you're not putting that monster—"

"I wasn't referring to my dick, baby. I was thinking more along the lines of a butt plug or a small dildo." I cup myself. "Not this bad boy."

She narrows her eyes. "And you just happen to have one of those in the cabin?"

I shrug. "I might."

"I don't believe you."

"Okay, I don't. But I can order one and have it shipped to the cabin."

She laughs. "You're impossible. Okay, I agree to your terms, as long as it's not too big."

I'm thinking she gave in way too easily on our bet, and that makes me think I'm about to get snookered.

17

Sophie

I grew up playing pool with my brothers every single weekend of my childhood, and well into my adulthood. We had a pool table in the basement rec room, and that was my brothers' favorite place to hang out. My sisters and I would join them, and of course we'd insist they let us play too.

When you're playing with four hotshot brothers, you have to get good or you'll get trampled.

So, I'm good at playing pool—especially eight ball.

Dominic racks the balls and invites me to break. It's a good, solid strike, and I sink two balls right off the bat. And that starts my run of the table.

He stands back, his arms crossed over his chest, and shakes his head as I sink one ball after another.

And then I miss what should have been a simple shot. "Shit!"

He laughs as he chalks his cue. "Stand back, baby. Now it's my turn."

And then he clears the rest of the table and tries to sink the eight ball, but just misses.

Ha!

"Eight ball, corner pocket," I say, and I make the shot, winning the game.

He comes up behind me and cages me against the pool table, his hips pressed against my ass, his arms on either side of me, holding me contained. His erection digs into my backside. "How about best out of three?" he murmurs in my ear.

The deep, dark growl in his voice sends a shiver through me, and I swear to god my ass starts tingling. All I can think is that I *want* him to win our bet. "All right. You're on."

While he's setting up the table for our second game, I head to the bar to pick up refills—a beer for me and another Coke for him. He meant what he said about not drinking tonight. Not here in town at least. I guess he considers himself *on duty* as my babysitter. I actually wish he would drink some alcohol, because then he might loosen up a bit and miss a few shots.

By the time I finish off my third beer of the night, my aim isn't quite so steady. He easily beats me in our second game.

We're tied, one to one. The next one who wins, wins the bet, and I honestly think about throwing the whole thing because I'm a very perverted woman.

But it ends up I don't have to throw the third game, because he trounces me fair and square. Maybe the three beers had something to do with it.

"So, you win," I observe, leaning against the table.

He steps forward and presses up against me, his hands settling on my hips. "Yes, I did." The smug bastard sounds pretty pleased with himself.

The heat from his body sinks into mine, making me lightheaded. I'm tempted to jump up on the edge of the table and wrap my legs around him. The idea makes my head spin. "I might be a little bit drunk," I confess.

He laughs. "You think so?"

"Mm-hmm." I slip my arms around his waist and lean my head against his brawny shoulder and sigh. "I also need to pee. Badly."

We give up the table to a couple of guys waiting their turn, and Dominic walks me down the back hall toward the restrooms.

"I'll wait out here," he says as I get in line for the women's room. He leans against the wall opposite me, his arms crossed over his chest.

All I can do is stare at his arms, at the inked designs on his skin, at the huge muscles filling out the sleeves of his t-shirt. And I'm not the only one staring. So are the rest of the women standing in line—and they're not being too subtle about it.

Back off, girls. He's mine.

Dominic, who misses nothing, meets my gaze with a roll of his eyes, making me snort with laughter.

Yeah, I'm a little, teensy bit drunk. But I'm having fun tonight, and I wouldn't change a thing. I just hope he takes me back to the cabin right after this and has his wicked way with me.

Finally, it's my turn to shuffle into the ladies' room. I find an empty stall and pee. When I'm done, I wash my hands, and as I'm drying them on a paper towel, I notice an olive-green landline on the wall in the corner of the restroom.

No way.

I walk over to the phone and pick up the handset, not expecting to hear an actual dial tone. To my surprise, there is one. *Holy shit!* A working phone. You've got to be kidding me.

I punch in Amber's cell number.

A moment later, her phone rings, and she answers breathlessly. "Hello?"

"Amber, hi!"

"Sophie? Oh my god! Where the fuck are you? I've been trying to reach you for days! I called Shane, and all he said is that you went out of town for a while."

I lean against the wall, one hand cupped over my other ear to block out the chatter around me. "Sorry, it's noisy here. I can barely hear you," I tell her. "Look, I only have a minute. Dominic will be wondering where I am. I just wanted to let you know that I'm safe. I don't know when I'll be able to come home, but you don't need to worry. I'm fine."

"Where are you? Why did you leave? Is it because of the shooting?"

"Yes. I'm not in Chicago anymore. In fact, I'm not even in Illinois. I'm sort of in a... witness protection program."

"Oh lord," she says. "That's crazy."

"I know, right? Hey, I've got to go because if I don't show soon, my babysitter is liable to come looking for me. He has no respect for the sanctity of women's restrooms. I'll call again if I get a chance. But please don't worry. I'm fine. And I miss you."

"I miss you, too! Please come home soon," she says.

"I will, as soon as I can. Gotta go now. Bye!"

"Call me later! Bye!"

After hanging up, I look behind me, half-expecting to see Dominic glaring at me, but it's just a line of women waiting their turn to pee.

When I step back out into the hall, he's standing exactly where I left him, looking annoyed.

"Took you long enough," he says as he pushes away from the wall. "Ready to go?"

I hear a new song starting, another one of my favorites. Lady A's *Need You Now*. "Oh my god, I love this song!" I rock up on my toes and get in his face, more than a little unsteady on my feet. "One last dance? Please?"

He looks torn. "It's getting late, Phee. I think we should go home."

Home.

I love the way he says that.

I slip my arms around his waist and nestle up against his warm, immovable body. If we were at home right now, I'd be climbing him like a monkey. "Just this one song. I promise."

He exhales a heavy breath. "Just one."

"Yes!" I take his hand and lead him back into the main room, toward the crowded dance floor. Then I loop my arms around his neck as he pulls me close.

This song always makes me so damn weepy, and the alcohol isn't helping. I tighten my arms around him and press my aching breasts to his chest. It feels so good I can't help moaning.

He responds by tightening his hold on me. "You're drunk."

I rest my head on his chest and smile. "I know."

As we sway slowly to the music, I slip my arms around his waist, then up beneath his t-shirt so I can stroke his bare skin. He smells so damn good, I could cry.

My pussy starts heating up, crying out for attention, and as I shuffle in his arms, I feel the slippery wetness growing. "When this song is over," I whisper, "I want you to take me home and fuck me until I can't walk."

I didn't think he could hear me over the music, but suddenly his arms tighten around me. I can feel his heart pounding beneath my cheek, and his breathing is a bit heavier now. *I guess he did hear me.*

When the song ends, we release each other.

"Time to go," he says in a gruff voice. He takes my hand and leads me toward the back door.

A dark-haired guy in cowboy boots, blue jeans, and a red-

and-blue plaid shirt intercepts us. "Hey, baby. Where you goin' so soon? How 'bout a dance?"

Dominic steps between us. "How about a broken arm?"

Startled, the guy takes several hasty steps back. "Whoa, dude. Calm down."

I start giggling, unable to help it. The look on Dominic's face is murderous. "Come on, honey," I tell him, linking my arm through his. "We need to go home and do some online shopping, remember?"

He backs away from the cowboy and, taking my hand, leads me out the rear door.

* * *

When we get to the Bronco, Dominic walks me to my door and fishes his keys out of his pocket. I watch him unlock the door.

"You're so old school," I say, laughing.

He looks at me. "How so?"

"You use a key to unlock your car door. My BMW has keyless entry."

He leans forward and kisses my nose. "I'm happy for you. But this is a nineteen eighty-eight gem, made long before all the fancy bells and whistles were invented. And I'm okay with old school." He opens my car door and motions me inside.

"Would you really have broken that guy's arm?" I say, as I attempt to climb up into my seat. It's a long way up, and I don't make it the first time.

He cups my ass and easily hoists me up into the SUV.

I settle onto my seat and reach for my seatbelt. "You really are an ass man, aren't you?"

He grins. "Yep. And fortunately for me, you have a glorious ass."

My cheeks burn, and I can't help grinning. "I'm not entirely sure if that's a compliment or not."

"Oh, it is," he says. "Trust me, it is."

He walks around the back of the vehicle to the driver's side, then opens his door and climbs inside.

I catch him staring at me. "What?"

He shakes his head. "You are so fucking gorgeous." And then he leans over, threading his fingers into my hair, and pulls me close for a kiss. His mouth is hungry on mine, almost fierce with need.

A wave of heat rushes through me, settling between my legs. I squirm in my seat, pressing my thighs together. The pressure on my clit feels so good. I feel so needy right now. "Please tell me we're going home to have sex."

His eyes darken. "If we make it that far. I might just fuck you right here in the parking lot."

That sounds intriguing. "I've never done it in a car before."

"Seriously? You've never fucked in a car?"

I shake my head. "And I suppose you have?"

He laughs. "Damn near every Friday and Saturday night when I was a teen. And more than a few times since then."

He turns in his seat and glances around the dark parking lot. "You haven't lived until you've fucked in a vehicle, Phee."

He reaches over to unfasten my seatbelt. Then he climbs over the center console and into the backseat. Trying to get comfortable, he stretches out as much as he can, but there's hardly enough room for his long legs.

Dominic pats his thigh. "Get back here, baby."

My pulse kicks into high gear. He can't be serious. We can't have sex in a parking lot. Someone might see us. "You're kidding, right?"

"Oh, hell no. It's time for you to get your backseat cherry popped."

18

Sophie

While I'm climbing awkwardly over the console and into the backseat, Dominic unzips his jeans and frees his erection.

Good god. I stare at the size of him. No wonder he's such a tight fit.

"Climb aboard, baby," he says, grinning like a damn fool. He's loving this.

I waver on the seat beside him. "I don't think there's enough room." There's not even enough room for him to stretch out his legs.

He pats his thigh once more. "Drop your britches and straddle me, cowgirl."

He's definitely enjoying this way too much.

I glance out the windows. The parking lot is mostly full, but thankfully the one light pole back here isn't working, so it's quite dark. Right now I don't see anyone around. But still... someone could pull into the parking lot or come out the back door of the tavern at any moment.

"Dominic..."

He reaches out and unfastens my jeans and lowers the zipper. Then he starts tugging my jeans and panties down.

"But my boots."

"Leave them on. Just shove your pants down to your ankles."

I flinch when I hear a car horn in the distance. "I don't think this is a good idea."

He slides a long finger between my legs and chuckles. "Your body says otherwise, baby. You're wet as hell."

He's already got my jeans and panties down past my hips, mid-thigh. The cool night air against my heated skin makes me shiver. He reaches into his back pocket for his wallet and withdraws a condom packet, which he waves in front of my face before tearing it open with his teeth. I watch, mesmerized, as he rolls the condom down his thick length.

After shoving my bottoms to my ankles, he pulls me onto him so that I'm straddling his hips, my knees digging into the seat on either side of him.

He grabs my hand and wraps my fingers around the base of

his cock. "Put me inside you."

My pulse is pounding now, and if I'm going to be honest with myself, hell yes, I want this. The thought of taking him here in the car, out in public, is so damn hot. His cock is straining, hot and throbbing in my grasp.

I brush the head of his cock against my clit, and pleasure bursts inside me. Just the merest touch, and I'm already throbbing. I think he senses this because his finger is suddenly there, between my legs, stroking my clitoris, first drawing teasing little circles around it and then pressing harder as he massages my most sensitive spot.

"Oh god," I moan, rocking myself against his touch. I close my eyes, wanting to wallow in the intensity and wishing that finger was deep inside me.

"Open your eyes, Phee." His voice is rough and demanding. "Look at me."

I do as he says, and I'm shocked at the heat and fire in his gaze. He's just as turned on as I am. *What is it about the two of us?* We only have to be in the same room, and we want each other.

"Tell me what you want," he says, clearly taunting me. "Say it."

"I want you inside me."

"My finger, or my cock?"

"Jesus, Dominic." I position him so that the head of his cock is pressed against my pussy. Then I sink down on him, slowly, gasping when the broad head of his erection pushes inside me. Already, he's stretching me, but it feels so damn good to be taken like this, consumed. I want all of him, every single inch.

I lift up slightly, then lower myself, again and again, sinking deeper each time as my wetness coats him and eases the way.

His hands are on my hips, gripping me securely and coaxing me down onto him. "That's it, baby. Every bit. You can do it."

By the time he's halfway in, I can feel the stretch, the slight burn, and it's exquisite torture. I'm biting my lip and trying not to whimper, but it's messing with my head, making me feel *owned* by him.

He groans. "Jesus, Sophie, you're killing me." Then he clamps his hands on my hips and bucks up into me, shoving himself deeper.

I cry out at the intrusion, shocked at the pleasure of being filled so completely. "Dominic." His name is little more than a breath.

But he's all the way in now. I'm sitting with my thighs flush against his, his coarse hair brushing against my sensitive, bare skin.

He glances down at the place where we're joined, and I follow his gaze. The sight of us makes my heart pound. My lips are spread wide open by his cock, his dark pubic hair a stark contrast to my bare flesh. Male and female. Ying and yang.

He reaches down to stroke me, then he slips the tip of his thumb between my swollen lips to tease my clit.

I start moving on him then.

He raises his gaze to my face. "Look at me," he says, his voice sharp.

I obey, unable not to. His gaze is dark and intent, and there's so much emotion there. I study his expression, the heat in his eyes, the flaring of his nostrils, the dilation of his pupils, the flush of color high on his cheeks. His erection throbs hard inside me.

His warm hands slide up beneath my top and into my bra, his palms cupping my heavy breasts. When he brushes his thumbs against my nipples, lightning streaks down my nerves to my pussy, making me ache.

"I will make you forget every man who's ever had you," he says. "Do you hear me?"

Silently, I nod, unable to form a single coherent thought. This is not some casual sex in the back of his vehicle. The realization floors me.

And then he's moving inside me, rocking his hips up into me. His hands return to my hips, and he holds me steady for his thrusts. He's doing all the work, and his strength—his ability to lift me so easily and pull me down—astounds me.

My arousal soars higher and higher with each thrust, and I'm climbing so quickly. I moan and whimper shamelessly, loudly, unable to help myself. It's so good I can't think straight.

I hear a car door slam shut, then voices not too far away. "Shit!"

"Ignore them," he says, slamming into me over and over, increasing his speed and not giving a fuck that we may or may not have an audience.

It's so dark I can't see where they are, or how close they are, or if they've seen us. Dominic is past caring as he powers into me, harder and faster, his chest billowing as his lungs heave.

His thumb is suddenly back on my clit, rubbing and teasing me relentlessly. "I want to hear you scream for me, baby," he says, panting hard from exertion. "I want you to scream your head off for me."

I gasp. "I can't. There are people—"

"I don't care. Let me hear you."

He pushes my top up, along with my bra cup, and exposes my left breast. And then his mouth is on me, hot and hungry, and he sucks my nipple into this mouth. He laves the tip with his tongue, and then he's suckling hard, drawing pleasure through me like a siphon.

I grab his shoulders, my nails digging into his muscles. The harder I grip, the louder he groans. I must be hurting him, but he doesn't complain. If anything, I think he likes it.

My orgasm slams into me like a freight train, taking me by surprise. Forgetting about any possible audience, I shriek loudly, my wails high and desperate. Then I feel the powerful buck of his cock inside me as he comes right along with me.

He throws his head back on the seat, his neck muscles taut, his eyes squeezed shut, and he roars as he empties himself into the condom, bucking wildly into me, over and over with every pulsating spurt of his release.

He pulls me down on him so that he's seated fully inside me, and wraps his arms around me, holding me to his broad chest.

I swear I can feel his heart slamming into his ribs. His hands slowly caress my back, moving up and down as he soothes me.

In one deft roll, he turns us so that I'm lying along the backseat and he's kneeling over me. He's still inside me when he starts to move again, more gently this time, which is good because I'm already sore.

We both groan at the pleasure of his steady strokes, as he slides easily through my wetness. I can't believe he's still hard.

I run my hands down his arms, marveling at the definition of his muscles. "Dominic, you should pull out. The condom."

He groans, dipping his face down to mine. "I know. But this feels so *good*." He kisses my forehead, the tip of my nose, and then finally my lips. "I want to stay inside you forever."

As a car pulls into the lot, bright headlights sweep the backseat of the Bronco, lighting up the interior of the vehicle. I hear an engine shut off and car doors open.

"Dominic!" I hiss, smacking his shoulder. My post-orgasmic euphoria has been swiftly displaced by the fear of being caught.

He chuckles, making no move to pull out.

"Dominic! I mean it. Get your ass up."

Moaning, he carefully withdraws and returns to his seat to remove the condom, quickly tying the open end. "I need something to put this in."

I scramble up into a sitting position, wriggle back into my panties and jeans, and fix my bra. Then I reach into the front seat and grab a napkin from the glove box.

"I can't believe we did that," I say, as I watch him take care of the condom.

"I can't believe you made me stop. I could have gone again."

"Someone pulled into the lot."

"Who cares? When we get home, I'm going to fuck you on the front porch swing. I'll get you over this fear of being seen."

I swat his thigh. "You wouldn't dare."

He gives me a side glance, looking far from cowed. "Oh, baby, don't put it past me."

19

Dominic

As I pull out onto Main Street, I reach for Sophie's hand. "You have to admit that was hot."

She's still blushing. "Someone might have seen us."

"So? I doubt it would've been the first time a couple got caught making out in a parking lot."

"We weren't *making out*, Dominic. We were *fucking*. Big difference."

I bring her hand to my mouth and kiss the back of it. "Come on. Admit it. It was hot as hell. I've never heard you screech so loudly. You were even louder than the time you saw the snake."

She tries to pull her hand away, but I link our fingers and rest our hands on my thigh.

She smiles reluctantly. "Yes, it was hot, but don't let it go to your head. I don't go around fucking in the backseat of cars."

I've never asked Sophie how old she is, but I'm sure she's in her early thirties. How is she still single? She's gorgeous, smart, funny. Physically, she's a goddess. Sexually, she's a dream come true.

"Why hasn't some lucky bastard put a ring on your finger before now?" I ask her.

Her smile falls as she breaks our gaze. She turns to face forward in her seat.

Obviously, I hit a sore spot. "Why is that a difficult question?" When she shrugs, I squeeze her hand. "Try answering."

"It's not easy being my size," she admits.

"Which means what, exactly? You're tall, so what? I find that a definite plus."

"It's not just my height. I'm big all around. I'm no twig, obviously."

I scoff. "You're a gorgeous woman with beautiful curves. I want to roll around with you all the time, preferably naked in bed. The Bronco's now a close second."

She giggles like a schoolgirl, and it makes my heart thump.

God, I love to hear her laugh.

"I was engaged once," she says.

By the tone of her voice, I can tell it's not a happy memory. "What happened?"

She shrugs. "I broke it off."

"Why?"

"Because he made me feel bad about myself far more often than he made me feel good. In the end, I realized it wasn't a healthy relationship. Since then, I've dated on and off, but it never turned out well. I went several years without dating at all, until recently. Amber talked me into going on a blind date. That was the night Kent Martinez was killed."

"And obviously that didn't turn out so well either."

She glares at me, clearly not amused.

"Sorry," I say. "Too soon?"

She rolls her eyes. "A man *died*, Dominic. Show some respect."

"Do you want to get married one day?"

She nods. "Sure. I see the kind of relationship some of my siblings have with their partners, and I want that too. I want that level of unconditional love."

"Shane and his wife seem happy," I say.

"Very." She smiles. "Beth turned his world upside down. I think he's still reeling from it."

"When's their new baby due?"

"September. I need to be home before then."

"We'll see. It depends on the court schedule. But don't count on it."

She gives me a look. "I can't miss the birth of their baby."

"Sorry, Phee, but I'm sure they think your life is more important than you being present at the birth."

"Sorry, *Dom*, but I'm not missing it."

I grin at her. "*Dom*, eh? Do you want me to be your dom?"

She pulls her hand from mine. "Of course not. If you try to tie me up, I'll castrate you."

I laugh. Why does every damn conversation I have with her feel so good? Even when she's complaining, it's fun.

"Fine, be that way," I say. "But you're missing out." I glance over at her to find her eyeing me warily. "What?"

"You'd like to tie me up sometime?" she asks.

I shrug. "Sure. It'd be fun."

"Would you let me tie *you* up?"

I grin, knowing she's intrigued. "Has anyone ever restrained you? Tied you or handcuffed you?"

She shakes her head. "No."

"Then don't knock it until you've tried it."

"You haven't answered my question, Dominic. Would you let *me* tie *you* up?"

"Sure. Why not? But only if you promise to ride me like a naked cowgirl. And you'd have to keep your boots on. That would be hot." When I catch her studying me, I say, "You're considering it?"

She tilts her head coyly. "Maybe."

Her answer is cautious, but I can tell she's mulling it over.

"Being restrained heightens the arousal," I tell her. "Being controlled, overpowered... by someone you trust, of course—someone who would never hurt you under any circumstances—is hot as hell."

"Are you speaking from personal experience?"

I laugh. "No one has ever restrained me, baby."

"But you'd let me?"

As we approach the turn-off to our lane, I look in the review mirror again to make sure no one is following us. There's been no one behind us since we left the tavern.

I toss her a quick look just before I make the turn. "If it would get you to agree to it, then yes, I would."

The drive up our little mountain is slow going. The deeply rutted road is partially washed out. Owen and I keep the lane in this condition on purpose to try to slow down the approach of anyone who has no business coming up here.

I keep one eye on the road, and the other on the rearview mirror. I know no one followed us from town, but it's a deeply-ingrained habit, and I see no reason to break it. Better safe than sorry.

We pass by the turn-off to Owen's cabin, then continue on uphill. Sophie's white-knuckling the door handle.

"Relax," I tell her, both of my hands securely gripping the steering wheel as the vehicle shakes and shudders. "I've made this trip a thousand times."

"It'd be easier to get up this road if you paved it."

"We don't want it to be easier. That's the point."

When we arrive at the cabin, I park the Bronco and hop out. There's enough moonlight tonight that we can see our way just fine to the cabin's porch.

Sophie climbs up the steps, and I'm right behind her.

I point at the swing. "We have a future date with that porch swing."

She laughs. "We are not fucking outside."

"Oh, yes, we are," I say. I can't resist teasing her.

I can tell she's tired, so I unlock the door, push it open—setting off the alarm—and let her precede me inside. I follow her in and turn off the alarm.

"God, I'm tired," she says, heading for the stairs.

"Wait." I snag her wrist and pull her into my arms. "I just wanted to say thanks. Tonight was fun."

She smiles up at me. "Even the dancing?"

"Yeah, even the dancing."

When she rises up on her toes to give me a light kiss—a thank-you kiss—my heart kicks in my chest.

I could get used to this... the two of us living together. I know it's only temporary. We've been thrown together until it's time for her to return to Chicago. That time will come, but whether it's weeks away, or months, there's no telling. The longer, the better, as far as I'm concerned.

But inevitably there will come a time when Shane says she needs to return to Chicago. A time when I have to take her back. Let her go.

Hell, I'd happily stay here with her indefinitely if she wanted to.

She kisses me again, only this time it's different. It's not a thank-you kiss. It's an I-just-had-you-and-I-want-you-again kiss.

I tighten my arms around her and drop a kiss on the side of

her neck. God, she smells good. "Are you heading up to bed?"

"No, not yet. I want to change into something more comfortable and sit outside on the swing for a while. It's nice out tonight. But first I need a quick shower."

She does a little shimmy, and I laugh as realization hits me. She's soaking wet from sex in the Bronco.

"A shower sounds good," I say. "Mind if I join you?"

Linking our fingers, she leads me toward the bathroom. "I'd love that."

*　*　*

After showering and changing, into PJ shorts and a tank top for her, a pair of sweatpants for me, we sit out on the porch swing and relax. She has a glass of red wine in her hand, while I finally get to drink a cold beer.

I'm tempted to follow through on the idea of having sex outside on the swing, but the truth is, I want to wait until I can have her in my bed again. I want to be *on* her, cradled between her luscious thighs, and I want to thrust, long and slow, into her sweet body for as long as I can hold out.

As we swing quietly, my arm over her shoulders, her head tucked sleepily against me, my chest tightens. I'm buzzing inside, my nerves vibrating, but I don't think it's from one beer.

There are words buried inside me that want to come out—confessions, declarations—but I can't do that to her. I can't ask her to consider giving herself to the bastard son of a mobster.

She deserves so much better.

"Tell me about your parents," she says, her voice quiet.

I never talk about them to anyone, but there's something in her voice that compels me to make an exception. "What do you want to know?"

"Tell me *their* story."

"Their story is a tragedy. I'm not sure you want to know."

"I want to know about *you*, and where you come from, and that starts with your parents."

I sigh. "Franco loved my mom, desperately. He was in an unhappy, arranged marriage, and when he met my mom, he fell head over heels in love with her. At least that was the story my mom told me. And like I told you, when his wife found out about the affair, she ordered Franco to get rid of my mom or she'd have her killed."

Sophie shudders. "Do you think she really would've done that?"

"Probably."

"Is Franco's wife still alive?"

"No. She died a few years ago. She was ruthless though. Franco didn't want to risk anything happening to my mom, so he let her go. She was six months pregnant with me at the time. He never saw her again. I didn't even meet Franco until after my mother died. He attended her funeral, and I had no idea who he was. He tried to talk to me after the service—I was ten years old—but once I realized who he was, I refused to talk to him. I blamed him for my mom's death. I blamed him for *everything*.

But now, in hindsight, I realize he did what he had to do to protect her. He made a deal with his wife, and he stuck to it."

"Did you ever see him after that?"

"Yeah. I was about fifteen years old when he approached me at a high school football game. I was sitting in the bleachers with some buddies when he came up and sat behind me. He asked me to join him—his family, his organization."

"Did you know he was involved in organized crime?"

I laugh bitterly. "Oh, I knew. My grandparents made sure I knew it all. They hated him with a passion. They blamed him for seducing my mom and for getting her pregnant."

"What did you tell him?"

"I told him no. I said I'd rather die than be part of his world. And I've told him the same thing ever since, every time he's asked me."

"I'm so sorry."

"My integrity—my honor—is all I have, and I'd rather die than lose it."

She kisses my shoulder. "What about Mikey? He's your half-brother."

"Mikey's a mean son of a bitch, and he's not capable of running that organization. The men don't respect him." I link our fingers, wanting to change the subject. "Enough talk. Let's go to bed."

She sits up and turns to face me, studying me for a moment before reaching out to cup my cheek.

Her thumb brushes along the edge of my cheek. "I'd love to."

* * *

The next morning, I wake up early and go downstairs to put on the coffee. My goddess is cranky if she doesn't get her caffeine soon after waking.

When the coffee's percolating, I sneak out to the shed to call Shane for a quick update. I need to know what's going on back in Chicago. I want to be on top of any impending doom or trouble headed our way. Because no matter how idyllic things are here, I never lose sight of the fact that the Alessio organization has put out a hit on Sophie. I have no idea what the bounty is, but I'm sure it's enough to draw hitmen from both coasts.

"The district attorney's office is still putting their case together," Shane tells me. "The judge presiding over the case ruled that Mikey was a flight risk, so he remains behind bars. My attorney is making damn sure he stays there. Franco's men are still searching for information on Sophie's whereabouts. They've harassed her neighbors, her clients, even her friends, but luckily no one's been hurt. They broke into Sophie's condo and ransacked the place. It's completely destroyed. And they stole her friend's purse on the street—in broad daylight. That's the extent of it so far."

"Her friend doesn't know where she's at, right?"

"No. In fact, no one knows where you guys are besides me and our brother Jake."

"Good. Keep it that way. And thanks for the update."

"Hey, how's my sister?"

"She's fine."

"Is she giving you any grief?"

"No, she's an absolute angel."

Shane laughs. "And you're a comedian. I grew up with Sophie. I know how she can be when she doesn't get her way."

I chuckle. "I'm sure she's mellowed out since then."

We end the call, and I head back into the cabin, up the stairs, and crawl back into bed with my sleeping beauty, who's soft and warm and smells so damn good.

She shivers when I wrap her in my arms. Then I tuck my face into the crook of her neck and breathe in her sweet scent. When she moans sleepily, my cock hardens.

"You awake?" I ask.

She stretches. "Mm. Do I smell coffee?"

I pull back the covers and settle between her thighs. "I'll make you a deal. You can have coffee if I can have a taste of your pussy."

And then I use my tongue to coax her into a screaming orgasm.

20

Sophie

I could get used to this... being awakened every morning with a hot guy between my legs going down on me like he's on death row and I'm his last meal. Afterward, he brings me breakfast in bed—pancakes smothered in melted butter and real maple syrup.

"Are you trying to butter me up for something?" I ask him, as I proceed to shovel a forkful of pancakes into my mouth.

He lies beside me on the bed, his head propped on his hand as he watches me eat. "I don't think I'd have to try this hard. You're pretty easy. I just did you in the backseat of my vehicle last night."

Laughing, I ball up my napkin and throw it at his head.

He catches it and tosses it back.

I give him a bite, and he helps me finish off the pancakes. Then we both go downstairs and take a shower.

Once we're dressed, I clean up the kitchen—wondering how one man can make such a mess? Dominic goes out to the shed to get out the lawn mower—*how domestic*. While I'm doing the dishes, he cuts the lawn around the cabin.

I watch him from the kitchen window, admiring the way his shoulder and arm muscles bunch and flex as he pushes the mower. I can almost picture us with a house in the suburbs... me taking care of a baby while he's outside doing the yardwork.

When the kitchen's tidied up, I carry a cup of coffee out onto the porch so I can sit on the swing and admire him going about his work.

There's a nice breeze today and not a cloud in sight. The birds are out in full force, chirping away. Surrounded by the lush greenery on all sides, we're nestled in sweetly. I feel settled here, very much at home and relaxed. I've always thought of myself as a city girl. I could never understand why my sister Hannah felt compelled to run off to live in the mountains out west, but now I think I get it.

I could get used to living like this—just the two of us, far from the pressures of civilization. Far from murder investigations and organized crime.

I don't like to think about the future. At some point, they're going to want me to return to Chicago to testify against that snake Mikey Alessio. I know he's Dominic's half-brother, but I just can't make the connection. The two men are nothing alike. Mikey murdered an innocent man in cold blood, while Dominic is one of the most honorable people I've ever met.

After noticing me watching him, Dominic turns off the mower and walks across the yard to join me. He climbs up the porch steps and stands towering over me, looking hot and sweaty and handsome as hell. "You look pretty sitting there."

I smile. "You looked pretty out there cutting the grass."

Propping his hands on his hips, he grins. "I'm glad you think so. It's a nice day. How about taking a walk with me?"

I finish the last sip of my coffee. "I'd love to."

"I'll wash up and put on a clean shirt," he says, heading inside. "Put on jeans and boots. It's a bit of a hike where we're going."

While he's getting cleaned up, I change into clothes more suited for hiking, brush my teeth, and put my hair up in a ponytail.

When we meet downstairs, he's putting some supplies into a backpack—bottles of water and some protein bars. He has a gun holstered to his chest and a hunting knife in a sheath attached to his belt.

After locking up the cabin, we set out, taking a different trail this time. It's barely marked.

"I hope you know where you're going," I say as I follow him along a narrow, overgrown path.

"I do."

We trudge along, going uphill the whole way. It's not long before I feel the strain in my thighs. The terrain starts to become more and more rocky, and there are some steep climbs that require me to use my hands to grab hold of tree roots protruding from the ground and rocks to pull myself up.

"Are you sure you know where we're going?" I ask as I heave myself up a steep hillside.

He stops and reaches back, offering me a hand. Easily, he pulls me up and in front of him so he can press his palms to my ass and literally push me up the incline.

"Is this better?" he says. "I wouldn't want you to break a nail."

"Shut up. My legs are killing me. You didn't tell me this was going to be a major workout."

"Stop complaining. It's worth the effort. You'll see."

Finally, the terrain levels out and it's easy going again. Dominic lets me walk in front, and when we turn the bend, there it is.

"Oh my god," I breathe.

"Nice, huh?"

"Nice doesn't even begin to cover it."

In front of us is a waterfall cascading over a rocky outcropping high overhead, at least fifty feet above us. At the base of the waterfall is a pristine pool of clear water. It's a lovely little clearing in the woods, drenched in sunlight.

"Dominic, it's gorgeous."

Coming up behind me, he puts his hands on my shoulders and brushes my ear with his lips, sending a shiver down my spine. "No, *you're* gorgeous."

I reach back and smack his shoulder. "Stop it. I bet you say that to all the girls you bring up here."

He turns me to face him. "Baby, you're the *only* girl I've ever brought up here." He touches his nose to mine and whispers, "In fact, you're the only girl I would ever consider bringing up here."

My heart lodges in my throat as we gaze into each other's eyes. I'm bursting with emotions, and there's so much I want to say to him. How I appreciate what he's doing for me. How I recognize the sacrifices he's made for me. How *happy* I am just being with him.

Abruptly, he steps away and drops his backpack to the ground, removes his gun holster and knife, then starts unbuckling his boots.

I stand there like an idiot, watching him undress.

He peers up at me as he tugs off his socks. "What are you waiting for?"

"What do you mean?" But I'm pretty sure I have a good idea where this is going.

"Get naked, girl. We're going swimming."

"Skinny dipping? Are you kidding?"

He shrugs. "Just get naked."

When he's fully undressed, he stands there staring at me, his hands on his hips and his penis jutting out from his body, half-erect. "I'll give you two minutes to get your clothes off," he says, "or you're going in with them on, and trust me, you don't want that. You'll have to walk back down this mountain in wet clothes, and you will chafe like hell."

"You wouldn't dare."

He grins. "Oh, baby, just test me."

I am not about to put him to the test. Still, the idea of undressing outside in broad daylight is a bit unnerving.

"You have two minutes to decide," he says, "and then I'm tossing you in."

I quickly remove my boots. "I can't believe I let you talk me into coming up here. You should have told me that getting naked was part of the deal."

He laughs. "If I'd told you, you wouldn't have agreed to come up here."

"Exactly! Have you ever heard of *full disclosure*?"

Once I'm naked—thank god it's a warm day, and the sun is beating down, warming my skin—he pulls me close and we stand beside the water.

He steps back so he can see me—all of me. I hold my breath as he runs his hands down my arms, then back up to my shoulders. He skims his palms down my chest, over my breasts, cupping and weighing them with his hands. Then his hands slip down to my hips.

My heart is pounding, but I keep my chin held high, refusing to show him how insecure I feel at his blatant perusal.

"What's wrong?" he says.

I look away. "This makes me uncomfortable."

"Why? It's the perfect day to take a swim."

"Not the water. I mean standing here with you staring at my body."

He looks at me like I'm crazy. "What are you talking about?"

I gesture at my body. "This—being naked in broad daylight."

"Why is that a problem?"

"Because!"

He lifts my chin and makes me look at him. "Because why, Phee?"

I gesture to my body again, to my wide hips and soft belly. "This!"

He grabs my hands and holds them out to my side, exposing me completely to his hot gaze. "Sophie McIntyre, you have a body that makes men weak in the knees. God knows you make *me* weak in the knees. Why is it so damn hard for you to get that through your head?"

I stare up at him, my own vision starting to blur through unshed tears.

He shakes his head, looking bewildered. "You have absolutely nothing to be self-conscious about."

As if to prove his point, his erection prods me in the belly.

He gazes down at his cock, which is doing a fine job of defying gravity at the moment. I look, too, aroused by the sight of it.

"See what I mean?" he says. "He looks happy." He takes my hand. "Now, come swim with me."

I nod. "All right."

He dives headfirst into the center of the pool, cutting cleanly through the water. He surfaces a few yards away and slicks back his hair.

As I cautiously wade into the water, I ask him, "How deep is it?"

"About ten or twelve feet in the center."

One step at a time, I feel my way across the soft, sandy bottom. The water is surprisingly warm, probably because it's in the sun all day long. I work my way into the waist-deep water and lean against a warm boulder.

He swims over to me, coming to stand beside me. Then he hoists himself up and out of the water to sit on the boulder. Water runs down his muscular body, streaming over his ridged abdomen.

As I turn to face him, I realize I'm at the perfect height. I nudge his knees apart and step between his legs.

"What are you doing?" he says, keenly interested as I move in closer.

I wrap my fingers around his erection and gaze up at him. "Returning the favor."

* * *

The next morning, back in our comfy bed, I wake up feeling deliciously sore. After we got home from our hike up to the falls, Dominic pushed me on my hands and knees onto our mattress and fucked me doggy style until I couldn't see straight.

I reach between my legs, my fingertips brushing my mound, and I discover an unpleasant reminder that it's been a while now since my last waxing back in Chicago. *Shit.* And there's nowhere in this small town where a girl can get a full wax.

Dominic stirs, groaning as he stretches like a big cat.

"Where's the nearest big town?" I ask him. "Someplace big enough to have a full-service beauty salon."

"There's a beauty shop right here in town."

"Yeah, but they're not *full-service.*"

"What does that mean? Is that a code for something girly?"

"Yes. Waxing services."

He chuckles. "The nearest *big town*—big enough to have something like that—is at least an hour away, so forget it."

I nudge his shoulder. "Dominic, I'm serious."

"So am I. The answer's no. You have a razor. Use it."

"I can't."

"Why not? You shave your legs and your armpits. Why not your pussy?"

"Because I'm afraid I'll cut myself. Last time I shaved it, I injured myself."

"Oh, hell, I'll do it."

A very unladylike snort escapes me. "You are *not* shaving me down there."

"Why not? I'm good with a razor." He raises his hands in the air. "See? Steady hands."

"Dominic, no."

He rolls over onto his side, facing away from me. "Fine. Then live with what Mother Nature gave you."

"You'll have to live with it too, you know."

He shrugs. "Don't care. It's fine either way."

"Well, it's not fine to me. I want it done."

"Then do it yourself or let me do it, but I'm not taking you to a bigger city."

I consider his offer. "You'd really do it for me?"

"Of course." Another show of his hands. "I've got hands like a surgeon."

Half an hour later, I'm lying in bed, naked. Dominic is positioned between my legs with a can of shaving cream, my pink razor, and a warm wet cloth.

"Relax, Phee," he says. He squirts shaving cream on his fingers and lathers it up, and then he gingerly paints my mound with it.

My legs are shaking, and I fist the sheet as my heart races.

"Sophie, come on," he says as he strokes my hip. "I'm not going to cut you."

Gently, he runs the razor through the shaving cream, once, twice, a third time. "See? Piece of cake."

It kind of feels good, so I start to relax.

With each stroke of the razor, he wipes the blade on the wet cloth and repeats.

"How about a pattern?" he muses.

"What?"

"You know... a landing strip? Or a heart shape right above your clit? Or, better yet—" he runs his finger downward, from below my belly button to the top of my labia "—how about an arrow pointing right here, so I can always find what I'm looking for."

"Oh my god, no. Just shave it all, please."

"Hair or bare, it's all good to me," he says as he resumes his work.

True to his word, he shaves me perfectly, with not a single scratch. After he's done, he gets a fresh wet cloth and wipes me clean. Then he places a gentle kiss at the top of my mound. "All done."

"Do you want me to shave you?" I ask him, biting back a grin. "A little bit of manscaping?"

"Don't even think about it," he says as he gathers up the supplies.

21

Sophie

For the past few days, we've been playing wargames out in the woods. I feel like Katniss from *The Hunger Games*. Dominic's been fanatical lately about these ridiculous drills.

Can I load my gun blindfolded? Yes.

Can I hit a paper target at one hundred yards with the rifle? Probably not, but my aim is definitely improving.

Can I find my way to Owen's cabin in the dark of night? Let's find out, shall we?

Right now, it's dark out, with only the moon to light my path as I traipse through the woods. My three-eighty is tucked into the holster around my waist, and there are extra rounds in my pocket.

"This is stupid, Dominic," I say loudly, grinding my teeth.

Silence.

So I keep going.

And then I hear the water in the creek, moving fast, and I know I'm getting close. We've had quite a bit of rain lately, and the water level is up.

Shit! I have to cross that damn fallen tree trunk by myself in the dark. "God, sometimes I hate you," I mutter.

"What was that?" he says, sounding amused.

"Nothing."

I climb up on the trunk and carefully walk across it, taking tiny steps, my arms extended like a gymnast walking a balance beam.

"I hope you're happy!" I yell. "If I fall in this creek and get swept away, only for my body to be discovered miles away, you'll be sorry!"

I *think* I hear his soft laughter, but I can't be sure over the sound of rushing water.

Miraculously, I make it to the other side, hop down, and continue following the stupid deer trail through the dark woods. God, I wish I at least had a flashlight, but he said that would be cheating.

Finally, after what feels like an hour—when it's probably only been twenty minutes—I step into a small clearing. Owen's seated on a log bench in front of a fire, roasting marshmallows.

"Are you making s'mores?" I say. My evening is finally looking up.

"Yes, ma'am," he says. "Want one?"

"Hell yes, I do." I join him at the fire, taking a seat on the log opposite his.

"Where's Dominic?" he says.

"Out in the woods playing boy scout. I hope he gets lost."

Owen laughs. "Not likely."

"I'm right here," Dominic says, emerging from the trees. "And I heard that."

Owen chuckles and then points at a plastic cooler. "Grab a beer, buddy."

"You're not giving her sugar, are you?" Dominic says, scowling as Owen hands me a long stick with a marshmallow stuck on the end.

"Afraid so," Owen tells him.

"Great," Dominic says. "Then you can deal with the mood swings."

"Ha, very funny," I say, as I hold my marshmallow over the flames.

Dominic twists off the cap on his beer bottle and joins me on my log. "You didn't fall in the creek," he says. "I'm impressed."

I bump his shoulder with mine. "Shut up before I shoot you."

Owen pops a toasted marshmallow into his mouth. "I take it the honeymoon is over."

"Never," Dominic says as he puts his arm around me and

pulls me close.

*　*　*

We stay long enough for me to make two s'mores. It was worth the trek down here just for the marshmallows, graham crackers, and chocolate. Dominic has a second beer, forgoing the sweets, and I drink a bottle of water.

"We should get back," he says, as he finishes his second beer. "It's getting late."

We walk back together, with Dominic taking the lead, as I follow close behind. This time, he helps me across the tree bridge.

Once we're back at the cabin, we both get ready for bed and head upstairs.

Right after I climb naked into his big bed, he says, "I'll be right back." He leaves the room and returns a moment with something in his hands.

As the light is off, I can't quite tell what he's got. "What's that?"

He holds it up, letting it dangle in the air. "The belt from your robe."

My stomach flutters before it does a somersault. "What are you planning to do with that?"

"Hold out your wrists," he says as he approaches the bed.

"Why?"

"You sure ask a lot of questions. Just do as you're told."

"No way," I tell him.

"You said you'd try it."

"I know, but—"

He loops the soft strip of material around both of my wrists and pulls it taut. "No buts." Then he drops a kiss on my nose and whispers, "Trust me."

He positions me on my belly, and then I watch, mesmerized, as he secures the strip of cloth—and my wrists—to the headboard. I pull on the belt, but there's no give. My belly starts quivering.

As I listen to the sound of him undressing—his shirt falling to the floor, his boots coming off with loud thuds, his socks, his zipper going down, his jeans shoved down his legs and off—my body heats with excitement.

The room's not totally dark. There's enough moonlight filtering through the curtains to give some light.

The bedframe creaks as he climbs on the mattress behind me, out of sight. Then his hands clamp onto my hips, and he lifts me so that I'm on my knees facing forward, my arms resting on the bed.

My ass is in the air, my head on a pillow. I pull on the belt to test the strength of the knot, but it doesn't budge. I'm not afraid. Of course I trust him. But I am intrigued about where this is going.

A shiver runs down my spine, and I start shaking. "Dominic."

"Shh."

Kneeling behind me, he spreads my knees wide apart and

then moves in closer. I feel his fingers as he strokes between the lips of my sex, taking a moment to tease my clitoris.

"Just relax," he says in a low, calming voice. "Relax and let go. You're fine."

I feel so vulnerable like this—unable to see him, with my ass up in the air. His warm hands grip my hips, stroking my flesh as he presses his cock against me, the thick length wedged between my butt cheeks.

"Don't even think about it," I warn.

"Hush." He smacks my hip lightly and begins to run his hands over my ass and down my thighs.

I pull on the belt again, as if it might have magically loosened, but no such luck. I'm nervous and shaking and turned on, all at the same time.

And then his fingers are there, between my legs, stroking me and spreading my arousal.

He chuckles. "Someone's wet."

"Oh, shut up," I say.

A moment later, when I feel his tongue on me, I cry out. Then his finger is there, teasing my clit, and his tongue joins in. He goes down on me like a ravenous beast until I'm whimpering into my pillow.

When my legs start shaking uncontrollably, and the belt restraining my wrists still won't give an inch, my mind spirals into a needy, overstimulated place. He pinches my clit and pleasure explodes in me, like fireworks.

I cry out loudly as my empty pussy spasms. I need him inside me, filling me—now. "Dominic, please!"

I hear him rip open a condom packet and quickly sheathe himself. A moment later, the head of his big cock pushes through my wet, swollen tissues. He leans into me, pressing deeper inside me, deeper and deeper, until his thighs are finally flush with mine.

I press my face into the pillow and gasp at the sudden fullness. He feels even bigger at this angle.

Groaning, he grabs a fistful of my hair and pulls it, lifting my head back. As he leans over me, he angles my face toward his and kisses me.

He rotates his hips and groans as he grinds into me. "God, you are so fucking tight."

He releases my hair to grip my hips and hold me in place as he begins to thrust. Between his hold on me, and my wrists being tied, I can't move, and it only heightens my arousal.

I press my face into the pillow and moan as pleasure radiates through me. When he reaches beneath me and rolls one of my nipples between his finger and thumb, pleasure shoots from my nipple to my clit, like an arc of lightning, and I cry out once more.

He starts moving then, his hand returning to my hips. He holds me in place as he starts to thrust, slowly at first, and then picking up speed. My body softens for him, only too happy to accommodate him.

The force of his thrusts rocks me, sending me inching forward on the bed. I feel so exposed, so open to him, and it feels shockingly good.

Soon the pleasure builds between my legs, higher and higher. I'm panting and whimpering. When a second climax hits me, my sex clamps down on him, squeezing him hard. He cries out, his shout low and hoarse, and as I'm coming, I feel him thrust deep and hold himself there. I can feel the power of his ejaculation, the heat and throbbing of his cock inside me.

When he pulls carefully out of me, I collapse onto the bed, no longer able to support my own weight. I hear a rustling behind me as he deals with the condom. Then he lies down beside me, his arm going around me, his lips in my hair.

"My god, that was incredible," I say, still panting. I tug on the belt. "Aren't you going to untie me?"

Breathlessly, he laughs. "I don't know. I kind of like you like this."

I groan. "You better untie me."

"In a minute," he says, cuddling close. "Just let me enjoy this a moment."

22

Sophie

The next evening, as we sit at the kitchen table eating a late dinner, I contemplate telling Dominic how I feel. I realized last night just how much he means to me. There's no other man on Earth I would ever let tie me up. That has to mean something.

We really haven't had a serious heart-to-heart discussion about our feelings, or what we're doing. This isn't a friends-with-benefits type situation for me, and I don't think it is for him either.

I've never been happier, or felt more loved, than I have since

Dominic whisked me out of Chicago. We haven't known each other all that long, and yet I feel closer to him—and more committed to him—than I have to any other man.

I want to see where this goes. That is, if he's interested. If he shares my feelings. There's only one way to know. "Dominic?"

He sets his beer down. "Yeah?"

I sigh, not sure where to start. "Um, I was wondering—"

A sudden ear-shattering screech blares over the walkie-talkie sitting in its charging cradle on the kitchen counter. I jump in my seat. Dominic shoots to his feet.

The static clears, and then we hear Owen's sharp voice come over the radio. "Dominic, you there? Pick up!"

Dominic jumps up from his chair and grabs the radio handset, clicking on the mic. "Roger. What's wrong?"

"You're about to get company," Owen shouts, breathless. "A sedan heading your way. I'm coming."

"Copy," Dominic says curtly. He ends the call and tucks the walkie-talkie into his back pocket. Then he turns to me and says, "Grab your rifle, all the ammo you can carry, and get up to my room. Just like we practiced, Sophie."

My stomach sinks like a stone as a wave of nausea rushes through me. "You can't be serious."

"Move!"

Flinching at his bark, I run for the armory to grab my rifle and a stack of ammo boxes. He follows me in, quickly gathering more weapons and ammo. When I race up the stairs, he's right behind me, just like we practiced.

We hunker down near his bedroom window that faces out over the front yard. This is the best vantage point because we can see exactly where the lane comes up into the yard. But the sun has already set and is well behind the trees now, so we can barely make out the yard.

I crouch against the wall as Dominic pulls back the curtains and opens the window. A cool breeze rushes inside, bathing my hot face.

Dominic looks at me, his expression hard. "We've practiced this. You know what to do. When they get here, you shoot anything that comes out of that car."

"We can't just shoot them! What if it's a friend, or someone from town? Or someone who's lost?"

"Honey, no one comes unannounced up a rural mountain road in the dark—not unless they have a death wish."

"What if it's Shane?"

He laughs. "Shane, of all people, knows better than to do that."

"This is insane," I mutter as we crouch near the window, our rifles in position. "Someone could get hurt."

Dominic grabs my shoulder, squeezing hard. "Listen to me. Somebody *is* going to get hurt, do you hear me? But it's not going to be you or me. It's going to be *them*. Trust me, baby, they're here for one reason only, and that's to kill. Got it?"

"But how did they find us? We're out in the middle of nowhere."

"I don't know, but obviously they did."

And then we hear the sound of tires crunching on gravel, grinding and spinning as the car struggles to get up the road. Slowly, a black sedan pulls into view at the top of the lane and stops abruptly.

They're running dark—no headlights on.

My stomach churns. "Dominic," I whisper.

"Shh."

This can't be happening.

The car doors open, and four men exit the vehicle, all dressed in black, their faces covered by black ski masks. It's like something out of a movie.

"Just like we rehearsed," Dominic says quietly. "You take the ones on the left. I take the ones on the right. We'll meet in the middle. No one left standing, got it? Aim for the torso. You can do it. You have amazing aim for a girl."

I choke back a laugh. Only Dominic could make me laugh at a time like this.

I stare in disbelief as the men crouch behind their vehicle in a huddle. One man rises up behind the car and points a pair of binoculars at the cabin.

"Dominic?"

"Shush, baby. You've got this."

In this moment, all of his stupid training and drills make perfect sense. I feel bad for giving him a hard time and making fun of him. He knew what he was doing all along. He knew this could happen. He knew they might come, and now they have.

And they want to kill us. Or, at least they want to kill me. And

Dominic could die in the process.

"I'm sorry," I say, my throat tightening painfully as I choke on tears. "I should have listened."

He leans over and kisses my temple roughly. "Shut up and focus."

And then the men, in formations of two, creep out from behind their car and begin to make their way across the yard toward us. They're all holding semi-automatic rifles directed at the cabin.

Surely, this is all some big cosmic mistake. It has to be.

The guy with the binoculars points up at the bedroom window and makes some kind of hand signal to his friends.

"Night vision," Dominic says with a growl. "*Fuck.*"

All four men spread out and open fire on the cabin. I hear glass shattering as the downstairs windows are obliterated.

We move back from the windows until the initial volley ends. Then, after motioning me to stay back, Dominic points his rifle out the window and fires one shot, then immediately ducks back behind cover. "One down. Three to go."

Just like that?

There are shouts outside, and then more gun fire. Dominic returns to his crouched position at the window and fires several more shots.

This is really happening. I move into position, just like he showed me, and point my rifle out at the yard. There are two bodies lying on the ground, unmoving. The other two men are now crouched behind a stack of firewood.

Dominic shoots me a quick look. "They're going to storm the cabin, baby. Be ready."

"How do you know that?"

"Because we've got them pinned down, and the only way to their objective is to get inside this cabin."

The thought of those men coming inside our private sanctuary sends chills down my spine. "Over my dead body," I say.

Just as Dominic predicted, the two remaining men split up and come running for the cabin door, from two different angles.

Dominic fires on the guy on the right, who's running in an erratic pattern, making himself a hard target to hit.

The other guy, the one on the left—my target—makes a wide arc as he tries to come up on the side of the cabin.

I sight him through the scope of my rifle and fire. He's running a zig-zag pattern, and my shot misses. I try again, and a third time, also missing. On the fourth shot, I hit him square in the gut, and he drops to the ground.

Dominic fires one last shot, stopping the fourth guy in his tracks.

The walkie-talkie crackles, and Dominic pulls it from his back pocket. "Owen."

"Nicely done, you two," Owen says.

"You're outside?" Dominic says.

"Just behind the treeline, near the shed. I was waiting to see if I was needed. If they'd gotten inside the cabin, I would have taken them out from behind. Turns out that wasn't necessary. You two handled it just fine on your own."

"Take care of the bodies, will you? And then we'll dispose of their car in town."

"I'm on it," Owen says. "You guys relax. How's Sophie doing?"

Dominic looks at me, noticing the tears on my face. "We're good, buddy. Thanks." And then he ends the call and lays the walkie-talkie down.

"Come here, baby," he says, as he rises to his feet and pulls me to mine.

He sweeps me into his arms and carries me to the bed, where he sits and holds me on his lap, gently rocking me. "I'm so damn proud of you."

"I killed a man." My words are garbled as I choke on my tears.

"Yeah. One who wanted to kill you first."

"I know, but—"

"Shh, no *buts*. He wanted you dead. You got him first. End of story."

Dominic holds me while I cry for a very long time.

* * *

Later in the night, well before sunrise, Owen returns to our cabin. He and Dominic talk quietly downstairs while I lie wide awake in Dominic's bed.

I can hear bits and pieces of their conversation, just enough to know that it has something to do with plans to get rid of the bodies and the car.

Finally, I hear the cabin door close, and then the sound of

Dominic resetting the alarm. Not that it's of any use as the downstairs windows are shot out.

Dominic comes up the stairs, his footfalls heavy on the wooden treads.

He walks into our room and pulls off his shirt. Then he drops down onto the bed, sitting on the side so he can remove his boots. He stands and shucks off his jeans.

I'm surprised when he crawls into bed with me. "Aren't you going with Owen?"

"No. I didn't want to leave you." With that, he crawls under the covers and pulls me close. He's naked, his body radiating heat like a furnace.

I curl up close to him, craving the feel of him against me. We cuddle together, our legs entwined, our arms wrapped around each other.

I still can't stop shaking.

He brushes my hair back from my face. "I meant what I said earlier. I'm so damn proud of you."

My tears start again, as if on cue. I can't help it. I killed a man tonight. A stranger. For all I know, he has a wife and kids waiting at home for him. I don't even want to ask what Owen plans to do with the bodies.

"Shh," Dominic whispers, his lips in my hair. "Everything's going to be all right, I promise you. When Owen's done getting rid of the evidence, he'll sleep downstairs tonight. Just as a precaution."

"When those men don't return, won't Franco just send

more?"

"No. He won't."

He sounds so sure of himself, but I can't imagine how he could possibly know that. He's lying to me. He must be. They're going to keep coming until I'm dead. *And Dominic's likely to die in the process.*

He kisses me, his mouth tender and reverent on mine. And then he holds me tight, almost desperately.

I'm half-asleep when I hear Dominic say, "I love you, Phee. Don't ever forget that."

I carry those precious words with me as sleep takes me under.

23

Sophie

When I wake with a start, the sun is shining through the bedroom windows. I reach for Dominic, but he's not there. His side of the mattress is cold.

Memories from last night come rushing back, filling me with a crushing sense of dread.

When I hear the crunch of tires on the gravel drive, I shoot out of bed, pull on my boots, and run downstairs.

"Dominic?" I call for him, but there's no answer.

Something's wrong.

Broken glass crunches beneath my boots as I peer out of the

shot-out windows. The Bronco is gone, and there's no sign of Dominic. It makes no sense. He'd never leave me here alone, unprotected.

"Dominic!"

As a vehicle comes into sight, my heart seizes. I was expecting the Bronco, but it's a silver Escalade with Tennessee plates. My heart starts pounding and I stare in disbelief as the huge SUV slowly approaches.

When it stops, the two front doors open. Shane steps out the driver's door. My brother Jake exists the front passenger seat. They're both armed, handguns holstered to their chests.

My cheeks grow cold as the blood drains from my face. The only reason my brothers would be here is if Dominic sent for them. And he'd only send for them for one reason—because he's gone.

I step out onto the porch as my brothers approach the cabin. Their expressions are reserved, telling me nothing.

I walk down the steps to the grass. "Where's Dominic?" I look around the yard in vain, half-hoping to see him coming around the cabin with a rifle in his hand.

Jake looks to Shane, and Shane keeps his gaze locked on mine. "Hey, sis."

Warning bells start clanging in my head, and my stomach roils in protest. I sink down on the top step as pain tears through me. "He's gone, isn't he?" *Dominic's gone.*

"I'm sorry," Shane says, as he joins me on the step. He puts his arm around me and pulls me close.

My throat tightens painfully. "Where is he?"

"On his way back to Chicago. He left in the night."

"Chicago? Why?" I shake my head. "He wouldn't just leave me here alone." The man I'd grown to... love... wouldn't just up and leave me.

I look up just in time to see Owen disappear into the trees, a shotgun strapped to his back.

Owen was here? Watching the cabin? Watching me?

Because he knew Dominic was gone.

"He wouldn't just leave me," I cry, choking on the tears clogging my throat. "He wouldn't."

"You were never in any danger," Shane says. "He had his friend watch over you through the night, until we arrived."

"None of this makes any sense. Why would he leave?"

Jake stands at the bottom of the porch steps, frowning. "He made a deal with the devil."

"What are you talking about?"

Shane sighs. "Dominic called his dad last night, after you two were attacked, and cut a deal."

I feel sick. "What kind of deal?" As soon as I say the words, I know.

Shane tightens his arm on me. "Dominic got Franco to agree to call off the hit on you."

"In exchange for what?" But I already know the answer.

Shane hesitates to answer. "In exchange for Dominic," he finally says.

He traded himself for me.

"Oh god, no." I lean forward, closing in on myself. I wrap my arms around my knees and hug them tightly to my aching chest. My head is spinning. Tears sting my eyes. "No, no, no. He can't."

Shane wraps me in his arms and holds me close. Jake comes to sit on my other side, his hand on my back.

When I was a little girl, my brothers always protected me. But there's nothing they can do to help me now.

"I'll go inside and pack your things," Jake says to me as he rises to his feet. "We need to get back."

"We're taking you home," Shane says. "To Mom and Dad's house. As long as Franco Alessio keeps his word, you'll be perfectly safe there in the compound until after the trial."

The rest is a blur. Shane walks me straight to the Escalade and helps me into the backseat. He waits there with me until Jake returns not long after with my meager belongings.

As Shane starts the engine and heads back down the mountain, my heart shatters into a million pieces.

* * *

The drive to a private airstrip in a nearby town is a mindless blur. All I can think about is Dominic and what he must be going through right now. I can't believe he made a deal with his father. That was the last thing he wanted to do. And it's all because of me. It's all my fault.

When we arrive at the airport, I spot one of Shane's company jets on the tarmac, waiting to take us back to Chicago. The crew—a pilot, co-pilot, and two flight attendants—is standing by the plane.

Shane parks the rented SUV, and we board the plane, along with the crew, and settle into our seats.

As I strap myself in, I keep hearing Dominic's words repeating in my head.

"My integrity—my honor—is all I have, and I'd rather die than lose it."

He sacrificed everything he stands for, everything important to him, to protect me. It's so unfair. I feel so heartbroken, so sick, I could scream.

Shane and Jake are seated across the center aisle from me, facing me. I catch them both watching me.

"How are Luke and Beth?" I ask Shane.

"They're fine," he says.

"And her pregnancy?"

"Everything's fine."

I smile. Shane's so sure his wife is having a girl this time. They chose not to find out the new baby's gender ahead of time—they want it to be a surprise. But since the beginning of Beth's pregnancy, Shane has insisted the baby is a girl.

"Jake, how about you?" I ask. "Everything okay at home?" Jake's married to his high school sweetheart, Annie, and he's the stepfather to a six-year-old boy, Aiden, and the father of infant twin girls.

Jake nods. "Annie and the kids are fine."

"Mom and Dad want you to stay with them until the trial is over," Shane says. "You'll be safe there. Jake has beefed up security at the compound."

I nod, though I really don't care where I go. Nothing can undo the damage that's been done—the sacrifice Dominic made for me.

"How did they find us?" I ask. "Does anyone know?"

Shane frowns. "We don't know. Have you spoken to anyone since you left Chicago?"

I shake my head. "No." And then I remember the night at the tavern. "Wait, yes. I called Amber once."

Shane's brow furrows. "Called her how?"

"On an old landline I found in the ladies' room in a tavern. But I was careful not to tell her where we were. I just wanted to let her know I was okay."

"Amber's purse was stolen two days ago, and with it, her phone. Did Amber put a passcode on her phone?"

I shake my head. "She says they're too annoying." I stare at Shane, studying the carefully neutral expression on his face. There's something he's not saying. "They tracked us through that phone call, didn't they?"

He nods. "Most likely. Her phone would have registered the number of the phone. They would have been able to trace that number to the tavern in Millerton, and from there, they could have asked around until they identified where you were staying."

My chest tightens, as do my lungs, and I can barely breathe.

"This is my fault then, isn't it?"

It is.

I did this.

I betrayed Dominic.

God, how he must hate me.

And I can't blame him, because I hate myself too.

24

Sophie

When our flight arrives back in Chicago, Jake drives us straight to our family's compound. A while back, Shane bought a brand-new residential development just north of downtown Chicago. It's a gated community, with private security. My parents built a home there, as did Jake and his wife, and my sister Lia and her fiancé, Jonah Locke. Beth's mother, Ingrid Jamison, has a house here as well.

My parents have been trying for a while now to talk me into building here. Now, I'm moving in with them, at least temporarily.

It's a bittersweet reunion when we arrive.

Immediately I notice that security has been beefed up significantly at the gate, and I know it's because of me. Once we're through the gates, which are manned twenty-four-seven, we head straight to Mom and Dad's house.

Jake pulls into their driveway and shuts off the engine.

"Hannah's here," Shane tells me. "She flew in from Colorado this morning to be here when you arrived."

Hannah.

My middle sister.

"I'm pretty sure the whole family is here," Jake says, chuckling. "So be prepared."

As I step out of the vehicle, the front door to my parents' house opens, and Mom and Dad step out. It's just the two of them. The rest of the family is probably lying in wait inside.

As I walk slowly up the driveway, Mom runs down to meet me. The minute I feel her slight arms around me, I break down sobbing. A moment later, my dad is there, wrapping us both in his strong arms, holding us close as Mom and I both cry.

My dad says, "Good job, boys. Thanks for bringing our little girl home." I smile in spite of myself. There's nothing *little* about me.

"Now let's get you in the house," my dad says, and he walks us inside.

It's officially a McIntyre family reunion. Everyone's here—my parents, my four brothers and two sisters, plus all their kids, spouses, and significant others. Sam and Cooper are here, as well. They might as well be family. Beth's brother, Tyler Jamison—the homicide cop who responded to Kent's shooting—and his boyfriend, Ian, are here. Even Beth's mom, Ingrid, is here.

Everyone I care about is here—except for Dominic.

Just imagining where Dominic is right now—what he's doing, how he's coping—is unbearable. I'm sure he regrets ever hearing my name.

I hug everyone. I accept their well wishes and heartfelt sympathies for what I've been through. And the entire time I feel like an undeserving imposter. Because no matter what I went through, it's nothing compared to what Dominic is now forced to face.

I wish those men had killed me back at the cabin. My death might have spared Dominic.

I excuse myself to go upstairs to the guest room where, I'm told, my clothes and personal items from my condo are waiting for me.

Once in my room, I close the door and collapse onto the mattress and let the tears fall. Hot, scalding tears that accomplish nothing. No matter how many tears I cry, it won't undo the harm I've done to Dominic.

"My integrity—my honor—is all I have, and I'd rather die than lose it."

But he wasn't able to keep his oath or preserve his honor. He sacrificed it—for me.

"You idiot!" I cry. "Why did you do that? You should have just let them kill me."

When there's a knock at my door, I wipe the tears from my face. "Come in."

The door opens slowly, and my sister Hannah pokes her head inside. Her long brown hair is pulled back into a single braid. She's dressed in jeans, a t-shirt, and hiking boots. Just seeing her makes me tear up again.

As she walks into my room, she gives me a sad smile. "Do you feel like talking?"

I nod and wipe my damp cheeks. "Sure. Come on in."

Hannah and I are close. For a long time, we were the only two girls in a family of mostly boys. It wasn't until years later, that our parents unexpectedly had twins—Lia and Liam—thereby giving us another sister, as well as a baby brother. But for a long time, it was just me and Hannah trying to cope with three rambunctious, hot-headed brothers.

She sits beside me on the bed and slips her arm around me.

Hannah and I couldn't be more different—a girly-girl and a tomboy—but we love each other dearly. And it's been months since I've seen her as she lives out west, in The Rocky Mountains, where she studies wild wolf populations.

I lean into her, grateful for her strength. "I can't believe you came back to Chicago."

Hannah hates the city with a passion, and she doesn't come back very often.

"Dad called me last night to tell me you were coming home,"

she says. "I had to come see you for myself. I had to see that you were okay."

"I'm fine, thanks to Dominic."

"I heard Dad asking Shane about somebody named Dominic. Who is he?"

"He's the one who got me out of Chicago and kept me safe when the mob put out a hit on me. That is, until they found us."

"Where is he now?"

I shrug. "I'm not sure." My eyes brim with tears.

"Sophie, what happened?"

"He traded his freedom for my safety. I didn't even get to say goodbye. Or tell him that I love him. Now I'll never get a chance to tell him."

Her arm tightens around me as she lays her head on my shoulder. "It's never too late to tell someone how you feel." She reaches into her back pocket and hands me her phone. "Call him and tell him."

"I don't know his number. I have no idea how to reach him."

"Shane will know," Hannah says, getting up. "I'll get the number."

After Hannah runs off to find Shane, a steady stream of people comes through my room—Lia, Beth, and Mom. Jamie's girlfriend, Molly. Jake's wife, Annie. All the womenfolk have come to check on me.

I'm an ungrateful wretch, though, because I just want everyone to leave me alone so I can cry and wallow in my pain.

A little while later, Hannah returns. She hands me an iPhone.

"What's this?" I say.

"Mom and Dad got you a new phone, to replace the one that got destroyed. Shane added Dominic's number to your contact list."

Hope surges in my chest when I realize I can call Dominic. Even though I'm afraid to face him, I'm even more afraid to not know where he is or how he's doing. I press the call button and wait.

His phone rings twice before my call goes to voicemail.

His voicemail greeting is short and to the point, but at least I get to hear his voice when the recording says, "Leave a message."

I end the call and look at Hannah. "It went to voicemail."

"Try again," she says.

I call a second time, putting it on speaker, and the same thing happens.

"Leave a message," she whispers.

"Dominic? Hi. It's me, Sophie. I'm back in Chicago, at my parents' house in Lincoln Park. I need to talk to you. I need to see you. Please. Call me, okay?" But as I hang up, I know he's not going to call.

If he's really with Franco, he won't call me.

"He's not going to call," I say to Hannah.

"Why do you say that?"

"He told me he loved me, right before he left to come back to Chicago."

"If he loves you, then of course he'll call you."

I shake my head. "He won't. He's still protecting me, now

more than ever."

25

Dominic

I knock on Franco's office door, hoping he's not there, or that he's busy and doesn't bother answering.

But no such luck.

"Come in!" he barks in his strong Italian accent.

I open the door and walk inside.

Franco Alessio is a big man, as tall as me, and twice as wide. His dark hair is cut short and heavily threaded with silver. I figure he's in his early sixties. His eyes are dark as night, and he has a few days' worth of scruff on his jaw, mostly silver. I got my height from him, but I got my brown hair and eyes from my mom.

His office is very old world, with the dark mahogany desk, matching bookcases, and wood-paneled walls. The bookcases are filled with leather-bound books, like what you'd expect to see in an attorney's office. I'm pretty sure the books are just for show.

There's a brass lamp on the desk and a fancy, stained-glass light fixture hanging overhead. Behind the desk, glass doors lead out onto a covered veranda, and there's a swimming pool beyond that—currently filled with pretty young girls in skimpy bathing suits, if they're wearing anything at all.

Franco looks up from his desk and smiles. "Dominic! Please, come in. Have a seat, son."

Reluctantly, I take a seat, hoping to get this meeting over as quickly as possible.

It turns my stomach to hear him call me that, but I don't correct him. I won't do anything that might endanger our agreement and put Sophie at risk. The only reason I can still function right now is because I know she's safe at her parents' house. Her family will look after her, I have no doubt about that. It just burns me that I can't be with her. It should be me keeping her safe.

As Franco watches me curiously, I force myself to snap out of it and say what I came to say. "I took care of your little problem over on Miller Street. The landlord and I came to an understanding. It's settled. He won't give your guys any more trouble."

He leans back comfortably in an old, brown leather chair and clasps his hands over his big belly. "I must say, I'm impressed. How did you get the old man to agree? He's been giving me fits for years."

"My methods are my own business." There's more than one way to skin a cat, and you don't have to break kneecaps to get someone to do something. I shrug. "Let's just say I made him an offer he couldn't refuse. It's done."

Franco's eyes narrow on me, and I suspect he knows I'm not being completely truthful with him, but he lets it go for now. "Fine. I'm glad to hear it. Results are what matter, right? Now, my son, what can I do for you? This is a two-way street, you know. You help me, I help you." He gestures at the pool out back. "Lots of pretty girls out there. Help yourself, eh? Take your pick."

There's only one thing I want from him. "Just keep your word regarding Sophie McIntyre. That's all I ask."

He nods as he brushes off my concern. "There's nothing for you to worry about. I gave you my word. No one will hurt the girl."

"Not the girl, not her family or her friends—not anyone she's associated with. She's completely off limits."

"Of course! Of course!" He gets up from his desk and walks to the wet bar, where he grabs two tumblers and a bottle of whiskey. He pours a generous shot in each glass and hands me one. "Let's toast to our new arrangement, shall we?"

He holds his glass out to me, and I touch mine to his.

"This is how negotiation works, Dominic. I get what I want;

you get what you want. As long as we *both* hold up our end of the bargain, our agreement remains in effect. Capeesh?"

I knock back the whiskey, and it sours my stomach. "Yes."

"Excellent." He swallows his with a grimace. "Then everything is good." He drops back into his chair. "I know you don't like getting your hands dirty, but sometimes it can't be helped." He hands me a photograph. "Look into this, will you? This punk dealer has been trying to make inroads into my territory. I want you to put a stop to it. The address is on the back."

I read the south Chicago address, recognizing the neighborhood. It's a rough one, financially depressed—more like desperate. Rising to my feet, I pocket the photo and head for the door, anxious to be gone. "I'll take care of it."

"Take some of the boys with you," Franco says. "You need to start building relationships with the men. They need to get to know you. Besides, you can have them do the dirty work if you don't want to. They won't balk."

Saying nothing, I leave the office. I leave the entire fucking building—a rundown warehouse on the southeast side of Chicago—and climb into my Bronco.

Once I'm a few blocks away, and sure no one is following me, I pull into a parking lot to check my phone messages. I see three calls from an unknown number. The thing is... it's not unknown. I know exactly who's calling me. I suppose I should block her, but I can't bring myself to do it. It's the only connection I have left to her. And right now, it's my lifeline.

"Hi, Dominic. It's me again."

As if I don't already know.

I don't know why she keeps calling when I refuse to answer or return her calls. But she does. Every day I have new messages from Sophie.

"I just finished having lunch with my sisters and my mom, and I came upstairs to call you."

There's a long pause, and then I hear what sounds like a sniffle.

Fuck. She's crying.

"I hope you're okay. I mean, I understand how awful this must be for you. I know it was the last thing you wanted to do." Her voice breaks, and now she's openly crying, her garbled words barely coherent. *"You shouldn't have done it. You should have just let them kill me. I never wanted you to sacrifice yourself for me."*

And then the call ends abruptly.

Damn it!

It's fucking torture to hear her voice and know she's nearby. It kills me to know she's hurting—suffering—and I'm not there to comfort her.

It's fucking killing me.

But I made my choice, and I won't let any aspect of this life touch her.

Ever.

No matter how much it's killing me.

* * *

I drive to the south side of the city, to the address on the back of the photo Franco gave me—an abandoned concrete apartment building. The windows are boarded up, and there's graffiti spray-painted on every possible surface.

After strapping my gun holster on, I walk around to the back of the building and find a door that's been jimmied open. I step inside, assailed by the strong odor of urine and feces.

A quick search of the ground floor reveals nothing. Up on the second floor, I find the punk I'm looking for. He's lying on a stained mattress, high as a kite.

He's a skinny, scrawny kid, barely out of his teens, with gang tattoos on his face and hands. Only I don't recognize any of the marks on him. He's not from a local gang. He must have run off, escaped, or been displaced from another gang—probably from the West Coast—and he's looking to gain a foothold here.

As soon as he spots me, he bolts, climbing out an open window and down the fire escape. I follow him out and chase him down in a back alley until I manage to pin him between two buildings. The alley reeks of urine and vomit.

"Whoa, calm down," I tell the kid as he backs himself into a corner. "I'm not going to hurt you."

He stares at the gun holstered on my chest. "What the fuck do you want?"

"I want you to stake out someone else's territory," I tell him. "If I catch you on Alessio territory again, I'm afraid you and I are going to have a serious problem. You gotta move on, pal. Don't make this hard on either of us."

"Or what?" he says, trying to sound like a tough guy. "You gonna make me?"

But I can tell he's scared. He's shaking.

I loom over him, letting my height do the talking for me. I hate using my size as a weapon, but sometimes it's effective. "Either you find somewhere else to do your business, or I break your leg. Your choice. I'll be back tomorrow, and if you're still here, you're going to wish you'd left when you had the chance. Is that clear?"

Eyes wide, he nods.

When I'm back in the Bronco, I can still smell the filth from that alley. I sure as hell hope the kid takes off, because if he doesn't, I'll be forced to follow through with my threat. So far I've managed to keep my hands clean, but I don't know how long my luck will last.

It's a good reminder of why Sophie's lost to me.

I'm no longer fit to touch the sole of her shoe.

* * *

That night, after I go back to my shitty loft apartment and drink myself into a stupor, I pass out on the sofa.

I dream I'm back in the cabin, waking to the smell of fresh coffee and breakfast.

"Good morning, sleepy head," Sophie says as she walks into the bedroom carrying a tray.

She's wearing a sheer white nightgown that does little to hide the rosy tips of her breasts. Her hair is up in a high pony, and a few curling tendrils hang down to brush against her cheeks. She's breathtaking.

She sits on the bed and sets the tray on the mattress. "How about breakfast in bed?"

All I can do is stare at her. *This is just an illusion, I realize. A dream. It's not real.*

I glance down at the tray. She's brought a plate of pancakes, with butter melting on them and drizzled with maple syrup, two forks, and two cups of coffee—one black and the other heavily doctored with creamer and sugar.

She picks up a fork. "Dig in, baby." She takes a bite, then frowns at me. "What's wrong? Aren't you hungry?"

I stare at her, wishing I could take a picture of her just like this. Sadly, I don't have a picture of her. I have nothing but my memories to remember her by, except for the voice messages I've saved on my phone.

In my dream, we hear a door slam downstairs.

Sophie frowns, looking frightened. "Are you expecting someone?"

Then we hear the sound of thundering footsteps as someone runs upstairs. Franco bursts into the bedroom, dressed in a black wool coat. He scowls at us, livid.

"You broke your fucking promise to me!" he snarls, pointing his big fat finger at me. And then he reaches inside his coat and pulls out a 9mm. "I told you there'd be consequences if you broke your promise."

In the dream, I shoot upright in bed. "No!"

And then he shoots her in the chest, at point blank range. As she falls back on the bed, I stare at the blood splattered on her face, in her hair. She stares up at the ceiling with a fixed gaze.

Jesus, I can't even dream about her.

I roll off the couch and vomit on the wood floor. I haven't eaten lately, so it's nothing but hot bile scalding my throat as it comes up. I lie where I fell, gasping for air, my head spinning.

No matter how hard I try, I can't get the image of her dead face out of my head.

After a trip to the bathroom to rinse the acrid taste of bile from my mouth, I grab my phone and sit on the sofa. Like a man obsessed, I play her voice messages again and cling to the sound of her voice.

"Dominic?" There's a long pause. "Hi." Another pause. *"I hope you're doing all right. I don't know what to say, other than I miss you so much."* Then she starts to cry. *"I guess if you wanted to talk to me, you would."* More muffled crying. *"I'm so sorry I ruined your life. Please forgive me."*

I don't know which message is worse. The one where she starts crying and then apologizes for ruining my life, or the one where she bitches me out for not taking her calls.

"Dominic, it's Sophie." In this one, her voice is clipped and direct. *"You're an idiot, you know that? I can't believe you traded yourself—your fucking freedom—for a client. What about all that bullshit you told me about your integrity and your honor? Huh? What about that? Look, tell your dad I said to fuck off. He knows* where to find me. Hell, I'll even make it easy on him. I'll come to him. How about that? Just give me the address. Let him kill me and get it over with. Then you can go back to living your own life, like none of this ever happened."

That one makes me laugh every time I listen to it. God, I love it when she's bitchy.

But my absolute favorite is the one where she's quiet, whispering. I think she was in bed when she left this message, because it came at three in the morning.

"Dominic?" A soft whisper. *"I miss you so much. That last night at the cabin, I had a dream that you told me you loved me. But sometimes I think it might not have been a dream. That you really said it. If you did, I'm sorry I didn't say it back when I had the chance. Because I do."* Even softer, quieter. *"I love you, too."*

Every time I listen to that one, my heart breaks all over again.

26

Sophie
Two months later...

Hannah and I sit on the swings on the playground in the center of the compound, right across the street from my parents' house. "I can't live with Mom and Dad forever," I say, rocking gently.

My sister pushes off and starts swinging hard and high, like the daredevil she is. "Shane's offered to build you a house here. Take him up on it. You can't go back to your condo, at least not until the trial is over. And even then, it might not be safe. You can't trust mobsters to keep their word."

"No, but I trust Dominic. If he believes his father will keep his word, then he will."

Just the thought of Dominic makes my heart hurt. A rush of longing sweeps over me, and my chest aches. I miss him so much. I miss everything about him—his presence, his strength, his humor. I miss the way he used to tease me. I miss the way he held me at night, as if he was afraid to let go.

My parents keep asking me what my future plans are, but the truth is, I don't know. I just don't *care* anymore. I don't care what happens to me. Sometimes I think I should just follow through on what I said to Dominic in a voice message—that I should turn myself in to his father and get this over with. I'd rather Franco kill me and Dominic be a free man than go on living like this.

The knowledge that he's suffering, day after day, being forced to do god knows what, haunts me—it's all my fault.

I kick off with my feet, setting my swing in motion, and the sudden movement makes me queasy.

Shit, not again.

I jump off the swing and puke in the grass.

Hannah jumps off her swing and rushes to my side. "Are you okay?"

Straightening, I wipe my mouth on the hem of my t-shirt. "I'm fine. I just... got dizzy there for a minute. I'm okay."

"Hey, bitches!"

We glance across the street to see our youngest sister, Lia, heading our way, dressed in black leggings and a matching tank top, her long blonde hair in braids. "I'm going for a run. Want to come with?"

"I'd love to," Hannah says. "I desperately need the exercise. Chicago is making me soft."

"You guys go ahead," I say. "I think I'll go back inside and lie down for a while."

Lia gives me a scrutinizing look. "You okay, Soph? You look a little green around the gills."

"She's fine," Hannah says, grinning. "It's just a little bout of morning sickness."

Lia's blue eyes widen as she looks from Hannah to me. "No way! Are you shitting me?"

I glare at Hannah. "Don't you dare even suggest it."

Hannah laughs. "Come on, Sophie. You've been tired and cranky for weeks, and this isn't the first time you've puked. Don't think I haven't heard you tossing your cookies in the upstairs hallway bathroom, which is situated right between your bedroom and mine."

My hand instinctively goes to my belly. "I can't be."

Hannah nails me with a knowing look. "Did you have sex about three months ago?"

I nod, feeling my cheeks burn. "Yes."

"Were you on the pill at the time?" she says.

"Not exactly. My pills got left behind in Chicago, so no. But we used condoms. Except for the one time we forgot. And there was one time when it almost slipped off too soon."

Hannah rolls her eyes toward Lia, who laughs.

"Mom's going to have kittens," Lia says. "Another baby! Yay! Maybe now she'll get off my case. Between you and Princess, we have enough new babies on the way to keep her occupied."

"Princess?" Hannah says, clearly confused. "Who's Princess?"

"It's Lia's nickname for Beth," I say.

I sit back down on the swing as Lia's words sink in.

A baby.

Dominic's baby.

As I rub my belly, I feel a tiny spark of joy. And in that moment, I realize that if it's true, if I am pregnant, I'm glad. "My jeans have been getting tight lately."

"There's only one way to find out," Hannah says. "We need a pregnancy test."

Lia turns back toward her house across the street. "Come on, bitches. I'll drive."

* * *

An hour later, we're all hovering in Lia's bathroom, staring at the little white pregnancy stick lying on the counter, waiting for my phone timer to go off.

Lia's fiancé, Jonah, appears in the open doorway and stares at the three of us.

Hannah's sitting on the closed toilet seat, Lia's sitting on the side of the tub, and I'm pacing. I'm way too nervous to sit.

"Hello, ladies," he says, eyeing the pregnancy test resting on the counter. "Is there something I should know about?"

"It's not my pee, if that's what you're asking," Lia says, sounding more than a little relieved.

"Whose is it then?" Jonah asks, looking expectantly from Hannah to me.

"It's mine," I say.

Jonah's dark eyes widen, but he refrains from saying anything more. "I'll just leave you ladies to it, then."

"Good idea, pal," Lia says, shooing him away from the door. "Go write a song."

The timer goes off, and we all step forward to look, the three of us staring down at the indicator. Then I pick up the box to double check the instructions.

"Damn, Sophie," Lia says as she stares at the stick. "You're knocked up."

The thought of a tall, sturdy little boy with brown hair and whiskey-colored eyes makes me smile. I may not have Dominic in my life, but it looks like I'll have a piece of him after all. He left me with a little souvenir.

That night, after peeing on two more sticks, just to be sure, I break the news to my parents. My mother, who adores babies and loves being a grandma, weeps tears of joy. My father isn't quite so sanguine about the whole thing, but he hugs me nonetheless and assures me that he and Mom will be here for me and the baby, every step of the way.

They don't mention Dominic at all.

We have a family Zoom call, and I break the news to everyone. Their reactions are a mix of surprise, excitement, and in the case of my eldest brother, Shane, shock and well-concealed anger.

Not two minutes after we end the Zoom call, my phone rings.

I'm not surprised to see it's Shane calling.

I sigh. "Hi, Shane."

"Tell me what happened."

I laugh in spite of the situation. "Your wife is about to have her *second* baby, Shane. I sincerely hope you know by now how this happens."

"Sophie, I'm serious. What happened between you and Zaretti? I'm assuming he's the father."

"Of course he is! What kind of hussy do you think I am?"

"Look, Sophie, I never pressed for details, but I know how upset you were when you found out Dominic had left you in Tennessee. And I know you've been depressed ever since you came back to Chicago."

"Get to the point, please."

"You and Dominic. How did it happen?"

"We had sex, all right? We had it in his bed, on the kitchen table, on the sofa, on the front porch swing, and in the backseat of his Bronco in a parking lot. There! Are you happy?"

Sighing, he mumbles something incoherent. Then he says, "It was consensual, right?"

"Oh, for crying out loud! Of course it was consensual. Do you think for one minute that Dominic would have hurt me?"

"Well, no. If I did, I never would have asked him to take you out of Chicago."

"Okay then. There you have it. I'm pregnant, and Dominic is the father. And you know what? I'm glad. Now I'll have something of him."

"I'll take care of this. I'll call him—"

"No! Don't you dare. He can't know, Shane. It would tear him to pieces to know he has a child he can't ever know."

* * *

A week later, I get a phone call from the assistant district attorney—Rebecca Murphy—who is part of the team that's prosecuting Mikey. They want me to testify before a grand jury. They'll decide if there's sufficient evidence to hold a trial.

When the time comes, Shane and Jake escort me to speak to the grand jury, and based on my testimony, the trial is scheduled.

Ms. Murphy comes to the house to meet with me, to go over my testimony and the procedures. My parents are there, along with Shane and his attorney, Troy Spencer, who's acting as my attorney. We all sit down at the dining room table.

As I'm the sole eyewitness, a successful prosecution hinges on my testimony.

Ms. Murphy describes the process, how I'll be brought in to testify, then escorted out of the courtroom. It should be a pretty straight-forward, cut and dry procedure. The prosecution is asking for life in prison without a chance of parole.

The whole time she drones on about the tedious details, I rest my hand on my belly and wonder if I'm carrying a girl or a boy.

Before she leaves, I ask her the one question about this case that has been haunting me most. "Why did Mikey Alessio kill Kent Martinez?"

She pauses in the process of closing her briefcase and frowns. "Kent was investigating several cases involving organized crime. He was starting to make life difficult for the Alessios."

"And so they killed him."

She nods. "We don't know if it was a sanctioned killing, or if Mikey was working on his own. Regardless, a good man is dead. Kent was a good friend."

"I'm sorry." Tears start forming in my eyes. Even though I didn't know Kent, I grieve for him, and for the unfairness of it all.

Ms. Murphy nods. "Sometimes, life's not fair," she says, as if she's reading my mind.

Shane escorts her to the front door, and I go upstairs to my room. I'm overwhelmed with emotions right now—something that happens to me pretty constantly since becoming pregnant.

It's also not fair that Dominic was taken away from me—from us—me and the baby. Dominic did nothing wrong, and yet he now has a child who is out of his reach.

* * *

That night, as always, I call Dominic and leave him a voicemail. His phone is still working—he hasn't changed his number or blocked me—so I like to think he listens to my messages. There's no way to know for sure as I never hear back from him. But, I'd like to think he's getting them.

"*Hi. It's me. The assistant DA stopped by today to talk about the upcoming trial. We went over my testimony and how the process will work. I'll be escorted into the courtroom by police officers. I'm not looking forward to seeing Mikey again. His face still haunts me. It's a hard face to forget. But enough about me. How are you doing? I hope you're okay. I can't believe the summer's almost over. Beth's baby is due soon.*"

And then I run out of steam, because thinking about Beth's baby makes me think about my baby, and that makes me think about how much I miss Dominic. And I can't tell Dominic about the baby. It would be too cruel.

I yawn and say, "It's late. I guess I'd better go to bed. Goodnight. Sleep well."

Even though I'll probably lie in my bed for hours, thinking of Dominic, missing him.

"I dream about you," I add quietly, speaking past a painful knot in my throat.

Do you ever think about me?

But I don't dare ask because I'm afraid the answer might be no.

I hang up before I start crying.

27

Dominic

There are nights I don't sleep. I lie awake thinking about Sophie, wondering where she is and how she's doing. She didn't go back to her condo—I know because I've been checking pretty regularly. And I haven't seen any sign of her coming or going from Shane's apartment building either. I can only assume she's still staying in their family compound in Lincoln Park, probably with her parents. At least I hope she is. That's the best place for her.

I live for her late-night messages. Every night she calls me around eleven. I stare at her name and number on my screen and wait for the ringing to stop as she's sent to voicemail. I itch to answer the call, just to talk to her for one minute, but I don't. I'd never risk her safety that way. I don't belong in her life anymore. I'm a two-bit criminal, and she deserves a hell of a lot better than that.

So, I save her voice messages and listen to them over and over, wishing she was here with me. Wishing we could be together.

Most of the time she sounds sad. But she keeps calling, night after night. It takes a lot of courage to reach out to someone when they're not reaching back.

I wonder if she hates me for leaving her. I'm sure she realizes I didn't have a choice. That night—after we were attacked—I called Franco as soon as Sophie fell asleep. I knew he'd send another carload of thugs to our location when the first group failed to report back. I couldn't risk another attack. And they'd have kept coming until they finally succeeded.

So, I took a chance and called him, offering him a deal.

I offered him the one thing I knew he wanted more than anything—me.

* * *

I walk a fine line these days. As Franco indoctrinates me into his organization, he gives me assignments. How I accomplish those assignments is left completely up to me—he doesn't try to micromanage me, thank god. I think he's smart enough to know that won't work. There are lines I won't cross, and he knows it. Even though I'm part of his organization now, it doesn't mean I've sacrificed all of my values.

So, I get creative and find ways to accomplish goals *without* breaking kneecaps. For the most part, it's worked out. I've only gotten my hands dirty a few times when it was absolutely necessary, and always well deserved.

I arrive at Franco's estate—he called me earlier in the morning and asked me to come. Apparently, there's something important we need to discuss.

I try to have as little to do with him as possible, while still upholding my end of our bargain. I won't give him any excuse to claim that I'm not keeping my word.

I drive through the gate onto his private property—an impressive estate in an affluent neighborhood west of the city. The armed guard recognizes me, of course, and waves me through. I park behind the house, in view of his six-car garage, and walk in through the rear door, past another armed guard.

"Mr. Zaretti," the guard says, nodding as I approach. He's a grizzled old guy with a strong Italian accent. He's probably been with Franco's organization longer than I've been alive. "Mr. Alessio's expecting you. He's in his study."

I nod to the old guy. "Thanks."

The house is full of people—Franco's men. I ignore them all and head to the study. I just want to get this over with, whatever it is.

When I reach the study, I knock.

"Come in!" Franco calls.

When I step inside, I see he's got his old guard in there with him—two of the older guys who basically help him manage the day-to-day operations of the organization.

"You wanted to see me?" I ask Franco, ignoring the others. "If you're busy, I'll come back later."

"No, no!" Franco lays his cigar in an ashtray. "We were just finishing up. Please come in, son. Have a seat."

The two men take that as a cue to leave. Without saying a word, they get up and walk past me, nodding at me on their way out.

"Sit, Dominic," Franco says, pointing at one of the chairs facing his desk. "We have much to discuss."

Once I'm seated, he steeples his fingers and studies me. "Mikey's trial has been scheduled," he says, getting right to the point. "I plan to be there in the courtroom to hear the testimony, and of course, to support my son. I want you there with me."

I hear a deafening roar, and it takes me a minute to realize it's the sound of my blood rushing in my head. Sophie will be there. I'd actually *see* Sophie—be in the same room with her, breathe the same air.

Franco's watching me closely, assessing my reaction.

"All right," I say, trying to appear unaffected. He already knows how I feel about Sophie, but I don't want to give him any additional ammunition to use against me.

"All right?" he says. "That's all you're going to say?"

I shrug. "What else is there to say?"

"The girl will be there, of course."

I give him a hard look. "Is there anything else?"

Slowly, he shakes his head. "No, just the trial. I want you there with me."

"I'll be there." Then I stand. "If that's all, I have work to do."

"That's all," he says, eyeing me curiously.

And I walk out.

I gave him my word I'd join his organization and learn the business. I never promised to like it.

28

Sophie

The assistant DA meets with us at my parents' house one more time before the trial is scheduled to convene, to go over my testimony once more, the procedures, and the process.

"Do you have any questions or concerns, Sophie?" Ms. Murphy asks me.

I shake my head. "No." I have a hell of a lot of concerns—like do I really have to do this? But they all seem pointless. I don't have a choice.

Troy Spencer lays his folded hands on the dining room table.

"Shane and Jake will also escort Sophie into the courtroom," he says to the DA.

Shane and Jake are seated at the dining table with us, along with my parents.

"That really won't be necessary," Ms. Murphy says as she clasps her hands in front of her, leaning forward as she eyes Troy. "The police—"

"Humor us," Troy says with a hard smile. "My client's brothers want to be there with her. And I'm sure you can... appreciate... the sensitivity of the matter. There's Ms. McIntyre's safety to consider."

The woman nods placatingly. "Yes, but the police are perfectly capable—"

"There's no *but*," Shane cuts in, his voice sharp. "My sister is pregnant, and I'm not letting her step one foot inside that courtroom without ample protection. Jake and I will be part of the security detail."

Ms. Murphy looks from Shane to Troy, and then to me. She ponders the impasse for a moment, and then she nods. "Fine."

Shane relaxes in his seat, although his arms are still crossed over his chest.

I'm overwhelmed with emotion, with my brothers' fierce desire to protect me. I don't know where I'd be without my family. Even Troy Spencer looks like he's ready to go to the mat for me.

My eyes water again, and I'm on the verge of tears. My emotions have been all over the place lately. One minute I'm crying, and the next I want to scream in frustration. When a wave of nausea overtakes me, I jump up from the table and hurry out of the room to the closest bathroom to throw up. Or at least my body tries to. As there's nothing in my stomach, there's nothing to get rid of.

My appetite has been nonexistent lately.

My nerves are shot.

I'm not sleeping.

I'm miserable.

Between lack of food and lack of sleep, I'm running on adrenaline. I just want to get this trial over with so I can try to put everything behind me and find a way to move forward. I have a child coming. I have to find a way forward, for the baby's sake.

When I come out of the bathroom, my mom is waiting outside the door.

Her soft blue eyes crinkle at the corners when she smiles. She touches my arm gently. "Are you okay, sweetie?"

The waterworks start up again, and wordlessly, she takes me in her arms and holds me tight.

My mom is petite, like Lia, and she feels tiny in my arms. But I know better. She may be small, but she's as fierce as a lioness, and she'll do anything for the ones she loves.

My dad appears a moment later, and he wraps his arms around the both of us, holding us securely. "Everything's going to be okay, honey," he says as he kisses the side of my head. "Your brothers won't let anything happen to you. It's going to be fine."

Unable to speak, I nod.

As my mom wipes her damp cheeks with shaky fingers, Dad leans over and kisses the top of her strawberry-blonde head. "Don't worry, Bridget. The boys have this."

I return to the dining room, to the discussion of the upcoming trial. But my mind is wandering all over the place. I can't help thinking about Dominic and how he's doing.

Once we wrap up the meeting, I say goodbye to Ms. Murphy and excuse myself, planning to head upstairs to my bedroom to lie down.

Mom offers to bring me some lunch.

"No, thanks," I say. "I don't feel like eating."

She lays her hand on my cheek. "I know you don't, honey, but you have to eat something." She gives me a sad smile. "You're supposed to *gain weight* when you're pregnant, sweetheart, not lose it. Your clothes are hanging on you."

"I know. But not right now. Maybe later, okay?"

* * *

Mikey Alessio's trial is a short one because I'm the only eyewitness to the shooting. The police officers who responded to the scene testify, as does Tyler Jamison. But I'm the only actual eyewitness who can point Mikey out as the one who pulled the trigger on the gun used to kill Kent Martinez.

I'm sitting in an antechamber at the courthouse with Shane and Jake, and with Troy. My mom and sister Hannah are with me, too.

I feel sick to my stomach, but I don't know if it's from morning sickness or simply my nerves. I'm scared to death to walk into that courtroom and face Mikey Alessio again. I'll have to look him in the eye while I point him out in front of a judge and jury. And I have to do that without getting sick in public.

When there's a sharp rap on the door, I stand and smooth my black sheath dress. Wearing black felt appropriate given the circumstances. Kent Martinez is dead, and his shooter is presumably going to prison for the rest of his life, if the DA gets her way.

"Are you ready?" Mom asks me.

I nod, lifting a hand to make sure my hair is still where it's supposed to be. I put it all up into a bun to keep it out of the way. I'm wearing black flats, pantyhose, and a dress, trying to look confident and professional, even when I don't feel like either.

My mom offers me a water bottle. "Do you want something to drink?"

"No, thanks." I give her a rueful smile. "If I swallow anything right now, it's liable to come right back up."

I block out everything as we walk down a wide corridor toward the courtroom. There are armed police guards spaced throughout the hallway and right outside the courtroom.

Shane is on my left, Jake on my right. There's an officer in front of us, and one behind. One of the guards opens the courtroom door for us and we file inside the room.

The courtroom is deathly quiet as we enter. Everyone's eyes

are on me—the judge, the members of the jury, the crowd seated in the gallery.

The deputy opens a wooden gate for us to pass through, and I'm escorted up to the witness stand, where I take a seat. My stomach is churning and my face burns as the deputy holds out a Bible and asks me to repeat after him, pledging I'll tell the truth and nothing but the truth.

Once that's over, I take a seat and glance up at the judge, a middle-aged African American man with close-cropped silver hair and a trim beard. He gives me a small smile and a reassuring nod.

As the prosecuting attorney starts asking me questions—first, easy ones, like my name and occupation—my gaze pans the courtroom.

And that's when I see him.

My god.

Dominic's here.

He's seated in the back row next to a man who has to be his father. They're the same imposing height. Even though their coloring is different, I can see the resemblance in their faces.

Dominic's hard gaze is locked on mine. His eyes are on fire, his neck muscles taut. Neither one of us looks away. We can't.

Then the DA calls my name, catching my attention.

I start to answer the hard questions when she asks me about that night. Exactly what happened, moment by moment, step by step—from the moment we stepped out of the elevator and into the parking garage, to the moment the car came speeding around the corner and the gun appeared through the open window.

I answer all her questions in excruciating detail.

And when she asks me if I can point out the shooter, I nod and point at Mikey Alessio.

As I meet his gaze, he stares a hole right through me.

"That's the shooter?" the DA asks. "That man right there?"

"Yes. He's the one who killed Kent Martinez."

And then a furor breaks out in the courtroom. The judge raises his gavel and slams it down on the bench.

And the whole time this chaos erupts, I stare at Dominic, and he stares right back.

Unflinching.

Unapologetic.

And sadly, unreachable.

We're only a hundred feet apart, and yet it might as well be a million miles.

After I answer the defense attorney's questions—he has hardly any for me—I'm excused. As I rise to my feet, a wave of dizziness overcomes me. I grab onto the railing and close my eyes a moment, hoping the room will stop spinning. And then my knees buckle, and I fall back onto my chair.

A murmur fills the air as the people in the gallery start talking in hushed tones. The deputy comes forward, helping me to my feet, and then Shane is there. He puts his arm around my waist and walks me toward the exit.

I glance once last time at Dominic, realizing this might be

the last time I ever see him, and I'm shocked to see tears streaming unchecked down his cheeks.

He stares straight ahead—not at me—rigid as stone and just as lifeless.

29

Dominic

I don't know how I made it out of the courtroom and to my Bronco in the parking lot. My mind is reeling, my body moving on autopilot.

Something's wrong with Sophie.

That thought keeps playing in my head, over and over, and I'm on the brink of an anxiety attack.

I was shocked by her appearance in court. She's pale, gaunt, just a shadow of herself. Clearly she's lost weight, and her eyes are framed by shadows. Where has my vibrant, vivacious goddess gone?

The moment I get to my SUV, I call Shane.

"I can't talk right now," he says curtly.

I can hear other voices in the background, as well as the sound of heavy traffic.

"What the hell is wrong with Sophie?" I yell into my phone.

"I'll call you when I can." And then he hangs up.

I just drive, unable to think straight. I drive and drive and drive, in circles, until finally my phone rings—it's Shane.

"What's wrong with her?" I say.

"Nothing's wrong."

"Don't bullshit me! She nearly passed out on the stand today."

"It was probably because of low blood sugar. She hasn't been eating much lately, but she's feeling better now. Our mom got her to eat something."

"Shane, please. Tell me. I have a right to know."

He hesitates. "Yes, you do have a right. More than you realize." And then with a heavy sigh, he says, "She's pregnant, Dominic."

I don't hear another word after that—not over the deafening noise in my ears.

* * *

Franco hands me a tumbler of whiskey. "Did you find out what's wrong with the girl?"

After Shane dropped his bombshell on me, I drove straight

to Franco's estate. I'm not sure why I came here, but it just seemed like the right thing to do. Maybe it's because I just heard earth-shattering news and needed someone to talk to. And whether I like it or not, Franco's the closest thing I have to family.

"Yes. She's pregnant," I say.

He looks dumbfounded for a moment. Then his expression turns irate and he slams his fist on his desk. "You got her with child? How could you have been so careless?"

The man has a point. We were careless. At least on one occasion, as I recall. "It doesn't matter now. What's done is done."

Exhaling hard, he brushes his hand over his face. Then he glares at me, and I swear he looks like a father about to read the riot act to his wayward teenage son. Only I'm not a teenager.

And then I remember where we were today. "I'm sorry about Mikey." It's true. I am sorry that Franco has a son who will likely spend the rest of his life in prison.

Franco shrugs. "He was a fool to do what he did. I warned him not to do it, and now he's suffering the consequences of his actions. He got what he asked for."

Cold, but also true. I've learned in a very short period of time that much of Franco's life is cold. "Still, I'm sorry," I say.

He nods. "I appreciate that. Now, let's talk about the fact that you knocked up your girlfriend."

"She's not my girlfriend."

Franco leans back in his chair, the leather creaking. He watches me carefully. "Lie to yourself if you want, but don't lie to your father. It's dishonorable."

Hearing Franco talk about honor makes me want to laugh. "If you're expecting me to renege on our deal, I won't do it," I tell him. "I won't give you an excuse to go back on your word—*that* would be dishonorable. It's not just her safety at stake now, but my child's. Your *grandchild's*."

The old man covers his face with his hands and breathes out heavily. He sits there for a long time, not moving, not talking. I sit back in my chair to wait him out and wonder what's going through his head. God help us both if that son of a bitch tries to renege on our deal.

When he finally drops his hands and meets my gaze, there are tears in his eyes—and I'm shocked.

"I loved your mother more than my own life, Dominic. When Angelica found out about our affair, she gave me an ultimatum. Either fire Mia or she'd have her killed. I never doubted that Angelica would follow through on her threat, so I did as she demanded. I fired Mia. I kicked her to the curb and never set eyes on her again. She was six months pregnant with you, and I never saw you with my own eyes until the day of your mother's funeral." He makes the sign of the cross. "God rest her beautiful soul."

Franco watches me with painful eyes. "I lost the love of my life, and in the process, I lost my first-born son. I wouldn't wish that kind of agony on my worst enemy, let alone on my own son."

My heart begins to pound as I watch him.

He nods to me. "Dominic, I release you from our agreement. You are free to live your life as you see fit."

Hearing those words makes my breath catch. "What about Sophie? What about her safety?"

He gives me a chiding look. "Do you really think I'd let anyone hurt the mother of my grandchild?"

My mind races, along with my pulse. I don't trust him—I don't trust *this*.

"Losing first your mother, then you, was the worst pain I've ever endured," he says. "Do you really think I'd want my own son to suffer the same fate? Of course not. Don't be an idiot." He points to the door. "Go! Go make an honest woman out of her."

I look him dead in the eye. "Do you swear that you will never raise a finger against Sophie, or allow anyone else to do so?"

He nods solemnly. "I swear it." And then he offers me his hand.

We shake.

It's more than a gentleman's handshake.

It's a vow, between father and son.

* * *

By the time I get behind the wheel, my hands are shaking and my stomach is in knots. The prospect of seeing Sophie again overwhelms me.

At the moment, I'm not entirely sure where she is.

I call Shane again. "Where is Sophie—right now?"

"She's at our parents' house in Lincoln Park. Why?"

"Call the guards at the gate and tell them I'm coming."

Shane chuckles softly. "It's about fucking time, Zaretti."

I drive north like mad to Lincoln Park. I know where her family's gated community is because I've driven by it dozens of times in the past couple of months, hoping to catch sight of her. My heart is in my throat as I pull up to the front gate.

Killian Deveraux steps out of the guard shack. I recognize him as one of the operatives on Jake's team. I don't know the tall Cajun well, but he seems like a solid guy.

I roll down my window. "Killian," I say, offering him my hand.

"Shane said you were on your way," he says as we shake hands. "It's good to see you, man. How've you been?"

I laugh. "Not great, but I'll be better soon, once I see Sophie."

He grins. "I heard about you two from Jake. Congratulations." Killian gestures to the guards inside the shack, and the gate swings open for me to drive through. "I guess I'll be seeing you around," he says.

It's a relatively new development with only a handful of houses. I don't know which house is her parents', but I can guess. There are six vehicles parked in front of one of the houses. That's got to be it. The McIntyres are closing their ranks to support Sophie.

I park just down the street and jog along the sidewalk until I reach the house. Before I can knock, the front door opens, and an older guy steps out onto the porch, closing the door behind him.

He's a brawny guy, about six feet tall, with brown hair liberally laced with gray and a matching beard. His hard eyes are a steely blue, a brighter shade than Sophie's, and currently they're narrowed on me.

I have a pretty good feeling I know who this is. "You must be Calum McIntyre."

The man nods, his jaw clenched and his eyes hard. "And you must be Dominic. Shane said you were coming."

I nod, wondering how much of a hardass her father's going to be. I can't blame him since I knocked up his daughter. "Yes, sir. Dominic Zaretti." I offer him my hand. "I'm here to see Sophie."

Before he can respond, the door opens, and a petite strawberry-blonde with freckles scattered across her cheeks and the bridge of her nose slips outside, her gaze darting between the two of us.

"You must be Dominic," she says, breathless as she peers up at me. She offers me her hand, and I shake it gently, careful not to hurt her. She's tiny.

"Yes, ma'am. I'm here to see Sophie."

"I'm Bridget, her mother. Come with me," she says.

When I move to follow her, Calum steps in my way, blocking me from entering. He doesn't look happy.

Sophie's mom elbows her husband. "Calum, don't be an ass. Let the man through."

He does as she says, although he still looks pissed, and I follow Bridget inside.

She leads me to the base of the staircase. "Sophie's upstairs in her room—the second door on the right. Go on up."

"Does she know I'm coming? Did Shane tell her?"

Bridget shakes her head. "No. She's been upstairs in her room since she returned from the courthouse. She's... resting. She's not feeling well."

"I could see that in the courtroom."

Bridget narrows her eyes on me. "Your job is to make our daughter happy. Is that clear?"

"Yes, ma'am. Crystal."

I start up the stairs, but she stops me. "Dominic?"

"Yes?"

"Welcome to the family."

Bridget's words ring in my head as I climb the stairs, taking them two at a time in my haste to get to Sophie. I stalk down the hallway until I reach the second door on the right. I pause a moment, collecting myself, and preparing for whatever reception awaits me on the other side of this door.

Will she welcome me, or will she scream her head off and threaten to castrate me for leaving her in the first place? I did what I thought was right, and best for her at the time, but now everything has changed so drastically that it all seems surreal.

I knock quietly, but there's no answer.

Carefully, I ease the door open and find myself staring into a darkened bedroom. The drapes are pulled shut. Light from the hallway shines on the bed, where I see a form huddled beneath the covers on a four-poster bed.

My heart is pounding.

After closing the door behind me, I cross the room to stand beside the bed. "Phee?" I whisper.

She stirs, half-awake and a bit disoriented. "Dad?"

I sit on the edge of the bed and lay my hand on her hip. "No, baby. It's me. Dominic."

And then, after turning away, she presses her face into her pillow and sobs.

It's not the reaction I was hoping for. Quickly, I strip off my boots and climb onto the bed to lie down beside her, spooning against her back. I wrap my arm around her and pull her close, tucking her against me.

I press a kiss to the back of her head. "I'm so sorry, Sophie. I never meant to hurt you. It was the only way I knew to keep you safe."

She doesn't reply. She just cries as if her heart is shredded and the pain's too much to bear.

I did this to her.

"Sophie, please talk to me. Shane told me you're pregnant. I called him after you left the courthouse today to find out what was wrong with you. You nearly passed out on the witness stand."

Gradually, the crying stops. I press my face to the back of her neck and kiss her damp skin. "I'm here," I say. "And I'm not going anywhere."

She rolls to face me. "What about your agreement?"

"Franco released me from it."

"Why?"

"Because you're pregnant."

She starts shaking, and I'm pretty sure she's crying again. It's hard to tell in this dark room.

I pull her close, hugging her to me, and let her cry. "I'm here, baby. I'm here."

She sniffs. "If you ever do something like that to me again, I'll castrate you, and this baby will be an only child. Is that clear?"

I laugh as I kiss her temple. "I had a feeling you'd say that."

30

Sophie

For a moment, I almost think this isn't real. That he's just a dream, or a hallucination. "You're really here?"

He rises up to gaze down at me. "Yeah, I'm really here."

I reach up to cup his face before stroking his beard and cheeks. When I thread my fingers through his hair, he dips his head and groans.

Then he kisses me gently. "I'm sorry you're not feeling well."

"It's your fault."

He grins. "It is?"

"Yes. You got me pregnant."

He brushes his nose against mine. "So that's what I hear." Then he rests his hand on my belly. "Is it really true? We're having a baby?"

"Yes. I'm about three months along, and sick as a dog."

He chuckles. "I'm sorry, I know that's not funny, but I can't help it. I'm just so happy."

"You're happy I'm pregnant?"

He nods. "I am. Are you?"

"Yes." I place my hand on his. "We're having a baby."

My throat seizes up and I feel sick to my stomach, but this time it's not from morning sickness. I have to tell him the truth. I take a deep breath and blurt it out before I chicken out. "It was all my fault, Dominic."

"What was?"

"That they found us. It was my fault."

He frowns. "Why do you say that?"

My eyes fill with tears. "The night we ate at the tavern, I found a phone in the ladies' room. I called Amber to tell her I was okay. I didn't tell her where I was, but later I found out that Franco's men stole Amber's purse. They got her phone. They must have traced the call to the tavern in Millerton. From there, they must have asked around and discovered our location. So, it's all my fault. I'm so sorry. I just didn't think—"

He presses his forehead to mine. "Shh. It's okay, baby. You didn't know."

"But I should've known. You *told* me not to make any phone calls."

He kisses me, his lips soft and gentle on mine. "In one of your voicemails, you asked me if it was a dream, or if I really told you I loved you before I left the cabin. It wasn't a dream, Phee. I said it because I knew I was leaving, and my heart was breaking." He kisses me again, so reverently. "I love you."

My tears spill over, running down the sides of my face and making it impossible for me to speak coherently. I try to get the words out. "I love you too." But they're garbled at best.

"I don't deserve you, Phee, but I'll do my best to make you happy. I swear it." He leans down and kisses my belly. "You and our baby. We're going to be a family. You're going to marry me, right?"

"Are you asking?"

"Hell no. I'm *telling* you. We're getting married."

"All right. Since you asked so nicely."

There's a quiet knock on the door, followed by a muffled voice. "Sophie? Honey?"

"Yeah, Mom?" I say.

"I'm keeping your suppers warm. Why don't you and Dominic come downstairs and eat?"

"Thanks, but I'm really not hungry."

Dominic nuzzles the sensitive spot behind my ear. "You need to eat, Phee. Let's go down. It'll be fun to watch your family glaring at me."

I laugh. "For getting me pregnant?"

"No, for breaking your heart."

I sit up and brush my hair back. "What you did was incredibly brave and selfless."

"I did what I had to do to protect you."

"I still don't understand why your father let you out of the agreement."

"Because he didn't want me to go through what he went through. He knows what it's like."

I frown. "Be careful, or I might start to like your dad."

"The jury's still out on that," he says. "Pardon the pun."

He climbs out of bed and tugs my hand. "Come on, baby. You need to eat."

I allow him to pull me out of bed. Then I take a detour to the bathroom to freshen up. When I come out, Dominic's waiting for me, leaning against the wall across from the bathroom. His arms are crossed over his chest as my youngest sister glares at him.

"I see you two have met," I say, grinning at the perturbed look on Lia's face.

"Not officially," he says, eyeing my sister cautiously.

Lia looks to me. "You'd better come down and eat something. Mom's pacing like a caged animal. Show her some mercy."

"That's the plan," Dominic says, holding his hand out to me.

I take it, and we walk toward the stairs.

Lia follows. "Watch your step, bigfoot. I'll be keeping my eye on you."

We walk into the kitchen, where my mom is fussing over my two young nephews, Aiden and Luke, who are seated at the kitchen counter having cookies and milk. Aiden's on a barstool. Luke's sitting in a highchair. Across the way, the sofas and chairs in the great room are filled.

It looks like everyone's still here.

"Honey!" Mom cries when she spots me. "How about some dinner? I made your favorite—chicken and dumplings."

"Thanks, Mom. I'd love some." While it's not exactly true, she went to so much trouble I'd hate to disappoint her. The least I can do is try to eat.

My mom cranes her neck to look up at Dominic. "Wow, you're tall," she muses. "I bet you could eat a bite, too."

"Yes, ma'am," he says. "Always."

The deep resonance of his voice sends a shiver down my spine, and I realize how much I've missed hearing it. I slip my hand in his, and he squeezes mine.

"Have a seat at the table," Mom says. "I'll get your plates."

Shortly after we're seated at the dining room table, my mom carries in two bowls of food, one for each of us.

"Try this for starters, okay?" she says as she sets a small bowl in front of me and gives Dominic a heaping one in comparison.

She returns a moment later with a cup of hot tea for me and a cold beer for Dominic.

"This has ginger in it," she tells me, referring to the tea. "It'll help settle your stomach."

After she leaves us to eat, I take a tentative bite of food and sip some of the tea, fully aware that Dominic is watching me like a hawk.

"How do you feel?" he asks.

"Okay so far." I take a few more bites and stop because I don't want to push my luck. "I think the tea is helping."

Shane, Jake, and my dad join us in the dining room. Dominic fills them in on Franco's gesture to release him from their agreement.

"Do you trust Franco to keep his word?" my dad says to Dominic.

Dominic nods. "Franco's never lied to me. I think he was sincere when he told me to go take care of the mother of his future grandchild. He sees Sophie and the baby as part of his family now."

My dad leans back in his chair, his arms crossed over his chest. "I'm sorry, but a mob boss considering my daughter and grandchild part of his *family* isn't a reassuring thought."

Dominic laughs. "I don't blame you, sir."

"What's your plan now?" Shane says, looking to both of us.

I shrug, having no idea how to answer that. I'm still trying to adjust to Dominic being here.

Dominic reaches for my hand. "We haven't thought that far ahead." He looks at me. "We'll do whatever Sophie wants. I just want her to feel safe and comfortable."

Shane turns to me. "The offer to build you a house here in the compound stands. I know I speak for everyone in the family when I say we'd all feel better if you'd accept."

"I'll think about it," I say.

The idea of having a house of our own has a lot of appeal, especially with a baby coming.

* * *

That night, after we both take showers and dry off, we climb into bed.

Dominic groans as he stretches. Then he turns to face me, a smile on his handsome face. "I never expected this."

I brush my hand over his chest, tracing the ridges of heavy muscle. When my hand slips down his abdomen, toward his groin, he catches it with a wry laugh. "I'm pretty sure your father would crucify me if he knew I defiled his daughter under his roof. In case you haven't noticed, I'm not one of his favorite people right now."

I pull my hand free and continue my exploration. "I'll crucify you if you don't."

Leaning close, he kisses me tenderly. "You're *pregnant*, Phee."

"So? What does that have to do with anything?"

"What if I hurt you or the baby? I can't risk it."

"You're not going to hurt me. Pregnant women have sex all the time. It's fine. I've spent too many nights alone in this bed, missing you and aching for your touch."

He growls in frustration. And then, before I can get another word out, his mouth is on mine—hungry yet gentle, controlling yet careful. His hand slides to the back of my head and he presses me down onto my pillow before he rises up over me, getting onto his hands and knees as he cages me in. His muscular thigh slips between mine, and he coaxes my legs open.

I run my hands down his chest, my fingers slipping south toward his erection. "Don't worry. You're not going to crush me."

He makes a noncommittal sound. "Can't be too careful." Then he kisses my belly. "We've got a baby growing in there."

"Are you okay with that?" We never once talked about children, or how we each felt about kids in general. Now, we're expecting one of our own. I've always wanted kids, but I have no idea how he feels about it.

"I never gave it much thought in the past. I never got serious with anyone, so the idea never entered my head." He lays his hand on my abdomen. "We're having a baby? Really?"

"Yes, really." I wrap my fingers around his erection, relishing how hard and hot he is. "Now please stop talking and fuck me because I've missed you and I need you."

He dips his head and grins. "Yes, ma'am. Let's just try to be *really* quiet, okay? I do not need to give your father more reason to dislike me."

"He doesn't dislike you."

"Oh, yeah? You wanna bet? If it weren't for your mom, I wouldn't have been let in the house."

I laugh. "Then I would have run away with you—again."

Dominic proceeds to make love to me, very carefully, and very quietly. He keeps shushing me when I get too loud, and then we both dissolve into quiet laughter.

By the time I come, and he follows right after me, we both have tears in our eyes.

Afterward, he wraps me in his arms. "Jesus, I love you," he says, his hot face pressed against mine.

We lie there quietly for a while, just letting our heart rates return to normal.

Dominic rubs my bare back. "So, what's next for us?"

I'm lying on my belly, still trying to catch my breath. He licked and stroked every inch of my body and made me come twice. Once with his mouth on my pussy, and once by thrusting slow and steady inside of me until I saw fireworks for a second time tonight.

"What do you mean?" I ask him.

"Where do we go from here? I mean literally, where do you want to go? Do you want to stay here with your parents? I'm okay with that, but it might get kinda awkward with your parents, if you know what I mean. You're not the quietest when it comes to sex. Do you want to go back to your condo? My loft apartment isn't an option. It's not someplace I'd ever want you staying."

I turn to face him. "I'm thinking about taking Shane up on his offer to build a house for me here, next to my parents' house. My mom has offered to watch the baby for me when I'm ready go back to work, so that makes the most sense."

He nods. "It'll take a few months to build a house, though. What do we do until then? Stay here?"

I laugh at the pained expression on his face. I can't blame him. He's a grown man; he probably doesn't want to live with his future in-laws. "As much as I adore my parents, I don't think the two of us living under their roof is a good idea. We need more privacy. We need a place of our own until the house is ready."

He brushes my hair back. "Your condo, then?"

I shake my head. "I don't want to go back to my condo. It represents a time in my life that wasn't happy. I'm going to sell it."

"Okay. Then where?"

"I want to go back to the cabin."

He smiles. "Really?"

"Yeah. We were happy there, and just starting to connect when all hell broke loose. I'd love to go back there and relax with you for a while, at least until the house is ready."

"That's fine with me, but what about your pregnancy? Don't you have doctors' appointments to go to?"

"Yes, but I'm pretty sure they have OB-GYNs in Tennessee."

"All right then. I'll call Owen in the morning and give him a heads up. In the meantime..." He puts his arm around me, his fingers brushing gently against the side of my breast. "I just need to hold you."

When I look into his eyes, I'm surprised to see fresh tears. "What's wrong?"

"I thought I'd never see you again, let alone be able to hold you, or love you. You have no idea how that haunted me."

I blink back tears of my own. "Same."

He leans forward and kisses me, and I taste the salt of his tears on his lips.

"No one will ever separate us again," he says. And then he presses his forehead to mine and tightens his hold on me. "I love you, Phee."

"I love you, too."

31

Dominic

The flight attendant hands me a cold beer. "Here you go, sir," he says with a courteous nod. He hands Sophie a bottle of chilled mineral water. "Captain says we'll be landing in ten minutes."

It's a short flight from Chicago to Destin, where there's a small private airport. Then it's a half-hour drive to the cabin. Shane was nice enough to fly us down on one of his company jets. For the next few months, until our new house in Chicago is ready, we'll live at the cabin.

While she's sipping her water, I turn in my seat to face her and press my hand to her belly. It boggles my mind to think we have a child growing inside her—*our child*. I never dreamed of meeting Sophie, let alone having a baby with her. It still feels so unreal.

I'm going to be a dad.

She lays her hand on mine and smiles. She's not showing yet, but according to her doctor, she's three and a half months along now. It won't be long before she has a baby bump.

"I wonder if it's a girl or a boy," I say.

She smiles at me. "Which do you want?"

"I don't really care. I just want a happy, healthy baby. A little miniature Sophie would be nice, though." Just the thought of a bossy little girl in pigtails makes me smile.

She strokes my hand. "Or a strapping little boy—a mini version of you. I keep picturing a little boy, but a daughter would be nice, too."

A few minutes later, the jet lands smoothly, and once the captain clears us to disembark, the crew lowers the exit steps. I go first, then reach back to hold Sophie's hand as she descends.

She swats my hand away with a laugh. "I'm perfectly capable of walking down a few steps, you know."

I leave her to her own devices, but I'm never more than an arm's length away, just in case.

Down on the tarmac, Owen's waiting for us with an Army green Jeep with a black hardtop.

"Where did the Jeep come from?" Sophie says.

"I asked Owen to pick up a spare vehicle for me to drive

when we're here. Something with four-wheel drive and plenty of clearance to handle the lane."

"Welcome back, guys," Owen says as he waits for us beside the Jeep.

He steps forward and kisses Sophie on the cheek. "Congrats on the baby. I'm happy for you guys."

She gives him a radiant smile and reaches for my hand. "Thank you. It was a bit of a surprise, but we're happy about it."

Owen grins sheepishly. "So, I guess I don't have a snowball's chance in hell with you, do I?"

"Afraid not," she says with a laugh, squeezing my hand.

"Not even in your dreams, pal," I tell him.

I open the back door for Sophie and help her inside. I know Owen's just joking, but still. Where she's concerned, I'm pretty territorial. And I suspect he does have a bit of a crush on her. I can't blame him for that. I imagine she's the first woman he's talked to in a long while.

One of the crew members carries our luggage to the Jeep, and Owen stows the bags in the back.

"So, how'd the repairs go?" I ask him as we head for home. He and I are sitting in the front, Sophie in the back. This time she has her mobile phone with her, and she's busy texting someone.

"Fine," Owen says. "I had all the broken windows replaced right after you left, and I restocked the pantry and cleaned out the fridge. You're good to go."

He lowers his voice. "So, your dad?"

"When he heard that Sophie was pregnant, he released me

from our agreement."

"Damn," Owen says, shaking his head.

I glance back at Sophie, who's listening in on our conversation. "He said he didn't want me to suffer the way he did."

"Stop it," she says, "or I'm seriously going to start liking your father."

"I wouldn't get too carried away if I were you," I tell her. "He's still a crime boss. He's not about to win a Father of the Year award."

Owen chuckles. "It's good having you guys back. I get tired of having only myself for company."

I drop Owen off in the lane, near his cabin. As he's about to step out of the Jeep, Sophie leans forward and says, "How about joining us for dinner this evening?"

Owen looks surprised. "Sure. I'd love to."

"Seven o'clock?" she says.

He nods. "I'll see you then."

As he walks into the woods, I get in the driver's seat, and Sophie transfers to the front. I drive us the rest of the way up to the cabin. This time, our arrival is under very different circumstances.

When the cabin comes into view, she smiles and says, "We're home."

I couldn't agree more.

* * *

The cabin is pristine inside. All the broken glass has been cleared away and new windows have been installed. There's no sign of the carnage that took place here not long ago.

After we unpack, we head downstairs to check out the pantry and the fridge. Sure enough, Owen restocked everything. There's even a fresh package of Oreo cookies, which Sophie snatches up, and an eight-pack of Pepsi bottles chilling in the fridge.

I come up behind Sophie as she's gazing out the kitchen window and wrap my arms around her, pressing a kiss to her shoulder. "That was nice of you to invite Owen for dinner."

She leans her head back on my shoulder. "He's always been there for us. It's the least we can do." Then she turns and wraps her arms around my waist. "We're lucky. We get another chance. Not everyone does."

"Yes, we are."

* * *

Owen shows up right on time, bringing with him a bottle of sparkling red grape juice for Sophie.

"It's nonalcoholic," he says as he hands it to her, a sheepish smile on his face. "You know, since you're pregnant."

She hugs him and kisses his cheek. "It's perfect, Owen. Thank you."

Owen and I grill steaks outside while Sophie sits on the porch swing sipping her bubbly grape juice. I glance back at her occasionally, just to check on her, and I'm glad to see a content smile on her face. She looks happy. Fortunately, her nausea has recently subsided, so she's been able to eat more. Her color has improved, and she's starting to fill out a bit.

"I'm happy for you, man," Owen says as he turns the steaks.

"Thanks."

He shakes his head. "Wow, a kid. That's kinda hard to wrap my mind around. And you—a dad."

"Yeah. It is for me, too. But I guess sometimes you just get lucky."

Owen laughs. "I don't suppose Sophie has any friends back home?"

I shrug. "She might. You never know."

The three of us eat dinner at the little table in the cabin. Owen is more talkative than usual. I think he's finally starting to come out of his shell. After leaving the military, he really closed himself off from the outside world. Maybe meeting Sophie, and seeing the two of us together, has made him realize there's plenty more possibilities waiting for him.

After a late dinner and a couple of beers, Owen says goodnight and heads back through the woods to his own cabin.

Sophie and I clean up the dishes and then head upstairs for the night. She's starting to tire more easily, and it's been a long day.

As we're lying in bed, both of us naked, skin to skin, I take Sophie's hand in mine and kiss the back of it. "Let's get married, Phee."

She laughs. "I thought that was the plan."

"No, I mean right away. Let's go into town tomorrow and make arrangements to get married by the justice of the peace. I don't want to wait any longer than necessary."

"But what about my family? And our friends? I can't get married without my family present. My mom would kill me, and so would my sisters. Amber would never forgive me. There's no way."

I squeeze her hand. "We'll have a big wedding later, anything you want, I promise. But right now, I just want to get a ring on your finger. We're having a *baby*, Phee. I want us to be married. I won't let my child be born out of wedlock like I was. I want him to know who his dad is. Please."

She turns to face me, her fingers gentle as they brush my cheek first and then my hair. "All right, we can get married. Just the two of us. Owen can be our witness. But then later, I want a big family wedding and a honeymoon somewhere spectacular. Somewhere with sun and sandy beaches and an incredible ocean view."

"You got it. Anything you want. I just want us to be husband and wife as soon as we can arrange it."

"Deal," she says.

I hop out of bed, open my rucksack, and pull out a small velvet box. Then I kneel beside the bed and hand her the box.

Her blue eyes widen as she carefully opens the box. Inside, there's a slim gold engagement ring with a sparkling, bright diamond. "It's beautiful," she says, lifting teary eyes to me.

I smile. "Can't get married without an engagement ring."

She leans forward and kisses me, her lips soft and warm. Instantly, I'm hard, and I wonder if it'd be considered tacky to interrupt a wedding proposal to have sex.

She slides the ring onto her finger. "It fits," she says, astonished. "How did you know my ring size?"

"I asked your mom."

She tosses the empty ring box onto the nightstand and pulls me up onto the bed. Her mouth is on mine a heartbeat later, hot and hungry, and it's clear that she doesn't think it would be tacky.

"Are you sure?" I ask her. I'm still not completely comfortable with the idea of us fucking while she's pregnant, but she assures me that it's fine.

"Yes, I'm sure," she says, pulling me between her thighs.

I slide my hands up her thighs, over her hips, and down to her ass cheeks, marveling at how soft her skin is. Her pussy is soft and smooth, freshly waxed. Smiling, I place a gentle kiss on her labia. "I guess now that we're back in Millerton, you'll have to let me shave you again."

She blushes. "Oh my god, that's right. I guess you'll have to do the honors."

"It'll be my sacred husbandly duty."

She bursts into laughter, and it soothes my soul to know she's happy. I'll never forget the heartbroken messages she left on my phone while we were separated. I saved them, and I'll keep them always to remember the rough patch we went through.

"Hey, what's wrong?" Looking worried, she reaches up to push back my hair. "Why are you crying? Isn't this supposed to be a happy time?"

All I can think about are those months we were apart. "I'm so sorry, Phee. I didn't have a choice. They would have killed you." That's all I can get out before I'm choked up.

"Shh," she whispers, leaning in to kiss me. "We're together now, and that's all that matters. I dare you to try to get rid of me now."

"Never," I say as I gaze into her blue eyes. "Never."

32

Sophie

The next day, we head into town to find out what we have to do to get married in this state. After filling out the paperwork and making an appointment for our ceremony to be held at the courthouse, we walk out hand in hand.

It's a beautiful late summer day, and I couldn't be happier.

"We need to get you a dress, right?" Dominic says. "And shoes."

"For you, too."

After grabbing some lunch at the diner, we hop back into

the Jeep and head to Destin, where we locate a wedding apparel store. It's just a small shop, with not much selection, but that's okay. We just need the basics—a suit for Dominic and a wedding gown for me.

While I peruse the dresses, Dominic gets fitted for a suit. There's nothing off the rack that will fit his tall frame.

I have better luck and manage to find a pretty, white wedding gown which looks like it might actually fit me.

After I try on the gown, which only needs a few modifications to fit me—*thank goodness we're doing this now and not after I'm showing*—I head over to the women's shoe department to find something suitable. I should have brought some shoes from home, but I never dreamed I'd have an occasion to get dressed up.

Looking over the shoe selection, I'm surprised to find a few pairs that fit. Usually stores have to order my size and have the items shipped in. I try on a lovely pair of white satin ballet slippers, a pair of cream-colored flats, and a stunning pair of silver heels—four inches of gorgeousness. I really want the heels, but every time I put on a pair, I get nothing but scowls from men.

"Find something you like?" Dominic says, as he comes up behind me.

I nearly jump out of my skin. "I'm beginning to think you *enjoy* scaring me."

He laughs as he slips his arms around my waist. "Sorry."

"I actually found a few pairs that fit," I tell him, pointing them out. "I should get the flats."

"What about the heels? They look pretty wicked." Then he whispers in my ear, "You'd look so fucking hot in those."

I turn in his arms. "Really? You wouldn't mind?"

"Of course not. Why would I mind?" He grabs the heels and sets them beside a bench.

I sit and try them on. Then I stand, four inches taller. Still, he's got a few inches on me.

Dominic looks down at the shoes and whistles softly. "Damn."

"You like them?"

"Hell yeah. Say yes to the shoes, baby—my new favorite fantasy is counting on it."

I start laughing as tears spill from my eyes.

"Fuck, what's wrong?" he says, looking all kinds of worried.

"Nothing's wrong." How do I tell him that every man I've ever dated *hated* me in heels because of how much taller they made me?

He grabs my arms. "Sophie, you're scaring me. What the fuck is wrong?"

"Nothing's wrong!" I repeat, throwing my arms around his neck and kissing him. "You're the first man who's ever *wanted* me to wear heels."

He shakes his head. "You've dated some real idiots, baby. Those shoes are hot."

* * *

A week later, dressed in our wedding finery, Dominic and I say our vows in front of a judge in the Destin courthouse. Owen stands at our side as Dominic's best man. Tennessee doesn't require any witnesses to sign the wedding license, but he joins us anyway.

I wish my family was here, and Amber, but I know I'll have plenty of time for a big wedding later on—and a honeymoon—once the baby is born.

Today is for Dominic, so he can rest easy knowing we're husband and wife.

After a brief ceremony, we head back to the cabin, where the three of us toast with sparkling red grape juice. Once Owen takes his leave, Dominic and I have a Zoom call with my parents and siblings.

My mom cries during the entire call, telling us how happy she is. Even my dad gets a bit teary eyed, although he refuses to admit it. Hannah sheds some tears too, and when Lia's eyes are suspiciously shiny, she pretends she got something in her eye. But she's not fooling anyone. In fact, all the females in the family are a bit emotional when we share the news.

Lia shakes her head. "First you get knocked up, and then you get hitched. You're on a roll, sis. Thanks for putting more pressure on me and Hannah."

Jonah laughs as he kisses Lia's cheek. "Your time is coming, tiger. Trust me."

Beth is blubbering on the call. "I'm so happy for you," she wails. "I'm sorry, but I can't help crying. I blame it on the pregnancy hormones."

Shane puts his arm around Beth, while he juggles a squirming baby Luke in his other arm. "I'm happy for you, sis." And then he looks at Dominic. "Congratulations, pal. I can't imagine a better man for a brother-in-law. Welcome to the family."

Epilogue

Sophie
Three months later...

"Put me down, Dominic!" I squeal as he sweeps me into his arms and carries me up the walk to our new front door.

The house was completed in record time—just three months—and today, we're moving in. I'm a little over six months pregnant and already as big as a house. I guess with two gargantuan parents, this child is destined to be a big one.

Dominic opens the front door and pushes it wide open so he can carry me over the threshold.

"You already carried me over the threshold at the cabin, you know," I tell him. "Isn't this a little overboard?"

"Nope. I'll carry you over every threshold we have for the

rest of our lives." He sets me on my feet in the foyer. "Welcome home, Sophie Zaretti," he says.

"That has a nice ring to it," my mom says as she joins us.

Dominic pulls me close and kisses my temple. "I think it does."

Mom holds her hand out to me. "Come on, sweetheart. I'll give you the grand tour."

We decided on a ranch-style house, with one main floor and a walk-out lower level. There are four bedrooms, four bathrooms, a kitchen, dining room, living room, and family room. The lower level has a home theater, a workout room for Dominic, and a home office for me. We opted for high ceilings throughout the house to accommodate Dominic's height.

At the end of the tour, we end up on the back patio, which is decorated with balloons, colorful streamers, a huge gas grill, my entire family, and then some.

My mom puts her arm around me and gives me a squeeze. "It's your homecoming party," she says, tears in her eyes.

There are folding tables set up around the yard, covered in white linen tablecloths, decorated with vases of fresh flowers and party favors.

My dad and Shane are cooking burgers on the grill.

Lia's chasing Aiden and Luke around the yard.

Dominic and I make our rounds, greeting everyone and thanking them for coming.

My mom is sitting with Jake's wife, Annie, holding one of the twin girls. Annie's holding the other. The girls are identical, and

I can't tell them apart.

"I have Emerly," Mom says, as she bounces the bright-eyed baby girl on her knee.

"And I have Everly," Annie says. Everly is resting on Annie's chest, sound asleep, sucking on her fist.

There's a commotion at the side of the house as several McIntyre Security employees arrive.

"Ooh," Lia says as she elbows Hannah. "Don't look now, but your sexy Cajun just arrived."

I turn to look just as Killian Deveraux, Charlie Mercer, and Cameron Stewart come around the corner of the house. They're part of Jake's surveillance team.

"He's not *my* Cajun," Hannah says, looking a bit flustered as she elbows Lia back. To me, she says, "I said *one time* that I thought he was good-looking, and she throws it in my face every chance she gets."

Lia grins. "I think your exact words were, '*Oh my god, that man is sex on a stick.*'"

Hannah smacks Lia on the shoulder. "I did not say that."

"Well, he is hot," I say, laughing. "You have to admit."

"Who's hot?" Dominic says as he joins us. "Who are you girls talking about?"

Lia points across the yard at the tall, dark-haired man. "Hannah has a crush on Killian."

"I do not," Hannah says with a growl, jabbing Lia once more.

"Speaking of hot Cajuns," I murmur, as Killian starts walking toward us. "One's coming this way right now."

"Oh shit," Hannah mutters, blushing.

"Hey, guys," Killian says when he joins us. He shakes hands with Dominic, then leans in to kiss my cheek. "Welcome back, Sophie. And congratulations, on both your marriage and your impending arrival."

I gently pat my burgeoning baby bump. "Thank you, Killian."

Killian's gaze drifts to Hannah. "Hello, Hannah. I heard you flew back for Sophie's return."

Hannah nods. "Killian."

"And this is my cue to leave," Lia says, hopping up from the bench. "I'm sure Jonah's looking for me." And then she's off like a rocket, heading across the yard. But obviously it's a ploy, because Jonah is deep in conversation with my brother Jamie and his girlfriend, Molly.

Killian nods toward the grill and says to Hannah, "The food's ready. Can I get you something?"

Before I can hear Hannah's response, Dominic takes my hand and pulls me to my feet. He presses his lips to my ear and whispers, "And that's *our* cue to leave. You come with me." Then, he leads me into the house.

"Why did you pull me away?" I tell him. "It was just getting good. I didn't even hear what Hannah said."

"Because they don't need an audience, that's why."

"Who doesn't? You mean Killian and Hannah?"

"Exactly."

"Really? But they hardly know each other."

"Baby, a man doesn't go out of his way to ask a girl if he can get her something to eat unless he's trying to make inroads with her. Why do you think Lia took off so fast?"

Dominic walks me inside through the kitchen door and down the hall that leads to the bedrooms. "Which bedroom is ours?" he says, as we pass several.

The first two bedrooms we pass are empty, but the third one—the biggest one—is fully furnished with a king-sized bed, along with the rest of my bedroom furniture from my condo. "It's this one," I say, pointing.

He sweeps me up into his arms again and carries me into our new bedroom. Once we're inside, he closes the door behind us, locking it, and carries me to the bed.

"Are you seriously going to carry me over every threshold?" I tease, laughing as he follows me down onto the bed.

"Yes," he says, getting on his hands and knees, looming over me. "Is it rude to sneak off for a quick fuck while there's a party going on?"

"Yes!" I laugh. "Very."

"Don't care," he says, dipping down to kiss me.

He reaches beneath my dress and presses his fingers between my legs, feeling the damp gusset of my panties. "Ah, Mrs. Zaretti, you're holding out on me. You're wet."

"I am *not* wet."

He slips a finger inside my panties and strokes me. "Yes, you are, baby. Very wet. Come here."

He coaxes me up onto my hands and knees and lifts my dress. Then I hear his zipper come down and the rustling of his clothes as he shoves his jeans down. He slides into me slowly.

Since I'm so far into my pregnancy, we've taken to having sex doggy style most of the time. It's just easier this way, and he doesn't worry so much about crushing me or the baby.

He pulls out all the way, then slides back in very carefully.

I press my face into a pillow and moan. "You don't have to be so careful, you know. I'm not that fragile."

"Yes, you are," he says, palming my ass cheeks. "You're with child. Hopefully the first of many."

He leans forward, covering my back, and drops a kiss between my shoulder blades. One of his hands slips beneath me, and he starts teasing my clit.

"Welcome home, Mrs. Zaretti," he says. "It took us a while, but we finally made it."

* * *

Thank you so much for reading *Collateral Damage!* I hope you enjoyed Sophie and Dominic's story. Stay tuned for more books coming soon.

* * *

If you would be so kind, please leave a review for me on Amazon. Just a short comment on whether or not you liked the book is all that's needed.

* * *

For news on future releases, sign up for my mailing list: www.aprilwilsonauthor.com

Books by April Wilson

McIntyre Security, Inc. Bodyguard Series:

Vulnerable

Fearless

Shane (a novella)

Broken

Shattered

Imperfect

Ruined

Hostage

Redeemed

Marry Me (a novella)

Snowbound (a novella)

Regret

With This Ring (a novella)

Collateral Damage

A Tyler Jamison Novel:

Somebody to Love

A British Billionaire Romance:

Charmed (co-written with Laura Riley)